The
Entity
Within

Also by Cat Devon

Sleeping with the Entity

The Entity Within

Cat Devon

St. Martin's Paperbacks

This is a work of fiction. All of the characters, organizations, and events portrayed in this novel are either products of the author's imagination or are used fictitiously.

THE ENTITY WITHIN

Copyright © 2013 by Cathie L. Baumgardner.
Excerpt from *Love Your Entity* copyright © 2013 by Cathie L. Baumgardner.

For information address St. Martin's Press, 175 Fifth Avenue, New York, NY 10010.

ISBN: 978-0-312-54780-6

Printed in the United States of America

St. Martin's Paperbacks edition / July 2013

St. Martin's Paperbacks are published by St. Martin's Press, 175 Fifth Avenue, New York, NY 10010.

10 9 8 7 6 5 4 3 2 1

To Jayne and Frank—
I am simply in awe of your generous spirit.

And to my other sister-friends—De, Donna,
Jimmie, Jill/Alison, Julie, Margaret, Susan,
and Suzette—who also helped me sucessfully
overcome my own demons. *Merci*.

I am forever grateful to you all.

Chapter One

"I don't want any trouble," Zoe Adams said as she eyed the two vampires staring at her from across the table at the All Nighter Bar and Grill.

One of the vampires, Damon Thornheart, had an extremely threatening aura about him. Everything about him was dark, from his inky black hair to his deep blue eyes. He was glaring at her as if he wanted to consume her for lunch.

Zoe tugged her red cashmere shrug more tightly around her as if it could protect her. This was her first interaction with vampires, and at the moment it wasn't going very well.

"*We* don't want any trouble," Zoe amended her earlier statement with a tilt of her head toward her grandmother Irma Adams, sitting beside her in a knockoff vintage Chanel suit. With her white hair and twinkling blue eyes, Irma was the epitome of elegant and classy grannies everywhere.

"We don't want any trouble, either," the non-glaring

vampire said. His name was Nick St. George, and he was the one who'd invited Zoe and her grandmother to this meeting today. Zoe had been nervous about the get-together, unsure of its purpose and uneasy about its possible outcome.

Looking at Damon now only increased Zoe's misgivings. He did not want her there, and he made no attempt to hide that fact. The sardonic gleam in his eyes conveyed the message that he planned on making her life very difficult—if he let her live at all.

"That problem back in Boston was not my fault," her grandmother piped up to say.

"We don't want any problems here," Damon growled. "No trouble. No problems. We like to stay under the radar."

"I understand," Zoe's grandmother said with a nod. "But all I did back in Boston was attend a motivational seminar given by Dr. Martin Powers."

"And what did *you* do?" Damon directed his question to Zoe.

"Nothing," she said.

"I find that hard to believe, witch," he growled.

Zoe held her head high. She'd been called worse. And the fact was that he was speaking the truth. She was indeed a witch. Actually, she came from a very long line of witches. The Adams women had more than a few blessings and more than one curse.

"Yes, I'm a witch," Zoe said, even though she wasn't very proud of that fact at the moment. There had been a time when she'd gloried in her powers and felt empowered by her magical abilities.

Her mother's death two years ago had changed all that. Now she just wanted to lead a quiet life.

But enjoying a peaceful existence was difficult to do with her grandmother around, because Irma was also a witch and not a very quiet one. Not that Zoe intended on sharing that bit of information at the moment. Oh, the two vampires knew Gram was a witch. They just weren't completely aware of *all* her escapades, and Zoe planned on keeping it that way.

"I'm a witch and you're a vampire," Zoe told Damon. "That's old news. *Very* old in your case."

Damon's glare intensified. He looked scary even to a witch.

Reminding herself that she'd said she didn't want trouble, Zoe dialed it back a notch. "As my grandmother said, what happened in Boston wasn't her fault." Gram had already told Zoe that she'd seen the motivational speaker in a TV interview on the local Boston TV station. He'd talked about his seminar, but what had caught her grandmother's attention was the fact that there was something strange and devious about his aura. Gram felt she had to attend to learn more. Once in the audience, she'd tried to keep an open mind, but when Dr. Powers started talking about how he had the secret to happiness and would only share it if paid a large sum of money, Gram hadn't been able to keep quiet. She hadn't cast any spells. Instead she'd spoken out, which was her constitutional right as an American, albeit an American witch.

"That's right. It wasn't my fault," Gram said in that über-cheerful voice of hers. "All I did was ask how anyone could be stupid enough to think that simply giving Dr. Powers money would give you absolute happiness. How was I to know my comment would cause a stampede?"

"As Vamptown's new head of security it's my job to make sure there aren't any stampedes here," Damon said.

"And I'm sure you're very good at your job." Gram patted his hand.

Looking like he wanted to rip her head off, Damon snatched his hand away.

Zoe downgraded this face-to-face meeting from bad to train wreck. Nothing in her experience had prepared her for this. She'd heard about vampires, of course. It was hard not to given all the movies and press they got. She could understand their need to keep things quiet. Most humans didn't believe vampires really existed, and that was the way they liked it.

The same was true for witches. That witch-burning disaster in Salem may have occurred over four hundred years ago, but the memory remained. Sure, there were plenty of websites and books about covens of Wiccans who practiced white magic instead of the darker magical elements, but no human was eager to have a witch move in next door.

Apparently few vampires were eager to have a witch move in nearby, either. Zoe had seen enough episodes of *The Vampire Diaries* to know that witches and vampires had issues. But then vampires didn't seem to get along with anyone other than vampires.

Damon appeared to be proof of that fact, although Nick had been extremely welcoming in Gram's time of need. And Gram's time of need was also Zoe's time of need. Her grandmother had always been there for her, so Zoe couldn't let Irma come to Chicago by herself.

Besides, Zoe had her own reasons for leaving the East Coast that had nothing to do with stampedes or motivational speakers. Her reasons were very personal and had to do with matters of the heart.

They'd had to leave their hometown of Boston in somewhat of a hurry. Zoe didn't know where they'd go, but Gram said she had a friend named Nick St. George whom she'd met at a local occult bookstore years ago and formed a bond with because of their similar interests. Nick had moved to Chicago, but he and Gram had kept in touch. He'd told her that if she ever needed help, he'd be there for her.

Gram hadn't told Zoe much about Nick—just that she trusted him. The bottom line was that their options had been limited so they'd had to accept Nick's invitation to stay rent-free in a house he was managing.

Zoe had only found out about the vampire element in the story this afternoon when they'd arrived in Chicago and were on their way to Vamptown. Not that the neighborhood's name was known outside of the vampire community. Zoe doubted it was known within the witch community, either.

Yet here she was, a witch in the middle of a vampire enclave. So much for living a quiet life.

They'd barely had time to drop their belongings at the brick house a few blocks away that was to be their new home when they'd been summoned to this meeting.

"If we can get back to the matter at hand," she said.

"I've informed Nick that I do not approve of witches moving into our community," Damon said. "It's too much of a security risk."

"What are you afraid we'll do?" Zoe said.

"Make trouble," Damon replied.

"I've already said—"

"I don't believe you," he said.

Nick spoke before Zoe could make a stinging response. "As I told you, Damon, I met Irma back in Boston when I resided there before coming to Chicago. We became friends. And as her friend, I invited her here when she needed assistance. End of story."

Zoe decided that Nick was nice . . . for a vampire, that is. Not that Zoe knew much about him. All Gram had said was that her friend Nick had invited them to come stay in a free rental in Chicago. No mention of the fact that the guy had fangs and drank blood. No mention of the fact that the rental sat in the middle of a place called Vamptown. The only thing that looked welcoming was the cupcake shop down the block from the bar.

Damon, on the other hand, didn't appear to have a welcoming bone in his entirely too sexy body. Instead everything about him radiated danger and power with a hefty dose of arrogance. This was not a man—er, a vampire—who followed the rules.

Thankfully, Nick appeared to be the one with the final say about whether Zoe and Irma stayed or left. And Zoe could tell that Damon hated that fact.

Even so, she detected no personal animosity between the two male vampires. But maybe she was wrong. While it was true that she'd always been good at reading people, reading vamps was entirely new territory for her.

Looking directly at her, Damon said, "If we could have a word alone?" He made it sound more like an order than a request.

No way did Zoe want to be alone with a clearly bad-tempered albeit attractive vampire. "I'm fine right here where I am," she said. She glanced over at Nick, looking for reassurance.

Instead he said, "Damon, why don't you show her the sports memorabilia by the bar?"

Nick's lack of support reminded her that she would do well not to count on a vampire, even one she incorrectly thought was nice. "That's okay. I can see the Blackhawks jersey from here," Zoe quickly said. "Not that we are fans back in Boston."

"But we're in Chicago now," Zoe's grandmother said, giving her a nudge. "And we don't want to seem rude to Nick. So let Damon show you the sporty stuff."

That better be all he showed her. She didn't want him flashing his fangs at her, trying to intimidate her. And what was with her grandmother throwing her to the lion's den . . . or in this case the vampire's bar? Zoe thought she could at least count on Gram to have her back.

"Afraid?" Damon's mocking look would have made a lesser witch leap to her feet just to prove she didn't fear him.

But Zoe was made of sterner stuff. She remained in her seat and calmly returned his mockery with some of her own. "Yeah, I'm just shaking in my boots. Can't you tell?"

"I can tell you twirl your hair around your index finger when you're nervous," he replied.

And she could tell he wasn't going to give up until she went with him across the room. Fine. It wasn't worth wasting her energy on arguing with him. She got up and strolled over to the bar, where he joined her.

Zoe started the interrogation with a question of her own. "Do any humans live here in Vamptown?"

"Some."

"And you don't . . ."

"Don't what? Eat them for lunch? Only on Tuesdays and Thursdays when they are the special on the menu."

She suspected he was mocking her. She sure hoped so.

"What about you, witch?" he said.

"I don't eat humans ever."

"Glad to hear it. That leaves more for us vamps to consume."

"You think this is very funny, don't you."

"Not particularly. Annoying as hell, yes. Funny, no."

"What do you have against witches?"

"Everything."

"That's no answer," she said.

"It's the only answer you'll get from me."

"What's the matter? Are you afraid I'll cast a spell on you?"

He laughed. "I'd like to see you try."

"It won't happen. I've given up the practice of witch-craft. Instead I run a legitimate business."

"Yeah, I read that you run some kind of soap busi-ness."

"It's not just soaps, it's bath and body lotions."

"Magical potions," he said dismissively.

"That's not true." She could tell by his expression that he didn't believe her. "Look, I didn't even know there were vampires in this neighborhood until we got here."

"Then you should have turned right around the mo-ment you found out."

"You don't know anything about me."

"Not true. I had you thoroughly researched. You and your grandmother."

Her heart dropped. No, he couldn't possibly know

everything. Only the other witches in their coven back in Boston knew everything, and they were bound by their own laws not to reveal a thing.

KEEP CALM AND CARRY ON. Zoe had the T-shirt packed in her belongings back at the house. She should have worn it today—but how could she have known she'd be dealing with vampires? As if moving halfway across the country wasn't bad enough, now she had Damon Thornheart to contend with.

So he'd had them researched. So what? All she had to do was stay calm. Stay calm and carry on. Oh yeah . . . and also lie. Big time. Because the truth could get them into a cauldron-ful of trouble.

Chapter Two

Damon clenched his fists. Witches. Why did they have to be witches? The only thing Damon disliked more than witches was demons. He *detested* demons. He merely disliked witches.

He knew how to deal with demons. Not only was he a vamp, but he was also a Demon Hunter. Sending demons back to the hellhole they'd crawled out of was the primary purpose in his afterlife.

His secondary purpose for the time being was to disrupt the facade of calm that the witch had displayed up to this point. He'd sensed Zoe's panic when he'd mentioned researching them.

"Is that fear I see on your face?" Ignoring the emphatic shake of her head, he continued, "Good. You should be afraid. Be very afraid."

Damon knew he was being rude and he didn't care. He'd never been known for his courtesy, but rather for his ruthlessness. That's why he was so good at security. He always got the job done, no matter what it took.

It was a shame that vampires couldn't compel witches the way they could humans. Then he could just get rid of Zoe by sending her and her grandmother packing right back to Boston.

Instead he'd had to listen to her claims that they wouldn't cause any trouble. Yeah, right.

Vampires weren't known for their patience, and Damon had long ago lost what little he had left. He was accustomed to the loner life of a Hunter. He took jobs like this one in Vamptown when business was slow and to keep up to date on the latest high-tech gadgets. He'd signed a one-year contract as head of security, which was the blink of an eye in vamp terms. Time took on a different meaning when you had an eternity.

Not that vampires were infallible. They could be killed by fire or decapitation.

Damon eyed Zoe, who kept her gaze fixed on the sports memorabilia on the wall by the bar. She was pretty if you went for long dark hair and porcelain-pale skin. She wore a black top and pants along with a red sweater thing that looked like it had shrunk. Even so, she clutched it around her body as if it could protect her from him.

Which was stupid. Nothing could protect her from him.

When she'd first walked into the bar, he'd noticed how tall she was and that she was not wearing those ridiculously high-heeled shoes women went for these days. She had long legs and nice breasts.

The most striking thing about her was her eyes. One was green and the other was blue.

She turned to face him. This was the closest he'd been to her. Before a table had separated them. Now there was little space between them. Her eyes mesmerized him.

"Is that a witch thing?" he said.

"What?"

"Your eyes." He reached out to shift a strand of her dark hair away from her face so he could get a better look.

Her eyes widened at his touch. He kept his expression stony, but inside he was startled by his reaction to the feel of her soft skin and silky hair. His fingers tingled.

Dammit, had she cast some sort of spell on him? He eyed her suspiciously. He never tingled. He got hard. He wanted sex. But he never tingled.

"Whatever you're doing, stop it," he growled.

"Doing? I'm not doing anything," she shot back. "You're the one who touched me."

"A mistake I won't make again," he said.

"Good. Glad to hear that. And no, my eyes aren't a witch thing. I mean, yes, it's true that several generations in my family have eyes like this, but so do humans."

"Your grandmother doesn't have eyes like that."

"My mother did."

"She's dead," he said.

Zoe took several steps back but kept her eyes on him. If looks could kill, hers would have reduced him to a pile of burnt ashes. She had some serious power locked up in that mild exterior. He wondered what it would take to make her lose control.

She jabbed her finger at his chest. "You're not fit to talk about my mother."

Even her finger jab made him tingle, and that angered

the hell out of him. Who did she think she was, telling him he was unfit? "Why? Because I'm a vampire?"

"Because you're arrogant and rude and mean."

"Yeah, so?"

"Those are not good traits," she told him.

"They are in a vampire."

"Nick doesn't seem to be like that," she said.

"He's already taken, so don't think you can seduce him into your bed."

Shaking her head, Zoe took several big steps even farther away from him. "That comment was completely inappropriate."

She sounded so prim and proper that Damon was totally turned on. The Hunter in him responded to her retreat, making him want to give chase. The vampire in him responded to everything about her.

She wasn't the first witch he'd ever come in contact with, so he couldn't blame his reaction on that. No, there was something about her specifically that he was finding incredibly sexy.

"Are you trying to cast a spell right now?" he demanded suspiciously.

"No. I already told you I've given up the practice of witchcraft."

"Witches lie," he said.

"Perhaps some do. I don't." Her gaze turned thoughtful. "What made you think I was trying to cast a spell?"

"Nothing." He wasn't about to admit that she got to him.

But she seemed to know anyway. "Right."

"Don't look so smug, witch."

"Don't look so angry, vamp," she instantly shot back.

Now Damon's eyes were the ones that widened. No

one ever spoke to him that way. He was feared on five continents. He'd escaped one of the levels of hell and had done more killing than he could keep track of.

Yet here she was, standing before him, refusing to back down. But she had shown fear when he'd talked about investigating her background. And she'd shown anger when he'd mentioned her mother. Those were both weaknesses that he was determined to check out. Because he wasn't about to lose in a power struggle with a witch, no matter how sexy she was.

"So did you and Damon work things out?" Gram asked Zoe once they'd returned to their rental house.

"You mean Damon the Demon?" Zoe said.

"Don't say that." Gram looked around nervously. "Demons are not to be messed with."

"They're not real," Zoe said.

"No? Vampires and witches are real. So are demons."

"Have you ever met any? I don't mean warlocks who are demon-mean. I mean a real demon."

"I've heard about them and that was enough," Gram said with a shiver. "How did we get on this horrible topic anyway?"

"You asked me about Damon."

"He seems nice, right?"

"Nice?" Zoe stared at her grandmother in disbelief.

Gram grinned and elbowed her like an adolescent girl at a sleepover. "I think he likes you."

"I think he wants to stuff me in a boiling cauldron or toss water on me like the witch in *The Wizard of Oz* and watch me wither away."

"He certainly was watching you, that's for sure," Gram said.

"He dislikes me and all witches, that's what's sure."

"Why would he dislike witches?"

Zoe shrugged. "He wouldn't say."

"I don't understand. We told him we wouldn't cause any trouble."

"I know. And speaking of that, he had us investigated."

Gram's face paled.

"It's okay." Zoe gave her a reassuring hug. "Our coven back in Boston is bound by our laws not to reveal our secrets."

"Right. If Damon knew the details, he'd have tossed us out immediately."

"But he is suspicious, so we have to be very careful," Zoe said.

"Certainly."

"And that means not drawing attention to ourselves."

"Unless it's your Bella Luna products we are drawing attention to, right?" Gram said.

Zoe was proud of the online natural botanical beauty line she'd started. Her business was still in its up-and-coming stage, but a popular artisan soap blogger had said the Bella Luna soaps were among her favorites, which had resulted in a nice boost in sales.

"I do wish you'd let me amp up your products a little," Gram said. "I could make the anti-wrinkle cream a real winner."

"No magic."

"Too late," Gram admitted.

"What did you do?"

"I used an unpacking spell to get your work area all set up with your creams and things. The upstairs apartment is perfect for your business. It has its own kitchen for you to work out new mixtures and soap combos."

"The soaps are the most popular items in our product line. I can hardly keep up with the demand," Zoe said.

"If you'd let me help you by tweaking a few of your items then you could afford to hire someone to help you. I hope you're not angry that I cast a spell to unpack things for you."

Zoe headed upstairs to check things out. Her grandmother's spells had been known to go astray in the past. Her mother's final spell had ended her life. Zoe no longer trusted magic to always do good.

Zoe couldn't afford to think of her mother at the moment. She had to stay focused. Looking around the large room that was the new home of her business, she gave a sigh of relief. Nothing was broken. Rows of muslin-wrapped soaps were neatly stacked on shelves. They were in alphabetical order from apple spice to wintergreen, a remnant from her days as a librarian back in Boston. She'd had to leave her job when the books had all started speaking to her at once. The cacophony had been deafening.

Zoe still wasn't sure what had caused that phenomenon. Sure, growing up she'd always had a close affinity with books, and sometimes she'd inadvertently make the characters of her favorite stories hop off the page and dance around her room—like the time at age five when she'd done the bunny hop with the Cat in the Hat from the book of the same name. But she'd never had her books screaming at her simultaneously, creating a deafening sound that made it impossible to think straight. The library had thousands and thousands of books, all of them screaming various quotes from within their pages or yelling her name. It was worse than the decibel level in the front row of a rock concert combined with the blast of shrieks from a haunted house on speed.

Gram swore she'd had no part in the occurrences at the library that had forced Zoe to leave. The incidents had continued even after Zoe gave notice, right up until she left the building. Thankfully no one else had been aware of the shouting books. Just her. She'd hated giving up a job she'd loved, but she'd had little choice. Zoe hadn't been to a library since then.

While her professional life was up for grabs, Zoe's personal life had been terrific. She'd fallen in love with Tristin Winters, a professor of paranormal activity at the local community college. She'd met him while still in library school. After two years as a couple, he'd proposed to her and she trusted him enough to tell him she was a witch. He'd been supportive and understanding. Given his chosen field of study, he'd known a great deal about witches and harbored no prejudice against them.

His requests for her to cast spells to help him economically had started innocently enough. Or so she'd thought at the time. His department had needed more funding, so she'd worked her magic on the lottery to allow him to win. It wasn't mega-millions, but it was a nice amount.

He said he'd donated it all to the college but that more was needed. He went on and on about the difference his work could make in the world of paranormal research and how he'd studied in Nepal and wanted to help the people there. She hadn't been a total patsy. She'd checked out his story; Tristin had indeed studied local legends and lore in Nepal. He'd shown her photos of himself with the locals. The faces of the children had been the breaking point for her.

So she'd applied her magic to Wall Street for him. Just a few stocks. Nothing meant to gain attention.

When her mother died and Zoe refused to use magic any longer, Tristin left her. He'd used her and broken her heart. Zoe's grief at the loss of her mother and the betrayal of her fiancé had nearly undone her. She'd wanted to give up.

Instead she turned to what had been a hobby before—making soap. At a time when her life had seemed out of control, she had been able to focus on creating her own recipes and mixtures for a line of botanical bath and beauty products that were pure and natural . . . and devoid of magic.

"Does everything look okay?" Gram asked her. "I don't want your business to suffer because of my mistakes."

"Having an Internet-based business means that I can pick up and move easier than if I had a bricks-and-mortar store," Zoe replied.

"Speaking of stores, did you notice the cupcake shop down the block from Nick's bar?"

"Yes. We will definitely have to check that out later."

"And did you also notice Damon's eyes?" Gram asked her.

"He sure noticed mine," Zoe said. "He asked me if it was a witch thing."

"What did you tell him?"

"That it isn't."

"Did you mention the curse?"

"That an Adams witch with two eye colors would never find happiness with a man? No, I didn't tell him." Zoe had also never told her ex-fiancé. "I should have put in the tinted contact lens I have to make my eyes match like I did when I worked at the library."

"Would you have gone with the blue or the green?"

"Green. I think they are more powerful."

"Damon's eyes are certainly powerful," Gram said. "Do you deny that?"

"No. He has very powerful expressive angry dark blue eyes. And yes, they are sexy. But dangerously sexy. This is a vampire we are talking about here. I am not about to play Little Red Riding Hood to his Big Bad Wolf."

Gram laughed and patted her arm fondly. "You always did have a thing for fairy tales."

"That's a make-believe world. We are dealing with real vampires here," Zoe said.

"And we are real witches."

"Why didn't you give me a heads-up before we moved here?" Zoe asked.

"We didn't have a lot of options open to us," Gram said. "We were pretty much banished from Boston. Our coven said we had to leave town because I'd created a scene unbecoming of a witch and you were still on probation for revealing the fact that you're a witch to Tristin. They didn't give us much time to make the move."

"I know, but you still could have warned me that we were moving into the middle of a bunch of vampires."

"I was afraid you wouldn't come."

"Damon is not happy about us living here."

Gram grinned. "That's an understatement." She reached out to stroke the long-haired calico cat perched on a worktable. "Isn't that right, Morticia?"

The cat purred her agreement as she tilted her head

so Gram could reach that spot behind her ear she
loved.

A gray short-haired cat jumped up on the other side
of the worktable. "Don't expect me to be so subservi-
ent," the cat said.

"I still can't get used to the fact that your familiar
speaks," Gram said with a shake of her head. "Bella
Plushallova is one of a kind."

"I can't get used to the fact that I was brought back
as a cat, and yes I am one of a kind," Bella said. "I was
once a Russian countess and now look at me. I have
been reduced to this."

"You are the familiar to Zoe, a wonderful witch. Be
thankful."

Bella regally lifted her nose in the air. "I did not ask
for this assignment."

"Well, we didn't ask for a familiar with attitude, either," Gram said. "Our coven decided you had to be
placed with Zoe after none of the other witches could
cope with your shenanigans."

The sound of pounding on the front door prevented
further feline-familiar-to-witch conversation.

"It's probably Damon ready to toss us out," Zoe said.

"Don't be such a Debbie Downer," Gram reprimanded her. "You go open the front door. I'll let you
deal with our company. I'm going to finish unpacking."

"What if it's Damon?" Zoe said.

"Don't upset the vampire," Gram suggested with a
pat to Zoe's cheek before disappearing.

"Definitely do not upset the vampire," Bella agreed
before leaping down and marching off, leaving Zoe
alone.

Chapter Three

Zoe went downstairs and opened the front door to find a young woman standing there with a box in hand. "Welcome to the neighborhood," she said cheerfully. "My name is Daniella Delaney." She opened the box's lid. "And I brought cupcakes."

"I can see that." Zoe looked around, half expecting to find Damon lurking somewhere nearby.

Satisfied that he was not waiting to pounce, Zoe returned her focus to Daniella.

"I'm the owner of Heavenly Cupcakes," Daniella said.

Zoe studied her. "You're part druid."

Daniella was clearly taken aback by Zoe's abrupt comment. "How did you know? Did Nick tell you?"

"No. Your aura told me. It's an unusually strong gold with tinges of bright royal blue, which is very rare and would indicate your druid heritage."

"Is that a problem?"

"Not to me," Zoe said.

"And you are a . . ." Daniella paused, clearly unsure how to complete the sentence.

"Soap maker."

"Right. Nick said you're also a . . ."

"A witch?" Zoe nodded. "That's right."

"Nick told me that you seemed surprised to learn about the vampires."

"True." Zoe suddenly realized two things simultaneously—that she was being a poor hostess and that the smell of those cupcakes was making her mouth water. "Oh my gosh. I didn't mean to keep you standing out here on the porch all this time. Come on in."

Turning around, Zoe realized that in the time it took for her to come downstairs and answer the door, Gram had completely unpacked the contents of the living room.

Daniella expressed her surprise. "You did a lot of work in a short amount of time."

"It's an Adams family trait," Zoe muttered, praying Gram wouldn't pull any more magic tricks while Daniella was here. While it was true that the cupcake maker knew Zoe was a witch, she didn't want Gram getting accustomed to always casting spells to meet their needs.

"The Adams family like the vintage TV show?"

"Not really. Don't expect to see the shark mounted on the wall with a guy's leg in it like on the TV show."

"I actually have a soft spot for fish mounted on the wall," Daniella said wistfully.

"You do?"

Daniella nodded. "You could say that a singing fish saved my life, but that's a long story." She nodded down at the cupcakes. "I brought red velvet. And with St. Patrick's Day coming up, I included mini mint along with a few Irish cream."

Zoe eyed the sweets before noticing the teapot on the coffee table. Gram's work again. Zoe really did need to speak to her grandmother about keeping the magic under the radar for now. Zoe took Daniella's lightweight coat and zebra-print silky scarf and hung them on the coatrack by the door.

"Please have a seat," Zoe said. "Would you like some tea?"

Nodding, Daniella sat on the couch and took the cup of tea that Zoe poured and then offered her. "I heard Damon gave you a hard time at the meeting today. Don't take it personally."

"It's hard not to," Zoe said, taking a seat on the couch beside her.

"I know."

"Did Damon give you a hard time when you first arrived?" Zoe asked.

"Actually I was born here. My family owns the local funeral home."

The news surprised Zoe. "So you grew up surrounded by vampires?"

"No. Well, yes, I guess I did. But I had no idea. I was totally in the dark. I left to go to college, and after my training as a chef I worked in New York City. I only met Nick when I opened my cupcake shop back in early October. And I only learned about the vampires shortly after that."

"Is that when you met Damon, too?" Zoe asked.

"No. Damon's only been here since mid-January."

"Yet he acts like he owns the place," Zoe muttered. "Sorry."

"No need to apologize to me."

"Nick seemed nice but not Damon. Damon already warned me that Nick is taken."

"That's correct," Daniella said proudly. "Nick is taken by me."

"Wow, I didn't think vampires and druids got along."

"I'm only part druid," Daniella reminded her.

"Right. You're a hybrid," Zoe said.

"Not that I go around bragging about that," Daniella said.

"Believe me, I totally understand. I don't go around bragging that I'm a witch, either," Zoe said.

"I do brag about my cupcakes, though." She picked up the box and held it out to Zoe. "Here, have one."

Zoe selected the red velvet. Taking a bite, she closed her eyes as the perfect blend of moist cake and cream cheese frosting hit her mouth. "Mmm, magical," she said before taking another bite.

Daniella beamed. "I'm so glad you like it."

"I don't like it. I *love* it. And could easily get addicted." Zoe eyed the remaining cupcakes and then studied Daniella. Had the cupcake maker used some secret kind of druid magic on her cupcakes to make them so delicious?

As if reading her mind, Daniella said, "It's not magic. I don't have any kind of magical abilities. Well, sometimes I get premonitions about the future, but that's it. Oh, and I can protect myself from evil vampires if necessary."

"How do you do that?" Zoe asked.

"It's a druid thing," Daniella said.

"So only druids can do it?"

"That's right. Only hybrid druids."

"Too bad," Zoe muttered. "There's a certain evil vampire I could use some protection from."

"Damon isn't really evil," Daniella said. "He just takes his job as head of security very seriously. We had an incident around Halloween that set everyone on edge."

"An incident?"

"Um, yes." Daniella paused to take a dainty sip of tea. "With a rival clan of vampires."

"Great," Zoe muttered. "So we're living in the middle of a turf war between vampires?"

"No, things have settled down and Damon's job is to make sure they stay that way."

"I'd like things to stay that way, too." Zoe finished her cupcake and dabbed at her mouth with a linen napkin printed with the Adams family monogram before asking, "How do you do it?"

"My recipes are top-secret."

"No, I mean how do you get used to living surrounded by vampires? You said your family runs the local funeral home. Do they know about the vampires?"

"No. My brother and father have no druid blood. They are human and it's safest for them not to know what's going on."

"What *is* going on?" Zoe asked.

"I can't answer that. But it's nothing that would involve you or your being a witch or a soap maker."

Could she trust Daniella? Maybe Nick had compelled her or something. Or Damon had.

"I can't be compelled by vampires," Daniella said.

Zoe squirmed uneasily. "Can you read minds?"

"No." Daniella laughed. "But I could tell by the

expression on your face that you were suspicious. If I were in your shoes, I would wonder if a vampire had compelled me. That's one of the first things Nick noticed about me. That he couldn't compel me. They can't compel witches, either, just in case you were wondering. Don't take my word for it, check it out on the Internet yourself. Or with someone you trust."

"This move to Chicago is turning out to be a lot more complicated than I thought," Zoe admitted.

"At least you're not here alone. You've got your grandmother. Oh, and a cat."

Zoe held her breath as Bella strolled into the room. She gave the feline a warning glare about not speaking in front of Daniella. Yes, the other woman knew about Zoe being a witch, but experience had taught Zoe that hearing a cat speak was another matter entirely. She didn't know why it always turned out badly. She just knew it always did.

"What's your cat's name?" Daniella asked.

"Bella," Zoe cautiously said. "She's very shy." That was her way of telling Bella to get lost.

Bella responded by coming closer and jumping onto the couch beside Daniella.

"Is she looking for some milk?" Daniella asked.

"She's looking for trouble," Zoe muttered.

Bella nodded.

Zoe leapt to her feet to prevent Bella from making a scene. The cat had caused trouble in the past, and she couldn't afford for her familiar to shoot off some comment like a loose cannon. She had to get rid of Daniella before that happened, even if it meant being rude. She glanced at her watch. "Look at the time."

Daniella rose as well. "I didn't mean to stay so long."

"That's okay," Zoe said. "It's just that we still have a lot of work to do to get settled in."

"Uh, you might want to close the lid on the cupcake box so your cat doesn't get into them." Daniella pointed to Bella, who was obviously eyeing the sweets.

"Right. I'll do that," Zoe said as she led Daniella to the door and handed over her coat. "Thanks so much for coming. Bye now."

Damon impatiently waited for Daniella down the street from the witch's house. "What did you find out?" he demanded.

"That Zoe seems very nice and she loves my red velvet cupcakes."

"That's it?"

"Oh, and she has a cat."

"Of course she does," Damon said. "She's a witch so she must have a black cat."

"It's gray, actually."

"That's it? That's all you've got for me?"

"What were you expecting her to say? I just met her. And I told you I wasn't comfortable spying for you in the first place."

"It wasn't spying. It was intel gathering," Damon said.

"She was worried that you'd compelled me until I assured her that vampires can't compel me. Or her."

"I wish I could compel her. It would make life easier."

"I guess you are just going to have to deal with her on an equal level."

"No way," Damon said. "Vampires are superior to witches."

"Says who?"

"It's a well-known fact."

"To you maybe."

Damon eyed Daniella suspiciously. "Maybe she cast a spell on you and that's why you weren't able to get more information out of her."

"I doubt that."

"I wouldn't put it past her. She's already put all the surveillance cameras in the house out of commission."

Instead of sharing his outrage, Daniella said, "Did you tell her about the cameras?"

"Of course not."

"Then how did she know about them?" Daniella asked. "I mean, they are usually pretty well hidden. And I certainly didn't tell her about them, because I didn't know they were even there in the first place."

"She's a witch," Damon growled. "She knows things." He turned on his heel and started walking away.

Daniella followed him, stopping him with a hand on his arm. "Where are you going?"

"To go talk to her myself," Damon said.

"She might not let you in."

"Oh, she'll let me in all right."

"Don't be a bully. Do not upset her."

"Right. Do not upset the witch," he said sarcastically. "Got it."

Damon removed her hand from his arm and walked away from her.

"Be nice," she called after him.

"Like that's going to happen," he muttered under his breath before taking the steps to Zoe's front door two at a time. Nice was not in his vocabulary. Nice didn't get you anywhere. It certainly didn't get you turned into a vampire or help you survive the torturous transformation.

Damon was all set to bang on Zoe's front door, but it opened before he could raise his hand. Zoe stood there wearing the same clothes she'd had on a few hours earlier at the bar and looking surprisingly good despite the startled look in those weird bicolored eyes of hers.

"How did you know I was out here?" he demanded.

"I didn't," Zoe said. "Daniella left her scarf. I was going to run after her to give it to her."

"There's no need." He grabbed it out of her hand. "I'll give it to her."

"Okay."

Zoe was about to swing the door shut when he put his foot out to prevent it. "Aren't you going to invite me in?"

"Why?"

"Because it's the polite thing to do."

"Says the rude vampire who doesn't want me here."

"You don't want to aggravate me," he warned.

"Ditto," she shot back. "Vampires can't cross a threshold unless they are invited in." She'd read that somewhere.

"Damon, how nice to see you again," Gram called out from the stairway. "Do come in."

Damon quickly moved inside before Zoe could slam the door in his face.

"Sorry I can't stay and chat but I've got more unpacking to do," Gram said. "You two sit down and have some tea."

Gram turned and made her way upstairs, leaving Zoe looking more pissed off than nervous.

"I can't imagine you drinking tea," Zoe told him. "It's not a vampire thing, is it?"

Instead of answering, Damon surveyed the room, noting the location of the hidden camera. It was still there in the corner of the crown molding. He also noted that the room contained a hell of a lot more furniture than it had in the earlier video coming in over the feed. In fact the room had been empty but now it had several large pieces of furniture in it, including a weird chair with writing all over it. It had a modern edge that was at odds with the rest of the place.

Well, maybe not. He was no expert on home decorating but even he could see that the heavy Victorian armoire looked weird compared with the rustic denim couch, which overpowered the dainty table with a teapot and two cups. There was a zebra rug in front of the stone fireplace.

"It's not real," Zoe said. "I don't believe in hurting animals."

"I hope you're not expecting me to make the same claim," he said sarcastically.

"I'm not expecting you to do anything."

"Oh, I plan on doing something, all right. Do you recall telling me that you aren't practicing magic anymore? That you and your grandmother wouldn't make any trouble?"

She nodded. For the first time this visit, a trace of nervousness flashed in her eyes before it was gone. He could hear her heart beat faster. Vampires had ultrasensitive hearing. When he concentrated he could practically hear the *swish-swish* of her blood rushing through her veins. He saw the slight tremble of her fingers.

Good. Damon wanted her scared.

But he wanted more than that. He wanted her lush mouth covered by his. He wanted her nude body beneath his. Which were only two of the hundred reasons he wanted her gone.

Chapter Four

Zoe refused to allow Damon to intimidate her. Not in
her own home. They were on *her* turf now.

Okay, so it was only a rental turf, but still . . .

And yes, they weren't paying rent, but that didn't
mean surly vampires could walk in and glare at her.
She'd had enough fangy angst for one day.

She raised her hands in the air in a mocking motion of surrender. "I get it. You don't want me here.
No need to keep pounding it home. Message received
loud and clear." She lowered her hands to place
them on her hips. "But I'm not going anywhere, so
get over it."

"It would be easier to get over it if you were half as
trustworthy as you claim to be."

"I don't know what your problem is—"

"My problem is *you*," he said, interrupting her.
"You're not even here twelve hours and already you're
spinning spells."

"What are you talking about?"

"Don't play dumb with me. You disabled the cameras with your magic so no one could see what you were up to."

"Cameras?" She looked around the room. "You're spying on us?"

"Most places in Vamptown have surveillance cameras."

"Why?" she demanded.

"For security reasons."

She didn't like his answer and neither did Gram's cat Morticia, who jumped onto the arm of the denim couch and hissed at him.

"That your cat?" he asked.

"Morticia is my grandmother's cat. That's my cat," she said as she hurried to scoot Bella from the creamer she'd been sticking her paw in. Scooping Bella into her arms, Zoe glared at him. "I can't believe you had the nerve to plant cameras in here. There has to be a law against that. Were you hoping to get some kind of kick out of watching the video?"

"I don't watch the video," Damon said. "Someone else does."

"And that's supposed to make me feel better?"

"I don't care how you feel," Damon said.

Morticia growled at him. Bella merely yawned. Zoe was well aware that her grandmother's familiar was being more protective than her own.

"What I care about is getting those camera feeds back online," Damon continued.

"Online? You mean you're posting them on YouTube or something?"

"They are linked to our neighborhood security system."

Zoe hugged Bella closer for protection. "I don't like it."

"I don't care."

"Does Nick know about this?"

"Yes."

"What about Daniella?" Zoe asked. "Does she know, too?" Something made her add, "And what's going on with the funeral parlor?"

Moving with vamp speed, Damon pinned her and her cat against the wall. "What do you know about the funeral parlor?" he growled with clear menace.

"Everything okay down here?" Gram asked from the stairway before joining them. "I see you met my cat Morticia." She moved closer to run her fingers over the calico cat's head.

Damon stepped away from Zoe and turned to face Gram.

"Wise move," Bella muttered.

He instantly turned to face Zoe. "What did you say?"

"Nothing." Leaning down, she whispered in Bella's ear, "Behave." She didn't want Damon knowing that Bella could speak. Zoe's general philosophy was that the less outsiders knew about her, the better. And that went double for vampires. Triple for Damon, in particular.

"I expect you're here about the cameras." Gram sighed.

Damon once again turned to face her. "What do you know about them?"

"Don't answer him, Gram," Zoe said before stepping between them to protect her grandmother from any possible vamp wrath.

"I'm assuming he already knows they're not working at the moment," Gram said.

"And I want that rectified," Damon said.

"Haven't you learned that you can't always get what you want?" Zoe countered.

Damon's smile was sardonic. "Haven't you learned that vampires *always* get what they want?"

"No."

"Then consider this lesson number one," Damon said. "I want those cameras working again right now, so remove whatever damn spell you put on them."

"It's not that easy," Gram said.

"I still don't know why you have cameras all over Vamptown. Are they in bathrooms, too? Bedrooms?" Zoe demanded.

"That's none of your business."

"Considering they might be in *my* bathroom or bedroom, I'd say it certainly *is* my business."

"We witches value our privacy," Gram said. "That's why I disabled the cameras as soon as I detected them. My decision. I'm sure you understand, Damon."

"I don't give a damn that you value your privacy," he said. "If you want to stay here, you will abide by our rules."

"And how many other outrageous rules are you going to come up with in your pitiful attempt to make us leave?" Zoe challenged him.

"As many as it takes. Now get those cameras working again."

"I'm not sure I recall how to do that." Gram sounded flustered as Damon towered over them both ominously.

"Stop bullying her." Zoe set Bella on the couch, where she curled up and watched them with an amused gleam in her eyes.

"Or what? You'll sic your cat on me?" Damon mocked.

Uh-oh. Bella did not like being mocked. In fact, it was one of the things sure to push her feline familiar buttons. Zoe saw the meltdown coming. Bella's eyes began to glow brilliantly. All sign of amusement was gone as the cat sat up and focused her attention on Damon.

"I know spells to make a vampire's privates shrivel up and fall off," Bella announced.

"That didn't come from me," Gram hurriedly said.

Damon went straight to Zoe. "Then it came from you."

Zoe wasn't sure what to say in answer to that. She glanced nervously at Bella.

Seeing that, Damon's sardonic smile returned. "Are you worried about your dainty feline? You should be. I eat cats for breakfast."

"Not this cat," Bella said. "Not if you value your privates."

Damon's anger flared. "Is this some kind of trick? A spell to make me think your cat talks? Do you think I'm so stupid I'd fall for that?"

"I think you are stupider than that," Bella said. "You're a vampire. You've been around a long time. You've never heard a cat talk?"

Understanding dawned in Damon's dark blue eyes. "It's not the growling cat. It's you. You're Zoe's familiar."

"A very powerful familiar," Bella said. "I don't want to brag but I have dealt with Russians, so vampires do not scare me."

"Then you are a stupid cat. Vampires are much tougher than the Russian mob."

"I'm talking about the Russian aristocracy. We all

have our pasts and our demons, don't we? Mine go back
to the court of Catherine the Great. What about you,
Damon?"

"I am not talking to a cat," Damon stated coldly.

"You've already been talking to her," Zoe pointed
out.

"I will give you thirty minutes to get the cameras
working," Damon said. "If not, I will be back."

"And we will bear the full brunt of your wrath,"
Bella mocked.

He lunged forward as if to grab the cat. Zoe instantly
moved to protect Bella but she had already put up a
protection shield.

"Thirty minutes." Damon's voice reflected his frus-
trated fury before he stormed out.

"What happened to not upsetting the vampire?" Zoe
asked Bella.

"He started it," Bella said.

Zoe was afraid he was going to end it as well.

Damon entered the All Nighter Bar and Grill and
headed for the premium bottle of blood kept in the re-
frigerated section beneath the bar. He tossed back a
glassful and immediately poured another.

He'd just been bested by a witch and her cat. Her
freaking *talking* cat. That was unacceptable.

The bar was empty aside from the owner, who
looked up from the steak he was finishing off. Nick's
mating with Daniella the half druid had resulted in
Nick being able to consume food, but he tended not to
do so in front of other vamps.

Damon knew all about Nick's situation. Having sex
with Daniella had changed Nick's world forever, and

not in some sappy sentimental way but in a matter-of-fact immortal life-changing way.

Damon couldn't imagine what he would have done in Nick's place. Would he be willing to increase his powers but decrease his life span? Because the reason Nick could eat that steak was that he was no longer immortal.

Sure, Nick would live longer than most mortals, as would Daniella. But he was forever changed.

Damon valued his own immortality. Would he have made the choice that Nick had? Doubtful. Very doubtful, as in no way.

Damon rarely paused long enough to think about things like this. He preferred action to introspection. He always had.

Did he miss being human? Not really. Did he miss eating a steak? Yes, but it wasn't worth the trade-off in his opinion.

Nick's choices and his relationship with Daniella were none of Damon's business unless they pertained to the security of Vamptown. Granted, he'd been hired after another outsider vamp named Miles Payne attempted to increase his own powers by kidnapping Daniella. When that plan failed, Miles had gone after Daniella in order to punish Nick, who had feelings for her.

Feelings were a vamp's downfall. Damon had no intention of following in Nick's footsteps. He had another path to travel and it didn't include falling for a female—witch, druid, or human.

"Did you fix the problem at the rental house?" Nick asked, shoving his empty plate aside and indicating Damon should join him.

Damon set his glass on the table with a noticeably irritated thud. "I told you witches were bad. They already messed up the surveillance system."

"Not the system, just the cameras in their house. And to be fair, I should have warned them about the security measures we take here in Vamptown," Nick said.

"They have no respect for authority. Allowing them to stay here is asking for trouble."

"Vamptown can survive two witches."

"And a talking familiar cat," Damon muttered.

"Really? I've heard of such things but never seen one. I'd like to see that."

Damon was not about to admit that the feline had threatened to put a spell on his privates. Humiliation fired his anger even more. His fangs emerged.

"She really got to you," Nick noted.

At first Damon thought Nick was referring to the cat, but then he realized Nick meant Zoe. "I don't like witches."

"You've made that clear. I assume you have your reasons?"

Damon nodded.

"Care to share them?" Nick asked.

Damon shook his head.

"Does it have something to do with you being a Demon Hunter?" Nick asked.

"It has everything to do with my being a Demon Hunter. A witch betrayed me not long after I was turned." Damon didn't like talking about that period of his afterlife, but even so, the memories were always there. The Civil War, or the War for Southern Independence as the southerners called it, was the most devastating war in American history, with nearly seven hundred thousand dead. A war that ripped families apart, including his own. His younger brother, Sam, had taken up the cause of the Confederacy while Damon had fought to preserve the Union. The ensuing bloodshed was something that stayed with him even when he'd left his humanity behind and become a vampire.

Damon could feel the muscles in his jaw clench. The Battle of Gettysburg had replayed in his mind millions of times. He'd had his doubts about the wisdom of the orders given by the men higher up the chain of command, but he'd been in no position to question them. Even so, he had no way of anticipating how bad it would be.

Nick interrupted his dark thoughts. "You were turned in the Civil War, right? The American one, not the English?"

Damon nodded.

"Is that when you became a Demon Hunter?"

Damon didn't like the attention being on him. "Yes. But you already know all this, don't you. I'm sure you had me checked out before you gave me the job of head of security."

"True," Nick said.

"Then why the inquisition?"

"I want to know how much your bad experience with that witch in your past is coloring your thoughts and decision making now," Nick said.

Damon didn't appreciate Nick's line of questioning. Damon wasn't the guilty party here. Zoe was . . . along with her witchy talking cat.

"My concerns are reality-based and specific to the current situation. Speaking of which, Zoe asked about the funeral parlor," Damon said.

Nick frowned. "What made her do that?"

"I don't know but I don't like it. How do we know she's not some kind of Trojan horse sent here to spy on us and gain access to our source of blood? She didn't even ask about our ability to tolerate daylight."

"Maybe she was afraid to ask questions," Nick said.

"She wasn't afraid to ask about the funeral home."

"What possible connection could she have to that place?" Nick demanded.

"To what place?" Daniella asked as she joined them.

"Your family's funeral home," Damon said. "What did you tell Zoe about it?"

"I only mentioned it in passing when I talked about growing up in this neighborhood without knowing I was surrounded by vampires."

"What exactly did you say?" Damon's voice reflected his impatience.

Daniella shrugged. "I don't remember exactly. I mentioned that my father and brother didn't have any druid blood. I didn't say I was adopted. I certainly didn't say anything about what's going on there."

"Did she ask you?"

"She may have. But not in a nosy kind of way," Daniella hurriedly added.

Damon rolled his eyes.

"I didn't tell her anything confidential. I don't even know all the details of how you process blood from the funeral home, and I really don't want to. It's not something I care to dwell on."

Daniella might not care to dwell on it, but Damon was well aware of Vamptown's special blood source. Doc Boomer, the vampire dentist/doctor/chemist, had developed a formula to revitalize the human blood they

received from the human-run funeral home. When he'd
first arrived in Vamptown, Damon hadn't believed their
claims that it was better than fresh, with additional
calcium for healthy bones, teeth, and fangs. Doc had
filtered out all the impurities. No germs, diseases, or
viruses. Not that it mattered, since vamps were immortal. But no one went looking for sickness. Even vamps.

Daniella's family was unaware of the side business
being run by the vamps, thanks to compelling when
required.

But Daniella knew. Not the details, as she'd said.
She knew enough, which was fine by Damon. Any additional info was on a need-to-know basis only.

Daniella eyed the empty plate in front of Nick.
"Weren't you supposed to save me some?"

"Let me make it up to you." Nick reached up and
pulled Daniella closer to kiss her with unabashed passion. She tumbled onto his lap with a laugh.

Damon had to restrain himself from rolling his eyes
at their public display of affection. He refused to imagine tugging Zoe onto his lap and kissing her. Instead he
kept his mind on business.

"I know Zoe's grandmother is a friend of yours,"
Damon told Nick. "But there are red flags showing up
on their very first day. First they use magic to block the
video camera feed, and then Zoe brings up the funeral
home. Did she ask you why we could tolerate daylight?" he asked Daniella.

"No. I think your hostility toward her threw her a
bit," Daniella admitted.

"Good." Damon wanted her thrown. He wanted her
thrown right out of Vamptown.

"I liked her," Daniella stated. "It was nice having someone a little unusual to talk to."

"You mean not human?" Damon said.

"The fact that she's a witch doesn't mean she's not human," Daniella said. "Does it?" She turned to Nick for confirmation.

Nick shrugged. "It's a bit of a gray area. I'm no expert on it."

"My point exactly," Damon said.

"And you are an expert on witches?" Daniella asked him.

"I'm an expert on how devious they can be." A century and a half ago, shortly after he was turned, Damon had ended up in New Orleans after the war. Eve Delacroix had been a dark-eyed beauty with a reputation for driving men beyond the edge of reason. But Damon wasn't a man any longer. He was an immortal vampire and a Demon Hunter, turned by powerful vampire Demon Hunter Simon Howell himself.

Simon had told Damon that he'd chosen him from the bloodied battlefield in rural Pennsylvania because of his courage in battle. Despite having been shot several times in the arm and shoulders, Damon had kept moving forward until his leg was nearly blown off and he'd collapsed. He was stubborn that way. He wasn't one to give up easily.

Damon had done the same thing with Eve. He'd been sure that he was the one who could win her. He hadn't known she was a witch at first, but even when he discovered that fact he hadn't been in any way unsure of his ultimate success.

She had been a hot seductress, well versed in the

erotic arts and acts. But she ended up betraying him in the worst possible way.

So, no, Damon didn't like witches. Didn't trust them. Didn't want them around.

Daniella reluctantly hopped up from Nick's lap. "I've got to get back to work. I really didn't get the feeling that Zoe is devious."

Before Damon could make a scathing reply, they were joined by Neville Rickerbacher, Vamptown's resident vamp super-nerd. He was a computer genius and a stock market whiz. Damon knew that Neville and his elite team made most of the money that kept Vamptown going using shrewd investments. Neville was also in charge of the neighborhood's surveillance system.

"The cameras are back online," Neville told them. "But they are now broadcasting Animal Planet. Here, look." He showed them his tablet.

Damon's growl made Neville shiver nervously. "Wait, now it's back to normal. Nope, back to Animal Planet."

"Still think she's not going to be any trouble?" Damon asked Nick. "I gave her half an hour to get the cameras going again, and this is her response."

"Zoe admitted she spelled the cameras?" Nick said.

"Her grandmother did it," Damon said.

"Well, that's another matter entirely," Nick said.

"Why?" Damon said. "What difference does it make which witch made trouble?"

"Come on, Damon. In the big picture, how bad is this minor thing? After all, Irma didn't know that the cameras were ours. Give her and Zoe a chance."

"How many chances do you plan on giving her?" Damon demanded.

"As many as it takes," Nick said.

Damon had no intention of being that generous.

"You couldn't have put up the protective spell sooner?" Zoe asked Bella. "As in when Damon pushed us against the wall?"

"No, I couldn't, because it's been decades since I'd been in such close contact with a man. You have no idea what that's like. I couldn't resist having that hot vampire body pressed against me. It felt sooo good," Bella purred.

"You've been a familiar long enough to know what your job is." Zoe shoved her dark hair away from her face in exasperation. "You're supposed to help me, protect and guide me."

Bella yawned daintily before replying, "He didn't kill you so what's the problem?"

"The problem is that you didn't have my back."

"The wall was at your back. He was against your front. And I threatened him later in the conversation. Vampires value their private parts," Bella said.

"How do you even know a spell like that? Most familiars—"

"We've already established that I am not like most familiars," Bella interrupted her to say. "As for the spell, we had Russian vampires at court who could get nasty and I had to use it once or twice."

"I need your help," Gram called from the back bedroom.

Zoe entered the room to find several spell books spread out on the bed.

"I can't remember how to undo the spell I did on the cameras." Gram sounded flustered.

"It's not in the family Book of Spells?"

Gram shook her head. "Just the standard one, which I tried." She opened the well-worn old book and recited the spell again.

What was done before,
Be done no more.

"Are you sure that didn't work?" Zoe said.

Gram nodded. "It's not specific enough. Maybe it's in here." She reached for a thin calfskin volume with gilded edges. "I don't remember seeing this one before."

"Gram, wait!"

But she'd already opened the book. A rush of cold dank air hit them along with a howl.

Zoe helped Gram immediately snap the book shut.

"That didn't sound good," Gram said.

"That definitely didn't sound good," Zoe agreed. The hair on the back of her neck stood up as she inhaled the smell of must and magic. Dark magic. Dangerous magic. "What just happened?"

"I have no idea." Gram reached for the book again.

Zoe stopped her. "Don't touch it." Even closed, the volume glowed with an unholy fiery light. "I've got a bad feeling about this."

She'd no sooner said the words than there came a fierce pounding on the front door. She opened it a moment later to find a furious Damon, who looked ready to kill as he growled, "What did you do?"

Chapter Five

"You gave us half an hour to get the cameras back up," Zoe reminded him even as she backed away from his obvious fury. "According to my watch we still have five minutes left."

"I'm not talking about the freaking cameras." Damon's voice was dangerously grim. "I'm talking about the demons."

"Demons? What demons?"

"The ones that just appeared out of the blue in the tunnels."

"I don't know anything about any tunnels or demons." Which was true, although her witch's sixth sense was warning her that this could be a result of the dark magic they'd inadvertently experienced a few minutes ago by opening that mysterious book.

"Oh my stars," Gram said as she joined them. "I sure hope it wasn't something I did."

Damon turned his attention to Gram. "What did you do?"

"Don't yell at her," Zoe said, rushing to her grandmother's side and putting a protective arm around her.

"Maybe it was the book," Gram whispered.

"What book? Show it to me," Damon demanded. "Before I break my promise to Nick about killing witches."

"It's on my bed," Gram said, heading down the hallway past the stairs to her bedroom.

Zoe bumped into Gram as she abruptly stopped, which made Damon bump into Zoe. He set her aside like a nuisance in his way. "Where is it?" He reached for their family Book of Spells but Zoe got there first and snatched it up to press it protectively against her chest—no easy feat, as the book was heavy and nearly a foot thick.

"No outsider is allowed to touch our family's Book of Spells," Zoe said. "It will burn your fingers off."

Damon didn't appear at all intimidated. "They'll grow right back."

"No, they won't. Besides, this wasn't the book Gram was talking about."

"That's right," Gram said. "It was a spell book I didn't recognize. But it's not here where I left it. Maybe it fell off the bed."

Zoe knelt down and looked under the bed. To her surprise, Damon instantly joined her on the floor. Both Morticia and Bella were under the bed, their fur standing on end.

"Demons," Bella growled.

Damon reached for the cat, but the protection spell prevented him from touching her.

"What did your damn cat do?" he demanded.

"Not me. The book," Bella said.

"Did someone come in here while we were in the other room and take the book?" Zoe asked Bella.

"It disappeared in a puff of smoke," Bella said.

"Bring it back," Damon ordered the cat.

"I didn't take it." Bella moved farther under the bed. "Demons."

Damon hauled Zoe to her feet. "I don't care if it was your possessed cat or you or your zany granny, but I want to see that book right now."

"Trust me, I want to see it, too," Zoe said.

"Trust you?" he scoffed. "Not in my immortal lifetime."

"Listen, the feeling is mutual."

"The difference is that I'm not the one who called forth a pack of demons."

"All my grandmother did was open the book. She didn't do anything else." Zoe tried to wiggle free. "And neither did I."

"Me neither," Bella called out from under the bed.

Damon held Zoe in place, his hands sliding down from her shoulders to her arms, thereby shackling her. "We could have seen what happened here if you hadn't messed with the surveillance cameras. But now there is no proof of what you did or did not do. How convenient for you."

"This is not convenient at all," she retorted.

"Damn right. Demons are not convenient. Do you know what they do? They possess humans and kill. They suck the brains out of witches." He tapped his index finger against her temple.

"Actually I think sucking brains is a zombie thing, not a demon thing, but I could be wrong," Gram said.

Seeing the look of fury growing in Damon's eyes,

Zoe said, "Gram, why don't you wait for us in the hall-way."

"Stay where you are. Both of you," Damon growled.

He made Zoe so nervous, her legs were shaking. She found the strength to pull away from him, but it took such effort that she ended up bouncing on the edge of the bed.

Damon towered over her but she didn't have the strength yet to stand and confront him again.

Placing a hand on either side of her, he bent over until his mouth was mere centimeters from hers. "You have no idea what you are dealing with here, little witch."

Staring him in the eye, she said, "I'm dealing with a pissed-off vampire falsely accusing me of calling forth demons." She tried to shove him away. It was like trying to move a tank. She ducked under his arm and stomped to the other side of the room.

Okay, it was more like a scurry than a stomp, but at least she'd put some much-needed distance between them.

"Whatever happened, it was an accident," she said.

"Fix it," he ordered, stalking her as she moved around the room.

"We need the book to do that," she told him.

"Find it."

"I don't even know who took it."

"So you say. But maybe you have it stashed here in the house."

He started dumping out the dresser drawers that Gram had filled with her unpacking spell earlier.

"You have no right—" Zoe said.

He cut her off. "I have every right. If you get in my way, you will both be banished from Vamptown immediately. Don't bother calling Nick," he said as Zoe reached for her smartphone. "He's already agreed with me on this matter. And get these surveillance cameras working again," he snapped as he dumped more belongings on the floor.

Looking nervous and remorseful, Gram said, "I'm working on it."

"Work harder. Meanwhile tell me what this book looks like."

"It's beige calfskin with gilded edges along the pages. It's not as thick as our family Book of Spells," Gram said. "We only saw the outside of the book. Once we heard the howl, I snapped it shut again. I don't know what's inside."

Without speaking, Damon moved on to the living room, which he ransacked with the same disrespect that he'd displayed in Gram's room.

His search was meticulous. Beneath furniture, behind it, inside couch cushions.

He went through the kitchen with similar thoroughness. There wasn't much to go through, as Gram hadn't unpacked those boxes yet. Damon ripped them open with vamp speed, rummaging through them.

"Be careful. That belonged to my mother." Zoe grabbed the ceramic soup tureen out of his hands.

He grabbed it back and tore the lid off to check it inside.

Finally satisfied that he'd covered the main floor, Damon announced, "The upstairs is next."

Zoe tried to get there before he did but could not compete against his freaky fast speed. He'd already wrecked half her workroom by the time she walked in.

Using his arm, he swept her soaps from the shelves, dumping them all on the floor.

"Be careful," she cried out as she saved a bottle of rare and very expensive essential oil from shattering on the floor.

It took a moment or two for her to realize that she'd used magic to prevent the bottle from breaking, freezing it in midair.

Damon noticed her relapse immediately. "So you don't use magic, huh? What do you call that?"

"Necessity." She wished she could freeze *him* in place.

"What's this?" He reached for an old book sitting in the middle of her worktable.

This time she didn't stop him. He swore as his fingertips were singed. "Shit!"

She opened the book for him. "It is an ancient book of recipes for making soap and lotions." Pointing to the botanical drawings, she said, "This book is much thinner than the one you are looking for."

Unconvinced, he made her show him every single one of the thirty-three pages.

"I can read Latin," he warned her.

"Goodie for you."

Damon speed-read all the concoctions written on the pages before moving on. She put her foot down when he confiscated her laptop.

"Give that back!"

"After our tech geek has checked it out," Damon said.

"There is personal stuff on there."

"Too bad."

Zoe felt tears coming to her eyes. She'd written her thoughts after her mom's death in a journal she'd kept on her laptop. The idea of someone else reading them was like being stripped bare for all to see.

A powerful and dark hatred for the vampire was taking hold deep within her. She'd never felt this way before. Not even when her ex-fiancé had dumped her.

No, this emotion was fierce and incredibly violent. She narrowed her eyes at Damon's condescending smirk—and an instant later the lamp fixture above his head burst into flames and fell to the floor, missing him by inches.

"Shit!"

"Kill the vampire." The words came from her lips, but the voice wasn't hers. "Death to the Demon Hunter."

She was levitating above the floor.

"Don't kill her!" Gram cried from the doorway. "She's been possessed by a demon, but I can fix it."

Pointing to Zoe, Gram recited the spell.

By forces of day and spirits of night
By solemn vow and powers strong
When evil lurks or harm be in sight
Be you safe from all evil forever long.

Zoe collapsed into Damon's arms.

"What happened?" she asked shakily.

"You just tried to kill me with a light fixture," Damon said.

She looked for confirmation to Gram, who nodded.

"What do you remember?" Gram asked.

Zoe said, "I felt this intense hatred toward—"

"Me." Damon finished her sentence.

She tried to scoot away from him, but he was not letting her go.

"I don't remember much after that," she said. "I heard Gram casting a spell."

Damon freed one hand to show her his smartphone. "The camera caught it all."

She stared at herself levitating off the floor. Shivering at the weird and terrifying image, she whispered, "That's never happened to me before."

"You probably never sounded like Darth Vader before, either," Damon said.

"I could hear someone talking but it wasn't my voice." She nervously looked around her workroom. "Where did the demon go?"

"Probably back to the tunnels. The demon slipped into your mind and fed off your anger and hatred for me."

"I don't hate you."

"Don't you?"

"No, I just intensely dislike you."

He let her go. "The feeling is mutual."

"Then why didn't the demon possess you instead of me?"

"You're a weak witch."

She wasn't sure if she should be insulted by his comment or not. She only knew for sure that she'd *never* had anything like this happen to her before. And that was saying something. After all, she was a witch and had been exposed to magic since birth, but nothing this dark and dangerous. Demonic possession was never something she'd ever worried about . . . until now. She was trying not to freak out, but it wasn't easy.

"I'm a Demon Hunter," he continued.

"I thought you were a vampire."

"I am. I am also a Demon Hunter."

"So maybe the demons are here because of you. I have no previous experience with demons. Gram doesn't, either. This is totally unfamiliar territory for me," she said.

"I didn't set any demons free," Damon said. "The two of you did that, recklessly disregarding the consequences. You don't know a damn thing about demons. One just took possession of your mind and there was nothing you could do to prevent it."

"That won't happen again," Gram said. "I cast a protection spell for her."

"I have to cast the same spell to protect you," Zoe told her grandmother.

"Do you remember the words?" Gram asked before repeating them for her.

Zoe nodded and recited the spell. So much for her claim that she would not be using magic here in Chicago. She could see the disdain in Damon's eyes, calling her out for being a liar.

She tried telling herself that her magic wasn't intentional or premeditated, but the truth was that she could have let that bottle of essential oils break. It would have cost her monetarily. But now that demons were involved everything was up for grabs, including her vow to be magic-free.

"We can give you a protection spell, too, Damon," Gram said.

He appeared insulted by her offer. "I don't need protecting."

"I still don't understand," Zoe said. "What was the demon trying to accomplish?"

"To possess you in order to use your magic, turning it dark and aiming it at eliminating me," Damon said.

Feeling sick to her stomach, Zoe wrapped her arms around her middle. "What do you mean 'possess'? Do you mean like spirits did to Whoopi Goldberg in the movie *Ghost*?"

Damon said, "They didn't possess your entire body. The demon slithered into your mind."

She clapped her hand on her ear. "You mean they entered through my ear and took over my brain?"

He shook his head. "Not literally speaking, no. We're not exactly sure how they do mind possessions."

"You're safe now," Gram reassured Zoe. "I should have put a protection spell over you the moment demons were mentioned, but I wasn't thinking straight."

"Were you thinking straight when you let the demons out?" Damon said.

"All I did was open the cover of a spell book."

Instead of answering, Damon completed his search of Zoe's work area while Gram removed the remains of the broken light fixture with a wave of her hand.

"If the book really is lost, don't you have a spell to return it?" he said.

"If it was lost, yes," Gram said. "But it was taken."

"And there's no spell for returning stolen property? I find that hard to believe," Damon said.

"I find this entire thing hard to believe," Zoe said. "First I find out we've moved into a neighborhood full of vampires—and now we've got a bunch of demons thrown into the mix."

"Thanks to your grandmother," Damon pointed out.

"It was an accident," Gram said. "Just like——"

Zoe cut her off. "It was an accident. Period."

But Damon was not easily distracted. "Just like what?"

"Nothing," Gram said.

Zoe nodded her approval of her grandmother's answer. Unfortunately Damon caught her.

"Did you release demons in Boston, too? Is that why you were booted out?" he demanded.

"We were not booted out. We were semi-banished. That's different."

"Why?"

"Why is it different?"

"No, why were you banished?"

"Semi-banished," she corrected him. "I told you earlier at the bar and grill that there was an incident with a motivational speaker."

"That's not enough to make your coven banish you. There had to be another reason," Damon said.

"I never said our coven banished us," Zoe pointed out.

"No one else would have the authority," Damon said. "The mayor couldn't banish you, as much as he might want to. Same for the governor."

"They both forgave me," Gram said.

"For what?" Damon demanded.

"Nothing."

Zoe was getting the mother of all headaches. Probably an aftereffect of demon possession. She'd have to Google that.

She had no doubt that Damon's ransacking her workplace had also ramped up her stress level.

Then there was her hormone level, which Damon had also knocked out of whack. There was no way she should find him the least bit attractive after his behavior. So why was she drawn to him? Had that demon messed with her mind?

"What are the aftereffects of demon mind possession?" she asked Damon.

"Most don't survive long enough to have aftereffects," he said.

"If that is supposed to make me feel better—"

He interrupted her. "It isn't." He looked around with those killer dark blue eyes of his. "Where's your bedroom?"

Her jaw dropped. Okay, just because she'd been thinking he was sexy didn't mean she wanted him in her bedroom.

Without waiting for her reply, he opened a door to his right. Bingo. Her bedroom. With her bed, a dresser, and nothing else.

He stepped inside and the sight of him, so dark and dangerous, beside her snowy white bed was strangely arousing. Was he trying to bring out her dark side the same way the demon had? Well, not *exactly* the same way, obviously, since Damon wasn't messing with her mind. Gram's protection spell guaranteed that.

But protection only went so far. Was Zoe really safe from a devilishly handsome vampire with a sardonic smile and bedroom eyes?

Probably not.

Chapter Six

The witch had only been in Vamptown a few hours and already all hell had broken loose. Damon couldn't believe it when they'd referred to a book of spells releasing demons. He'd been searching for just such a book for over 150 years.

He'd honestly started to doubt its very existence. Of course, the witches could just be scamming him. Having the book disappear was a little too convenient in his opinion.

Damon looked around Zoe's bedroom. There was a bed, a dresser, and nothing else. "Where is the rest of your stuff?"

She pointed to the closet.

He opened the door where her clothes were neatly hanging. She apparently liked red and black, as those colors were predominant. Maybe that was a witch thing.

"You've unpacked a lot in the short time you've been here. There were no moving trucks outside the house today. Obviously you used magic."

She glared at him with those witchy blue/green eyes of hers but said nothing.

"Or your grandmother did," he said.

He saw the truth flash across her face. "Keep my grandmother out of this," Zoe said.

"Hard to do when she's unleashed a horde of demons upon us."

"I told you. It was an—"

"Accident. Yeah, so you say. For all I know you could have put a cloaking spell on the book to make it invisible to me."

"Why would we do that?" she said. "Why would we want a horde of demons running around?"

"I don't know. But I will find out."

Just for the hell of it, he tried to compel her by looking deep into her eyes and softly saying, "Tell me the truth."

To his surprise, she did. "We did not intentionally call upon any demons. Your eyes are too sexy for words. So is your mouth."

Zoe clasped her hand to her mouth and slammed the door shut into her mind.

So she'd allowed him momentary access to her thoughts. She'd even spoken them aloud. But now when he tried to compel her again, he was met with the blank wall he'd expected from a witch.

He moved closer. "So you think I'm sexy?"

Zoe backed up until she bumped into her bed. "That's irrelevant."

"Not to me." He placed his hands on her shoulders. He could feel the warmth of her skin beneath his fingers. The sound of her heartbeat echoed in his mind.

The sexy swish of her pulse compelled him to lift her hand to his mouth. He licked her wrist.

He expected her to yank her hand away and stare at him with fear. Instead she grabbed his hand and brought it to her mouth and licked *his* wrist.

The feelings throbbing through him were powerful and totally new. Yes, he'd wanted women before. He'd wanted their blood. He'd wanted to bury his fangs in their veins and draw sustenance. He'd wanted to bury his body in theirs and have raw sex. But he'd never felt this fiery need. Not since New Orleans.

Dropping her hand, he pulled his hand from her tempting mouth and demanded, "Why did you do that?"

"Why did you?" she countered. "I'll tell you why. Because you wanted to intimidate me. And no way would I let you do that."

"So you thought you'd intimidate me?" He wasn't about to tell her that while she hadn't accomplished that, she had incited an unexpected reaction in him. "That will never happen."

"Never say never." Zoe flipped her long dark hair away from her face and sauntered out of her bedroom.

Damon was only a few yards from Zoe's house when the first demon attacked him, swooping down from the roof's gutter. Damon swiveled with vamp super speed and noted the look of hatred in the being's bulging red eyes before he buried his demon dagger in his assailant's throat. Quickly yanking the dagger out, he watched as the demon dissolved in a fiery cloud of sulfuric smoke.

The light color of the scales and the lack of horns on

his attacker indicated the demon had been a recent inductee into hell and not a long-term member.

Damon made it to the street before another demon flew out from beneath a parked car and latched his claws into Damon's leg. Slime slithered from the demon's putrid mouth as he tried to take a chomp out of Damon. This demon was still light in color but had horns, although they were nothing to brag about. Damon told him so before thrusting his dagger into his assailant's throat.

He barely had time to remove his dagger from that demon before another attacked. Blood streamed down Damon's leg as he fought this much stronger demon. One swipe of the demon's arm and Damon was sent flying onto the hood of a black Mercedes.

"That's going to leave a dent," Damon noted.

"Death to the Demon Hunter," the hatemonger proclaimed.

Damon leapt off the hood before the demon could pin him down.

Smacking his lips, the demon ran his claws through the pool of vampire blood that Damon had left behind on the car. The beast's eyes glowed red with rage as blood dripped from his claws back onto the car. He rushed Damon a millisecond later.

Damon was ready for him. He threw his dagger with expert precision. The demon was dead before he reached Damon.

Removing his weapon, Damon turned to find an older woman sitting across the street on the bench at the bus stop on the corner. He could tell by her scent that she was human. He could tell by the look on her face that she was utterly horrified. He rushed to her side to compel her.

Looking deep into her terrified eyes, Damon said, "Forget what you just saw."

She nodded her blind compliance.

While she did so, he instantly returned his dagger to its sheath. Demons had no blood in their bodies, but vampires did. Again using vamp speed, he yanked off his shirt and wiped his blood from the hood of the Mercedes. As he'd predicted, his landing on the hood had left a dent. Nothing he could do about that.

He was really pissed now. Yes, vampires were fast healers, but that didn't mean that wounds and broken bones didn't hurt at first. He cracked his left arm back into place.

Turning his head, he checked on the woman on the bench. The bus stopped and she meekly climbed aboard and took a seat.

Okay, so the human was taken care of, but the demons were another matter. And all because of the damn witches.

Damon watched the torn flesh in his leg quickly heal as he walked into the bar and grill and headed straight for the secret panel housing the voice-activated security system.

"To the Vamp Cave," he said. A hidden door opened, allowing him to enter the underground room filled with the latest cutting-edge computer equipment and flat screens displaying camera footage from numerous sites. This was Vamptown's communications and security center.

"I was attacked by three demons just between Zoe's

house and here. I had to compel the lady at the CTA bus stop to forget what she just saw," Damon said.

"I know." Nick gave him a look of approval. "I saw. You kicked some demon ass."

"That may be, but I couldn't find the spell book that unleashed the demons," Damon said before tossing his bloody shirt into the trash and tugging on a plain black T-shirt from the stash he kept in his desk drawer. Turning to Neville, he said, "Have you isolated the demons yet? How many are we talking about?"

"Four got out before we locked down the tunnels, lowering lead walls between sections."

"I killed three," Damon noted. "So that leaves one still on the loose. What about in the tunnels?"

"There are three down there at the moment," Neville replied. "That number has remained stable."

"Do we have any visuals on them?" Damon said.

Neville shook his head. "They destroyed the surveillance camera."

"Just like the witches did," Damon said.

Nick pointed to the screens. "They didn't destroy them. Irma temporarily incapacitated the cameras. I should have told her about the surveillance at our meeting. The cameras there are working again now."

Which meant that Zoe's grandmother must finally have remembered how to undo the spell she'd put on the cameras. At least that was one thing accomplished.

Damon returned his focus to the blank screen, which would have displayed a portion of the tunnel. "If we have no visuals, how do we know the number of demons in the tunnels has remained stable?"

"Heat sensors," Neville said. "State of the art. Installed just a few months ago."

At that point Pat Heller, the oldest resident of Vamptown given his claim that he'd been turned four hundred years ago, joined them. Pat was also a body artist and owner of Pat's Tats next door to the bar. With his gray hair held back in a ponytail, the vamp was commonly mistaken for George Carlin before he passed away. Or so Pat claimed, being pleased with the comparison as Carlin was Pat's favorite comedian. Since vampires remained the same as when they were turned, Pat's hair remained long and prematurely gray as it had been when he'd been bitten back in the 1600s.

Personally, Damon got more of a hippie vibe from Pat than a comedian vibe although the vamp did have his funny moments.

Looking around, Pat shook his head. "I leave for one weekend for the Vamps in Vegas conference and I come back to mayhem. I have to say I wasn't that surprised to hear we've got demons now. I was wondering when that would happen."

"What do you mean?" Damon demanded.

"You're a Demon Hunter. Why would you come to Vamptown to be our head of security? We haven't had any demons in these parts for decades," Pat said. "Half a century or more."

Damon resented his insinuation. "So you think I'm responsible for the demons showing up here?"

"Not responsible. No," Pat said, before adding, "But you are part of the puzzle somehow."

"What puzzle?" Damon said.

Pat shrugged. "I don't know yet. But it involves you and the witches."

"I only met them today."

"I realize that," Pat said. "But that doesn't mean

there isn't some kind of cosmic connection between you and Zoe."

"The only connection is that her grandmother released demons and I need to destroy them," Damon said.

"These aren't run-of-the-mill demons," Neville said, inserting himself into the conversation before nervously pushing up his glasses higher onto the bridge of his nose. Bits of duct tape held the earpiece together.

"How would you know?" Damon demanded. "As Pat said, Vamptown hasn't seen demons in half a century or more. You were turned forty years ago."

"I wasn't speaking from personal experience," Neville said, "but from their energy level and heat levels. They won't be easy to defeat."

"Demons never are," Damon said. "But that hasn't stopped me before. It won't stop me now. I need to get my hands on that book that released them."

"How do you propose to do that?" Pat asked.

"By sticking to the witches like white on rice," Damon said.

Pat's partner, Bruce, entered the Vamp Cave, holding a tray with two dainty teacups filled with blood. There was nothing dainty about Bruce. The vamp was built like a brick outhouse. Nevertheless he was a self-proclaimed fashionista. Pat had once described him to Damon as part Hulk and part Armani.

"Tea time," he cheerfully announced. Bruce's occupation before being turned was that of a clown, which made him happy all the time. Or maybe he'd been born that way. Damon wasn't sure. He only knew that he'd never met anyone as upbeat as Bruce. It wasn't a character trait Damon was fond of in the least. Not that

Damon had anything against Bruce. He just wished the vamp wasn't such a ray of sunshine.

"So what are we talking about?" Bruce asked as he handed one teacup to Pat and took the other for himself before carefully setting the tray down.

"Demons."

"Great." Bruce grinned. "*Demons* or the straight-to-DVD sequel *Demons Two*?" Seeing everyone's confused look, he said, "You're talking about movies, right?"

"No, we're talking about the demons in the basement," Damon said. "Or the tunnels, to be more accurate."

Bruce leaned forward with excitement. "Real ones?"

"Yeah."

"Shut the door," Bruce said.

"We have," Damon said. "The demons are locked in the tunnel. For now."

"For now?" Bruce repeated, suddenly nervous. "What do you mean by that?"

"They will find a way to get out sooner or later," Damon warned.

"How soon?" Bruce bit his lip.

"There's no telling, which is why I have to find that damn book," Damon said. "The witches are the key."

"There are two of them and only one of you," Bruce said.

"Which means you'll need help when you move in with them," Pat told Damon.

"Who said anything about moving in with them?" Damon said. The truth was that he hadn't actually formulated a plan yet. He'd been too busy fighting demons on the street and trying to locate the rest of their putrid kind.

Pat raised one gray eyebrow. "Did you have another plan in mind?"

"No." Damon had to admit that moving in made sense. Keeping closer tabs on the witches was the only way to monitor the situation. Clearly relying on the surveillance cameras was not sufficient—things could change in an instant.

"At least Zoe already knows you are a vamp," Pat said. "That should be helpful."

"Helpful for what?"

"Dealing with her," Pat said.

"Did you bring Zoe's laptop so I can go over it?" Neville asked.

"No. I was sidetracked when she tried to kill me." Seeing their startled looks, he explained. "She was possessed by a demon at the time."

Nick frowned. "And you're only telling us this now? You didn't think it was worth mentioning before?"

"It's been taken care of," Damon said. "Her grandmother put a protection spell on her and Zoe did the same."

"Who's watching the witches now?" Nick said.

Damon pointed to the screen. "I sent Tanya to stay with them."

"Heaven help us all," Bruce said.

Chapter Seven

"So you're a witch, huh?" Tanya gave Zoe the kind of dismissive look that the Dark Queen specialized in throughout the movie *Snow White and the Huntsman*. Tanya had been giving Zoe that look since Gram had made the mistake of inviting her in. After that, Gram had quickly returned to her own room, leaving Zoe to deal with their "guest." "Show me something witchy."

"So you're a vampire, huh? Show me something vampy," Zoe countered.

Tanya snarled and bared her fangs.

"Okay, then." Zoe took a quick step back. "That was fun."

"What's the matter?" Tanya taunted. "Are you afraid of me?"

"No," Zoe lied. "That's not it at all."

"Then why did you step away?"

"I don't mean to be rude but you could use some breath freshener," Zoe said.

"Like I'd believe anything a witch told me."

"You don't know a thing about me," Zoe said.

"I know all I need to know. If you think you can sell your wares here in Vamptown, you are sadly mistaken. I'm the owner of Tanya's Tanning Salon."

"Tanning beds are dangerous."

"So are vampires." Tanya bared her fangs again.

"Maybe you'd like to try one of my moisturizers . . . ?" Zoe suggested.

Tanya was highly offended. "Vampires don't age. We don't get wrinkles. That's why my boyfriend turned me. To keep me beautiful and young. So don't think you have a chance with Damon."

"Damon?"

"That's right. Keep your witchy mitts off him."

Zoe recalled licking his wrist. Remembered the taste of his skin on her tongue. She replayed the moment she'd sat on her bed and he'd leaned over her. "What did he tell you?"

"Everything."

The fiend. Zoe wanted to kick his vampire butt. Damon had some nerve talking about her to this slutty female vampire.

Okay, so Zoe had no idea if Tanya actually was slutty, but she sure looked the type. Skinny but oozing sex in a tight tank top, spandex micro-mini, and stiletto black boots. And yes, given her librarian background, Zoe should know better than to judge a book by its cover. But if Tanya walked like a slut and quacked like a slut, Zoe felt justified in labeling her one. Besides, the female vampire had been rude since she walked in.

"If it was up to me, I'd let the demons get you," Tanya said, flipping her hair over a tanned shoulder. "Not that I'm really here to protect you. I'm here to make sure you don't do another witchy thing to make trouble. Damon sent me."

"You can have him," Zoe said.

"I don't need your permission to get Damon."

"Get him? I thought you said you already had him," Zoe challenged her.

"I lost Nick to a cupcake maker. I am not about to lose Damon to a witch."

"I already said I don't want him," Zoe assured Tanya.

"Yeah, right," Tanya scoffed. "Every woman wants Damon."

"Not the smart ones."

"Are you saying that I'm stupid?"

"I don't know you well enough to make a determination like that," Zoe said in her best demure voice.

"Well, I know you well enough to know that I don't like you," Tanya retorted. "You act like you're better than anyone else."

"You should be relieved that I'm not interested in Damon."

"It's not like you'd be any real competition," Tanya said. "I mean, look at you. There's no way you could compete with this." She pointed to her model-thin body. "Unless you used black magic."

"I don't do black magic."

"You're a witch. Witches do black magic."

"Not all witches."

"Maybe black magic doesn't work on vampires. I'll have to ask Pat about that."

"Who is Pat?" Zoe said.

"He runs Pat's Tats Body Art Salon and he knows everything."

"Is he a vampire, too?" Zoe asked.

"Of course."

"And a Demon Hunter like Damon?"

"No," Tanya said. "No one is like Damon."

Zoe's curiosity was aroused. "What do you mean by that?"

"He's special."

"Because he hunts demons? What made him get into that line of work?"

"Why do you want to know?" Tanya asked suspiciously. "Because you're a demon's BFF? Is that why you unleashed them?"

"I didn't even know demons existed until a few hours ago," Zoe said.

"Then you're the one who is stupid, not me."

"Maybe I am," Zoe muttered. She certainly didn't feel like she'd made a brilliant move here. She for sure had not landed somewhere safe and secure. No way. Instead it felt like she'd left one bad situation back in Boston for another one here in Chicago's Vamptown.

With her librarian background, Zoe was an excellent researcher. She should have learned more about their new location before moving. But there hadn't been time. They'd had to leave in a hurry and this mess was the result.

Zoe didn't like to hurry. She liked to be thorough and precise, although there had been times in her life when she'd taken a leap of faith. A very few times. And they'd all ended badly. Which should have been a warning about moving to Chicago.

But Zoe had thought she'd be leaving all that behind. Yes, she was still a witch. There was no leaving that behind. It was as much a part of her as her height or her long dark hair. Wait, she could cut her hair or dye it. But there was no changing the fact that she was a witch. She could change what she did with that ability, however.

The last time she'd taken a leap of faith, she'd hooked up with Tristin Winters. She'd fallen for him big time. As a professor specializing in the paranormal, he'd been comfortable in her world before he knew there was anything unusual about her, aside from her bicolored eyes.

He'd said he loved her. That she was the woman he'd been waiting for his entire life. Her mother, who'd still been alive when he'd proposed, had warned Zoe to take her time and not do anything rash like tell Tristin that she was a witch from a long line of witches.

No human was supposed to know.

But Zoe had trusted Tristin. She didn't see how she could say yes to his proposal if he didn't know the truth.

So she'd told him. He'd taken the news incredibly well. And he hadn't made any demands on her. Not at first.

Tristin had been subtle at first. He'd been solicitous and sweet. Concerned and candid.

No one outside of her family and her coven knew Zoe was a witch. She'd never said a word to anyone else. It's not like the admission was a great conversation starter. Besides, it broke the covenant of their coven to reveal to a human the fact that she was a witch.

Tristin got that. He understood her. Or so she'd thought.

He'd requested her help when there had been drastic cuts in funding for his department at the college. When he'd wanted her to help him in the stock market, he'd told her about his earlier trips to research the legends of

Nepal and how he wanted to donate money to build
schools there and help more of those in need.

She hadn't agreed at first but had eventually taken
another leap of faith and done it. A sign of how much
she'd trusted him. That trust had been completely mis-
placed.

She didn't learn that fact until her mother's death.
Even now, two years later, she missed her mother and
felt the loss like a huge void within her. The dark side
of magic had resulted in her mother dying and Zoe
vowing she'd never use magic again.

Tristin's compassion and understanding had only
lasted a few days before he wanted her to cast another
spell to increase his finances—for the greater good, he
claimed. When she refused, he'd been furious and she'd
broken their engagement.

Gram had stepped in and zapped Tristin with a
memory spell to make him forget the fact that Zoe was
a witch.

The entire experience had been a lesson very pain-
fully learned. When their coven had eventually learned
that Zoe had confided her secret to a human, they had
been very angry with her. Zoe had been put on probation. Gram's run-in with the motivational speaker had
been the last straw as far as the coven was concerned.
Like vampires, witches preferred to stay under the radar.
The Adams witches currently had two strikes against
them. A third could be disastrous. So they'd been sent
away.

Not that there was any danger of history repeating
itself. Zoe didn't trust Damon at all. Besides, he already
knew she was a witch. He clearly had a thing against
her kind. But if he knew that she'd once trusted her

deepest secret to a human, he would most likely accuse her of being willing to reveal the fact that she was living among vampires, insinuating that she couldn't keep her mouth shut. Which wasn't true.

It belatedly occurred to Zoe that the surveillance cameras were working. "We're being watched, aren't we?"

Tanya looked around. "By the demons?"

Zoe pointed to the surveillance camera in the corner of the living room up near the crown molding.

Was Damon watching? Had he heard what she'd said about him? She tried to remember exactly what she had said.

"So tell me more about these demons you unleashed," Tanya said.

"I didn't unleash them."

"Right. The story is that your grandmother unleashed them."

"It's not a story. Did Damon send you over here to interrogate me?" Zoe demanded.

"What if he did?"

"Then I'll tell you the same thing I told him."

"The same story you made up."

"It's not a story. It's the truth." The expression on Tanya's face clearly indicated that she didn't believe Zoe. "Why would I want demons hanging around?"

"Because you're a witch."

"And all witches call upon demons?"

"I don't know. You're the first witch I've ever met," Tanya admitted.

"Then let me be the first to assure you that witches do not want demons around. Witches aren't evil."

Tanya just gave her a look.

"Okay, so maybe somewhere on the planet there are evil witches," Zoe said. "But *we* aren't. We're good witches."

"Now you sound like Daniella."

"She's not a witch," Zoe said.

"I know that. But she plays the songs from that musical *Wicked* when she's making cupcakes."

"I met her. She seems very nice."

"I'm the one who saved her, you know. When she was trapped down in the tunnels, I mean. I escaped and got help."

"What do you know about the tunnels?" Zoe asked.

"That's where the demons are right now. Bootleggers trying to smuggle alcohol during Prohibition built the tunnels. Not that I was alive during that time. I was turned in the '50s. Not my fifties, obviously. I was turned at the peak of my beauty. You're already past yours."

"I'm only twenty-eight," Zoe said.

"Yeah, but your eyes are different colors. That's weird."

"This coming from a vampire who runs a tanning salon," Zoe retorted.

"I don't run it, I own it."

"Well, that's an entirely different matter then," Zoe said sarcastically.

"Right. I know. I'm a business owner. A member of the Vamptown Council," Tanya bragged. "And the other business owners are not happy that witches have moved in. We don't want your kind here."

For a second, Zoe thought the growl came from her before realizing it emanated from Bella, who'd strolled into the room to sit at Zoe's feet.

"I don't like cats," Tanya said. "They sneak up on you."

"I don't like vampires," Bella said. "They sneak up on you and suck you dry."

Tanya growled.

Bella growled louder.

Tanya tried to reach for Bella but the protection spell prevented her from touching the cat.

Bella stuck her dainty pink feline tongue out at Tanya.

Zoe was tempted to do the same.

"That's black magic right there," Tanya said, glaring at Zoe. "I say we torture you to get you to remove the demons and then we get rid of you. Or maybe the demons could kill you first and then Damon can kill them. I like that idea." Tanya paused to look at the camera and preen a bit. "It's brilliant. Right, Damon?"

"No, it's not," he said from right behind her.

Chapter Eight

"What are you doing here?" Zoe said.

"Preventing Tanya from torturing you," Damon said. "Although there is something to be said for a good catfight."

"I find that comment offensive," Zoe said.

"As do I," Bella said. "Although back in the day at court I was known to battle a lady-in-waiting or two. But those days are over."

"Her cat talks," Tanya said.

"I know," Damon replied.

"That's black magic," Tanya continued. "Evil stuff."

"It's not black magic," Zoe corrected her.

"Like you'd admit it if it was," Tanya scoffed. "You can't trust her."

"I already know that," Damon said.

His comment aggravated Zoe no end. Granted, it was nothing new. Damon had told her more times than she could count that he didn't trust her. But saying it in front of Tanya made it worse somehow.

Remembering what had happened the last time she'd

felt intense dislike, Zoe deliberately tried to play it cool. Yes, she had a protection spell over her now, but even so she had no desire to tempt fate. Being possessed by a demon and levitating once was one time too many in her book.

If only they could figure out what had happened to the mysterious spell book that had unleashed the demons in the first place. But it was hard for Zoe to concentrate when she had to deal with angry vampires in her living room. Her rented living room.

"Thanks for your help, Tanya, but I can take it from here," Damon said.

"I think I should stay," Tanya said. "What if she tries her black magic on you? It would be safer if you had someone like me to watch your back." She ran her fingers over his shoulder and down his back.

"I appreciate the offer," Damon said.

"I'll bet you do," Zoe muttered.

"But I'll be fine," Damon said. "I've dealt with demons, after all."

"What if she calls up a bunch of demons to attack you?" Tanya said.

"I'll hack their hearts out," Damon said,

"And hers, too?" Tanya pointed to Zoe.

"Sure," Damon said.

"You and what army?" Bella growled.

"That cat of hers is dangerous," Tanya warned him. "Maybe she's really a demon in a cat's body."

"And maybe you're a demon inside a vampire's skeletal body," Bella shot back.

Tanya showed her fangs.

Bella yawned before lifting her left paw to daintily wash her face.

"We don't have time for this right now," Damon told Tanya. "Leave."

"This isn't over," Tanya hissed before stomping out on her four-inch-heeled boots.

Zoe wasn't sure if the female vampire was speaking to her or to Bella. Not that it mattered. Zoe knew that neither of them was on Tanya's buddy list. Zoe didn't know why Tanya was so upset with her. She could understand being miffed with Bella, but Zoe had tried to be polite. She'd even assured Tanya that she was welcome to Damon.

Which brought Zoe's attention back to Damon and the self-satisfied look in his dark blue eyes. "You heard our conversation, didn't you," she said.

"Of course I did," he replied. "I was standing right here."

"I meant before. Your cameras were spying on me."

"You seem to enjoy talking about me," Damon noted with a smirk.

"Tanya does. Not me."

"So you say."

"I told her she was welcome to you," Zoe reminded him.

"I know you did." He sent her a reprimanding look. "You shouldn't lie."

"I didn't lie," she shot back.

"Come on. We both know you did."

Zoe pulled her hair away from her face in exasperation before letting it fall loose again. "I do not know where that mysterious spell book went."

"I wasn't talking about the book."

"What then?" she said.

"You saying you're not interested in me."

"Conceited much?"

He grinned and shrugged.

His movement drew her attention to his broad shoulders. Damon might be sexy but he was definitely off limits. Okay, he was *definitely* sexy, and he got to her in ways she had not expected. Even now, she felt the spark between them. Maybe it was a vampire thing but she suspected it was a Damon thing. She didn't want to jump Nick and have sex with him the way she did with Damon.

She could tell by the knowing look in those damn bedroom eyes of his that he realized she was attracted to him, despite her best efforts to hide it.

She pointed to the camera in the corner. "We are not having this conversation."

"Fine." He leaned closer until his warm breath brushed her ear. "Talking about sex is overrated. Doing it is much better."

She stopped herself from giving a soft moan of excitement, but it took a lot of effort.

Damon abruptly stepped away. "Let's go back to the beginning. Why did you quit your job at the library?"

Zoe blinked. She was still recovering from him whispering about sex in her ear. "What?" She'd expected him to ask about the appearance of the spell book, not her past work history.

"You heard me."

"That's none of your business." Zoe used her best librarian voice. She was totally peeved that he'd used his seductive ways to distract her. She wondered what he'd do if she whispered something sexy in his ear.

"Ah, but it is. Everything about you is my business now that you've unleashed demons." He was looking at

her as if he wanted to consume her. Consume her as in
bite her and drain her of her blood or as in kissing her?
She couldn't be sure.

"You didn't like me even before that," she said.

"And I like you even less now."

His words hurt her. They shouldn't have. It was stupid to be upset. But she couldn't seem to help it. Was
she so vulnerable that the thought of anyone—even an
arrogant, albeit hot, vampire—disliking her made her
feel bad?

She should be glad he disliked her. She certainly
disliked him. Especially now that he'd said that. Fanta-
sizing about having sex with him in an erotic way
didn't mean she had to like him. In fact, it made her
like him less even if she wanted him more.

"Which is all irrelevant," Damon said. "Tell me why
you quit your job."

"Did your research tell you that I don't like being
bossed around?" she asked.

"I observed that much myself."

"How astute of you," she said sarcastically.

He smiled. "I thought so."

Zoe didn't want to tell him anything about her past,
her job, her ex-fiancé, or her mother's death. None of it.
Knowledge was power, and she didn't want him having
any more power over her than he already did. The sexual tension between them was hard enough to fight.
She didn't want to add anything personal to the mix.

"Things didn't work out for me at the library," she
said. "That's why I left."

"Your co-workers said that you seemed very happy
and that your resignation came out of the blue."

She felt violated by him questioning the people she'd

worked with at the library. Which wasn't really logical since he'd already gone through all her things in both her workroom and her bedroom. "My leaving the library had nothing to do with demons," she said.

"Why don't you let me be the judge of that?"

"Because I don't trust you."

"I don't trust you, either. What does that have to do with anything?" Damon said. "The bottom line here is that your grandmother's actions have put us all at risk. Accident or not. You owe me. You owe Nick. You owe all of the inhabitants of Vamptown."

Nothing like a ton of guilt to make Zoe break and start talking. "It was the books," she muttered.

He frowned. "The books?"

"Sometimes books talk to me. The characters come to life," she admitted. "Not because I did anything. It just happens spontaneously. But all of a sudden *all* the books in the library were talking to me at once. Screaming, screeching, and shrieking."

"What were they saying?"

"It wasn't like that exactly."

"Then what was it like?"

"Scenes came alive. I couldn't see characters but I heard thousands of voices reciting what was written inside their covers. It was deafening. Books would fly off the shelf and hit me."

"Sounds like you pissed them off," Damon said.

"I didn't do anything."

"Where have I heard that before?"

"It's the—"

"Truth. Right. Did someone else cast a spell to start the book attack?"

"No one in my family did."

"What about your ex?" Damon said.

"He's not a witch. Or a warlock."

"Maybe not, but he has studied magic and the history of witches very intensely. He's even written books about it."

Which was one of the reasons Zoe had confided in Tristin. She thought that he'd understand, given his background. And he claimed he had understood her and valued her and didn't think she was something bizarre or scary. She'd trusted him. A huge mistake on her part. Okay, enough about him. She had bigger problems to deal with now.

"Maybe you did something to aggravate some other witch in your coven and she retaliated with the book spell," Damon said.

"I don't aggravate others."

"You sure aggravated Tanya."

"That was your fault," Zoe said.

"Of course it was."

"She was staking her claim on you."

Damon eyes crinkled at the edges with something resembling laughter. His voice reflected more sarcasm than humor, though. "Vampires tend not to like talk of staking."

"Sorry," Zoe muttered.

"I don't belong to anyone," he said emphatically.

"Me either," Bella said from the couch, where she'd made herself comfy. "Oh, wait. I'm a familiar. So I guess I do belong to someone. I belong to Zoe. Right, I keep forgetting. I like my independence."

"Getting back to your former job—" Damon began.

Zoe interrupted. "I already told you everything. I don't intend to tell you anything else."

"What are you hiding?" Damon demanded.

Zoe didn't like sharing her issues. In fact, she hated it. She hadn't even told Tristin everything and she'd been engaged to him. No way was she baring her soul to a sardonic vampire who disliked her and distrusted her, even if he was as sexy as hell.

He obviously was accustomed to having his way with women. But she was no mere woman. She was a witch. A smart witch with a master's degree.

Okay, so nothing she'd learned in her library science classes had taught her how to deal with a surly hunky vampire. Too bad, so sad. Still, she was an Adams witch, and Adams witches . . . well, they did tend to get into trouble. But most of the time it was not their fault. And they usually were able to come up with a way out of the difficulties they were in.

Except for her mother. Even now, two years after her death, Zoe still didn't know all the details of what had happened that fateful night. She only knew that her mother had tried to cast a powerful spell and that something had gone terribly wrong. The doctors told Zoe her mother had died from a sudden cardiac arrest despite the fact that she had no prior signs of heart disease.

Gram had warned Zoe that digging deeper would put her at risk of suffering the same fate. Gram had also said that after losing her daughter, losing Zoe would end Gram's life. Then she'd cryptically added that these things had a way of taking care of themselves. And she'd sworn that no one else had taken Zoe's mother's life, that black magic was dangerous and deadly to anyone who attempted to harness its power.

Zoe wanted to ask Gram if there was any chance that demons had somehow played a role in Zoe's mother's death, but she hadn't had a moment alone to do so. Not that being alone would help when they were both under constant surveillance.

She refocused her attention on Damon, who was watching her closely.

"I already allowed you access to my thoughts for you to confirm that I had nothing to do with the demons being released. I did not have to do that."

"That was one brief flash."

"That's all it took. It was enough."

"Not enough to satisfy me," he said.

"I don't care about your satisfaction," she retorted.

He didn't say a word. He didn't have to. His look said it all. Suddenly it was all about sexual satisfaction. She pretended not to notice the erotic tension between them, but the heavy silence wrapped around her like a caress. She tried to shrug it off. When that didn't work she tried to be logical, but it was hard to think straight when Damon was standing so close and staring at her with those dark blue eyes of his.

She stubbornly refused to be the first to look away. This was one battle she was determined to win. Maybe if she imagined him more vulnerable, like in his underwear or completely nude.

Big mistake. She quickly turned those thoughts off. The images weren't as easy to erase. Once in her mind, they just stayed there.

She could do this. She could win this stare-off. She was a witch. Not that that seemed to be helping her any at the moment, and she wasn't about to use magic to help her win.

The corners of Damon's lips lifted slightly in that semi-smirk he was so good at giving her.

He was a vampire. Not to be trusted. He didn't like her. None of those things seemed to matter at the moment the way they should.

"Satisfied?" he asked in a husky voice that was both rough and sexy.

"Yes." She had to look away. She likened it to looking too long at the sun. She didn't want to go blind with desire or something. Maybe there was even a rule about not looking too long into a vampire's eyes. She'd have to Google that later.

"Well, I'm not satisfied."

"You both look ridiculous, staring into each other's eyes that way," Bella declared with a sniff. "You're old enough to know better. Especially you, Damon."

He growled at Bella.

Bella growled at him.

Zoe's stomach growled. Checking her watch, she noted that it was time for dinner.

She looked at Damon again, belatedly noticing that he'd exchanged the black shirt he'd worn earlier for a black T-shirt accentuating his broad shoulders, and that he was wearing black jeans instead of black pants. "You changed your clothes."

"That's right."

"Too bad I can't change mine."

"Why not?"

Zoe pointed to the camera. "Because those are everywhere."

"So turn the lights out."

"Aren't they equipped with special night-vision technology?"

"Yes."

"So turning of the lights wouldn't really help anything, would it?"

"You don't have to get so sensitive about it."

"I'm a former librarian who is now a soap maker," Zoe said. "I am not a stripper."

"Exotic dancer," he corrected her.

"I'm not that, either."

"I noticed that you left *witch* off your description of yourself. You are actually a witch who is a former librarian who is now a soap maker."

They were interrupted by a knock on the front door. Eager to avoid Damon, Zoe opened it immediately to find Nick standing on the doorstep. Zoe recognized his expression. She'd seen it a lot on Damon's face. It was the expression of a pissed-off vampire.

Great. Now she had *two* of them to deal with.

Chapter Nine

"I'm here," Nick announced curtly.

"Yes, you are. Is there a problem? Aside from the demons, I mean. Not that they aren't a problem." Zoe
paused to take a deep breath. "Are you here to evict us?"

Nick looked over her shoulder at Damon. "You
haven't told her?"

"I was getting around to it," Damon said.

"What's all this about?" Zoe demanded.

"Invite me in and I'll tell you," Nick said.

"I thought since you're the landlord, you could come
in anytime. I'm sorry. Come in."

"Where's your grandmother?" Nick asked.

"She got a headache when Tanya came so she went
to rest in her room."

"Tanya has that effect on some people," Nick said,

"A lot of them, I would think," Zoe muttered. Looking at Damon, she added, "That's probably why the two
of you get along so well. You make a perfect couple."

"We are *not* a couple," Damon denied.

"It's none of my business if you are."

"You're right. But we aren't."

Zoe shrugged. "If you say so."

"You could at least pretend to believe me," Damon said.

"Why should I?" she said. "You never pretend to believe me. Nick and Daniella are the ones who have been welcoming and polite."

"Daniella sends her regrets," Nick said. "She wanted to join us but I refused to allow it."

Zoe tried hard not to show it, but her feelings were hurt. "Why?"

"Too dangerous," Nick said.

"You think that my grandmother and I are dangerous?"

"I was referring to the threat of demons," Nick said.

"You think they'd come here?" Zoe said.

"They were already right outside your house a few hours ago," Nick said.

Stunned, Zoe stumbled backward and landed on the bottom step of the staircase. Now she was stunned *and* embarrassed. And scared. She'd opened the door before she knew that Nick was the one knocking. What if it had been a demon? Or two demons? Or a gang of them?

Yes, she did have a protection spell to keep her safe. She would rather not have to actually test its potency against demons, however.

Zoe accepted the hand Nick offered her. She stood and tried to look calm as she murmured her thanks for his courteous help. Unlike Damon, who stood there looking amused at her clumsiness.

"You didn't tell her about the demons attacking you?" Nick asked Damon.

"No, he didn't," Zoe replied.

"A couple of demons attacked me when I left. I took care of them," Damon said.

"What did they want?" Zoe said.

"To kill me," Damon said bluntly.

"They were after you?" she said.

He nodded.

"Not Gram and me?"

"You, too, probably. But they had to go through me first, and that didn't happen."

"Are there more out there?" Zoe tilted her head toward the front door.

"Probably," Damon said.

Nick was more forthcoming. "There is only one remaining demon unaccounted for. The rest are locked in the tunnels."

"The bootleggers' tunnels?" Zoe said.

"How do you know about those?" Damon demanded.

"Tanya told me." She nervously glanced around the hardwood floor. "Do those tunnels run under this house?"

Damon nodded.

Once again, Nick was the one who elaborated to soothe her panic. "But the demons are not locked in this portion of the tunnels. They are actually near the section beneath my bar and the dental clinic. I believe in keeping my friends close and my enemies closer."

"And which are we?" Zoe asked. "Friends or enemies?" She held up her hand before Damon could speak and shot him a quelling look. "I already know what your answer would be. I'm asking Nick."

"Friends," Nick said.

"Does that mean you're not here to evict us?"

"I thought I made that clear before."

"No, you didn't."

"We have company," Damon announced before pulling the front door open.

"I brought pizza!" Daniella said with such enthusiasm that Zoe grinned.

"That's great!" she said with equal excitement. She was starving.

"No, that's not great," Nick said even as Daniella came inside and headed for the dining room with the large pizza box in her hands. "I told you to stay home."

Daniella smiled at Nick, her cheerful demeanor unfazed by his disapproval. "I know you did."

"Then why are you here?"

"To introduce Zoe and her grandmother to Chicago-style deep-dish pizza and welcome them to the neighborhood," Daniella said.

"You already brought some of your delicious cupcakes earlier," Zoe said.

"Yes, but now it's dinnertime," Daniella said. "And I got to thinking . . . there is still at least one demon on the loose. I think I'd be safer here with you, Nick, than home alone in my little apartment." She cuddled against him and kissed him.

"That's disgusting," Damon said. Seeing Nick's angry expression, he explained, "I meant the cat jumping on the table."

"Is that the talking cat?" Nick asked.

"Wait, you have a cat that can talk? Really talk?" Daniella said.

"I'm not just a cat," Bella proclaimed. "I'm her familiar."

"And you shouldn't be on the table." Zoe hurried to lift her down.

"I smelled pizza," Bella said.

"Wow." Daniella was impressed. "Will you talk to me?"

"Bring me a cupcake next time," Bella said. "Chocolate is my favorite flavor. We can sit and have a nice chat. The tales I could tell you about Catherine the Great and her court."

Daniella's eyes widened. "You knew Catherine the Great?"

"I was one of her closest confidantes," Bella said.

"Were you her pet?" Daniella asked.

Bella's eyes narrowed with displeasure. "I was a countess, one of her ladies-in-waiting. I have never been anyone's pet. Although I wouldn't mind having Misha as my pet."

"Was he a Russian lord or count?" Daniella said.

"I was referring to the ballet dancer Mikhail Baryshnikov," Bella said. "I've never met him, but I would certainly like to."

"We are getting entirely off the subject here," Damon protested. "We need to discuss the security and surveillance issues for tonight."

"What are you talking about?" Zoe demanded.

"Nick and I will be spending the night here."

"Me too," Daniella raised her hand to add. "So you won't feel awkward about having two vampires watching over you as you sleep, Zoe. Not that they would actually be in your bedroom, right, guys?"

Vampire silence.

"They have a camera in my bedroom," Zoe said.

"How am I supposed to sleep knowing that I'm being watched? How am I supposed to put on a nightgown or pajamas with them watching me?"

"The cameras can't see in the dark," Daniella said,

"They are equipped with night-vision technology, which turns things green," Damon said.

"Like the witch in *Wicked*," Zoe said.

" 'They called one witch good and one witch wicked,' " Daniella quoted from the musical.

"I know which one I'd call you," Damon said, looking right at Zoe.

She looked right back at him. "I know what I'd call you, too, if I hadn't been raised not to curse."

Daniella frowned. "I didn't have surveillance in my bedroom."

"That was different," Damon said.

"What he means is that he doesn't care if we get eaten by demons," Zoe said.

"That's not true," Damon said.

"Right. My mistake," Zoe said. "They need us alive to try to retrieve the spell book."

"True," he agreed.

"Damon, tell her you won't let any demons hurt her," Daniella instructed him.

"I won't let any demons hurt her."

"Now say it as if you mean it," Daniella said,

"She won't believe me."

"Then do a vampire pinkie swear," Daniella said.

Damon looked aghast at the idea. "I don't even know what that is."

"Sure you do." She nudged Nick. "Tell him."

Nick remained silent.

Sighing, Daniella explained, "A pinkie swear is—"

"I know what a pinkie swear is," Damon interrupted her.

"This is just the vampire version and since you are immortal it means even more," Daniella reminded Damon. "Now you link your pinkie with Zoe's."

"No way," Zoe and Damon said in unison.

"The pizza is getting cold," Nick said.

"Oh, right. We can do the vampire pinkie swear later," Daniella said.

"Or not," Zoe muttered.

"I smell pizza," Gram said as she joined them. She was wearing her favorite flowing caftan in shades of aqua and green along with a hundred inches of freshwater pearls, which she had wrapped around her neck several times. Addressing Daniella, she said, "I don't believe we've met."

"I'm Daniella Delaney. I own Heavenly Cupcakes."

"Oh my. I had one of your creations earlier," Gram said. "The Irish cream was to die for. Well, not really. Not that I want anyone dying, I mean."

"Daniella brought us a pizza to welcome us to the neighborhood," Zoe told her grandmother.

"It's Chicago-style deep dish," Daniella said as she opened the box. "We'll need a big knife to cut this."

"Don't bother offering your demon dagger," Nick warned Damon.

"I wasn't about to," Damon denied.

"I'm not allowed to conjure sharp objects," Gram said. "Zoe made me promise."

"I'll get a knife from the kitchen." Zoe was eager to leave the room if only for a few brief moments. Given a choice, she would have stayed in the kitchen. But she didn't have a choice and she hated that fact. She hated this entire situation.

It didn't take her long to find a knife. She returned to the dining room and handed it to Daniella.

Standing beside her, Damon said, "I'll bet you were tempted to run that blade through me, weren't you, little witch?"

"Not at all," Zoe said. "It wouldn't hurt you."

"It would sting. I might even say ouch."

"You'd only say that to mock me," she countered.

"True."

"Too bad you can't eat," Zoe said.

"Now you're the one mocking me," Damon said. "I fed before I came, so you can relax."

Yeah, right. Like that was ever going to happen. There was no way she could ever relax with Damon around. Every additional second she spent with him increased the sexual tension between them by a thousand percent. She was more and more aware of those awesome dark blue eyes of his and the erotic shape of his lips. But there was no way she could act on her desire . . . or his. She'd seen him eyeing her. *Look but don't touch* seemed like a safe motto, but damn . . . a mere look from him was enough to make her body melt.

He left them around the table and went in the corner to work his iPhone.

"Damon, do join us," Gram said.

"He's a vampire," Zoe said. "He can't eat food."

Gram looked confused. "But Nick is eating."

Zoe had noticed that but was too polite to ask why.

"That's a result of Nick mating with me," Daniella

cheerfully explained, which made Nick nearly choke on his pizza.

"Need help over there?" Damon asked mockingly.

"No," Nick growled.

"The first vampire to mate with a druid hybrid will have his powers greatly increased," Daniella said. "We didn't realize that one of the side effects was that Nick could once again eat real food. He'd never had a hot dog or pizza. Can you imagine that?"

Which left Zoe wondering about Damon. He'd probably never had a pizza, either. She wasn't about to ask him or feel guilty eating in front of him. Or maybe he had. Maybe he'd been turned in the 1950s like Tanya, in which case he would have had plenty of chances to eat hot dogs and pizza.

But if Damon was turned in the 1850s, that was another matter entirely. Same for the 1750s. Hell, he could have been born in 1050 for all she knew. What was the politically correct way to inquire about such things?

Not that she cared when he was turned. It was none of her business really. She should just ignore him the way he was ignoring her.

He was totally immersed in whatever was on the screen of his phone as he pressed the tiny keyboard with incredibly rapid strokes. His actions drew her attention to his fingers, which were thin and artistic. Not dainty, though. Not at all.

"Having fun playing Words with Friends?" Zoe couldn't resist asking.

Damon lifted his head to give her a blank stare.

"Never mind," she muttered, focusing on cutting her pizza instead. It was so thick that she couldn't just pick it up and eat it like back in Boston.

"No one beats me," Damon said.

Which left her wondering if he really *was* playing or if he just had heard about the online game and was yanking her chain. She hadn't known him very long, but she already knew for a fact that he got a big kick out of pushing her buttons.

"It was so nice of you to all come over and make us feel welcome," Gram said.

"They're staying overnight," Zoe warned her. "To keep an eye on us."

"Really?" Gram clapped her hands. "It will be like a vampire-witch-druid-hybrid pajama party. What fun!"

"Next you'll be getting out Twister . . . no, I'm only kidding, Gram. Do not do that."

"Of course I wouldn't do it right now. We're still eating," Gram said. "But later . . ."

"No."

"Why are you against this Twister thing?" Damon demanded.

"It's a stupid game."

"Let me be the judge of that."

"It's great at parties," Gram said.

"We're not here to party," Damon said.

"That doesn't mean you can't have fun while keeping an eye on us," Gram said.

"The first night I stayed with Daniella, she made me watch a chick flick," Nick said.

"It was *The Proposal*," Daniella said. "You remind me of Betty White in the movie," she told Gram.

"It's the white hair," Gram said.

"And the mischievous look in your eyes," Daniella said.

Gram laughed. "I don't know about that."

Zoe knew all about Gram's mischievous streak. It might be a benefit in a regular senior but in a witch it became an occasional liability.

Once they'd finished the pizza, Gram offered to whip up a little something for dessert.

Zoe was already shaking her head before Gram had even completed her sentence. "Not a good idea."

"I'm not good at conjuring up cooks. I once tried for Emeril and for some reason got a set of T-fal cookware instead. And then there was the baked Alaska incident. All I can say is that I'm glad the ballroom had built-in sprinklers."

Morticia walked into the dining room at that moment, diverting Daniella's attention. "So you have another cat? Does this one talk, too?"

"No," Gram said. "But she communicates in other ways."

"Does she write notes?" Damon asked sarcastically.

"She probably could if she wanted to," Gram said.

"We didn't save any pizza for them," Daniella said.

"They've got Fancy Feast in their dishes in the kitchen," Gram said.

"I've gone from Russian caviar on golden spoons to cat food on the floor." Bella shook her head. "It's pitiful."

"We all have our burdens to bear," Zoe said.

"She is such a hard taskmaster." Bella looked up at Daniella with the soulful look she'd perfected from watching the *Puss in Boots* movie over and over again. That, *Turning Point*, and *Magic Mike* were Bella's favorite DVDs, and she'd often watch them nonstop.

"It must be very hard for you," Daniella said sympathetically.

Bella nodded her agreement.

"I'll bring you a chocolate cupcake tomorrow," Daniella promised her. Turning to Zoe, she said, "Can she eat that okay?"

"I'm down here," Bella said. "And I can eat it just fine. I would prefer caviar, but I'll make do."

Morticia sat beside Bella and copied her soulful look up at Daniella.

"I'll bring one for you, too," Daniella said.

"If you two are done begging, I'll clear the table," Zoe said. She was eager to take a break from Damon. He hadn't spoken up during the feline discussion but Zoe knew he listened to every word.

"I'll help you," Daniella said.

"No. You're a guest."

"Or a prison guard," Daniella noted. "I wouldn't blame you for thinking that way."

"I don't think that about you," Zoe said.

"She thinks it about me," Damon said.

"Which is why we need to insert a little fun into the evening," Gram said, and she pulled a box from thin air.

"That doesn't look like Twister," Daniella said.

"It's the witch version. Similar but not close enough to break any copyright laws," Gram said. Unfolding the mat, she set it on the floor. "Instead of colors we have symbols. The stars, the moon, the sun, and a purple triangle."

"The meaning of which is?"

"That I like purple," Gram said. "Now someone draws a card from this deck with one of the symbols. You only move your hands. Your feet remain here at all times." She pointed to the foot-shaped marks labeled

LEFT and RIGHT. "Two players are on the mat at the same time."

"Let Daniella and Zoe play it," Damon said.

"Great idea," Zoe said. "Vampires wouldn't be any good at this as it requires manual dexterity and flexibility."

Damon shot her a sardonic look. "Nice try, but I don't have to prove anything to you."

"Nick has great dexterity and flexibility along with super vamp speed," Daniella proudly proclaimed. "I don't know if you realize that vampires move really fast."

"Damon demonstrated that earlier this afternoon when he tore through the place searching for the mysterious book of spells because he thought we had hidden it somewhere. Part of him still thinks that," Zoe said.

"It's his job to be suspicious," Nick said.

"He's particularly suspicious of witches," Zoe said.

"Guilty as charged," Damon said without any remorse.

"We don't need them to play this game," Daniella said. "We can do it ourselves. Come on. It will be fun."

Zoe didn't know about that, but she knew from the challenging look Damon gave her that she wasn't going to back down the way he clearly expected her to. "We'll use the three-minute rule," she said. "The first one to touch the mat with anything other than your hands and feet within three minutes is out."

Zoe deliberately let Daniella win by touching her elbow to the moon-shaped symbol within the first thirty seconds.

Daniella was thrilled with the win and challenged Nick to play with her.

"No fair using vamp speed," Zoe warned Nick.

As she watched Daniella and Nick grappling and laughing, Zoe was struck by how much the two of them were in love. It was bittersweet to see because Zoe had thought she and Tristin were that much in love.

That memory stuck with her as she prepared for bed a few hours later. Gram had produced a screen behind which Zoe could change into red flannel pajamas while Damon stood by the door guarding her.

It had been one hell of a day. Nick was downstairs with Gram, which left Zoe with Damon.

"Hey, there," Daniella announced as she walked in after knocking. "I thought you might like some company."

"Don't you want to stay with Nick?" Zoe asked.

Instead of answering, Daniella said, "I know how uncomfortable it can be to have a vampire hanging over you. Well, it's uncomfortable if it's a strange vampire. I like Nick hanging over me now, but I didn't that first night. I don't have to change clothes. I can sleep in these lounge pants and top." Daniella hopped onto the bed and patted the space beside her. "Join me and we can play Angry Birds." She waved her iPad, which Zoe hadn't noticed before.

They'd barely played one game before Daniella fell asleep. Zoe gently removed the iPad from Daniella's hand while Damon took a white afghan throw from the foot of the bed and tucked it around her. His actions surprised Zoe.

Seeing her look, Damon stepped back and softly said, "She has to get up before dawn to make cupcakes."

Zoe nodded. She felt too vulnerable getting horizontal with Damon so close by, so she propped a pillow behind her and rested against the headboard in a sitting position.

"You should sleep, too," Damon told her.

"I'm just going to rest my eyes for a minute," Zoe said.

"You do that."

The next time she opened her eyes, pale sunlight filled the room and Daniella was gone. Damon was not. He was sprawled in a chair he'd brought in from her workroom, his intense gaze on her. She felt as if he were touching her with his eyes, which should have been creepy but was instead hotly arousing. Had he slipped her a vampire roofie or something?

"What did you do?" she asked suspiciously.

"Nothing," Damon said. "You fell sound asleep while you rested your eyes."

"He's right," Bella said from the foot of the bed, where she was curled up on the white afghan Damon had used to cover Daniella.

Zoe rubbed the crick in her neck before checking her watch. "The cable guy is scheduled to come this morning between seven and ten."

She got out of bed and headed for the attached bathroom before remembering the all-seeing surveillance cameras. "I am not taking a shower with a camera on me."

Damon typed some text into his smartphone. "You have ten minutes before the camera goes on again. And if you pull anything, your grandmother will pay the consequences."

She paused for a second by the closet to grab clean clothes and underwear before racing to the bathroom and locking the door. She used her own brand of

Sunshine soap, one of her favorite citrus blends, in the shower. The combination of orange, lemon, and pineapple along with touches of other fruits and spices made her feel energetic and ready to face the day most of the time. Knowing there was a sexy vampire right outside her bathroom door timing her before turning on the cameras might be more than even the Sunshine soap could handle, however.

She made it out with five seconds to spare. The stress of trying to hurry had her heart racing. She was wearing black yoga pants despite the fact that she was a yoga class dropout. Her V-neck knit top was a powerful red. Not trendy coral or dainty pink. No, this was kick-ass red and matched the polish on her toenails. Her fingernails were bare because she hadn't had time to paint them yet—she had been too busy dealing with vampires and demons to do that. She reached for her good-luck cameo bangle from the nightstand drawer and slipped it on before touching her neck to make sure the necklace she always wore was still there. The slim chain was the only visible part; she kept the rest hidden beneath her top.

Damon watched her, tilting his head as if he could hear her pulse.

Ignoring him, she marched downstairs and poured some Frosted Mini-Wheats and skim milk into a bowl for breakfast.

Nick and Damon consulted each other and their smartphones while Zoe ate. Gram didn't like getting up before noon.

"I'm leaving you in charge," Nick told Damon. "I need to get back to the bar. Be safe."

"I won't hurt him," Zoe said between bites of cereal.

"Very funny," Damon said before returning his attention to his smartphone.

He ignored her after that as she waited for the cable guy to show up. She spent the time making notes about possible new combinations for her soap line. Mint and lavender was a possibility. She didn't return to her workroom but stayed in the living room. She didn't want Damon messing around in her work space. Not because she had something to hide but because that was her sanctuary.

Eight o'clock came and went. So did nine and ten. Finally at ten thirty there was a knock at the door. "Who is it?" she called out.

"The cable guy" was the muffled reply.

She hurried to open the door only to have Damon leap forward and jam a dagger into the man's throat.

Chapter Ten

"You just killed the cable guy!" Zoe shrieked.

Damon was unremorseful. "He was evil."

"He was only half an hour late," she whispered. "That doesn't mean he was evil."

"True, but *this* means he was a demon." Damon pointed down to the body, where the guy's features changed from human to demonic before the body dissolved in a puff of smoke.

Zoe tried to stay calm while inside she was shaking like a puppy in a thunderstorm. "I didn't know they could do that."

"There's a lot you don't know."

Obviously. Just for clarification, she had to ask, "This doesn't mean all cable guys are demons though, right?"

"Right."

"That stinks," she said.

"You wanted all cable guys to be demons?"

"No, I was referring to the smell." She waved her hand under her nose.

"The stench of hell."

"And rotten eggs," she said,

"That smell is sulfur, as in fire and brimstone—also known as fire and sulfur," he explained.

Zoe's head was spinning. "If you don't mind, I need to sit for a moment." She sank onto the couch. "I'm not used to dissolving demons before lunch."

"Get used to it," he said.

"How do you do that? How did you get used to it? Have you always been a Demon Hunter?"

"No. I was a minister once."

Her jaw dropped. "Really?"

"Of course not. Do I look like a minister?"

"Then why did you lie?" she demanded.

"To see that look on your face," he said,

"What look?"

"The one of wide-eyed amazement. You do it so well."

"Yeah?" Zoe didn't take his words as a compliment. "Well, you . . . you *lie* well."

"Yes, I do." He nodded, clearly pleased by her comment.

"You still haven't told me how you became a Demon Hunter."

"That's right," he said.

"Are you ever going to tell me?"

"Perhaps."

His attitude angered her. "Don't do me any favors."

"Too late. I already did you a favor by killing that demon."

"You were just doing your job. That's what a Demon Hunter does, right? Kills demons? You were probably born killing demons," she said.

"I wasn't born a vampire."

"No?"

"No. I was human once," he said.

"I find that hard to believe."

"I was a soldier once and a law student before that."

"Yeah, right," she scoffed.

"It's the truth."

"Sure it is. If you're expecting that wide-eyed amazed look from me again, you're going to be disappointed. I'm not falling for another lie about your past."

"I don't care if you believe me or not," he said.

But she could tell that he *did* care, and that surprised her. It also made her think there was a possibility he was telling the truth. A slight possibility, granted, but a possibility.

"You were a law student?" she asked.

He nodded curtly.

She wasn't sure how he managed to make the nod indicate his impatience but he did.

"And a soldier?" she continued.

Again with the nod, but not quite as curt this time. She studied his expression. It wasn't a happy one. "Did you fight in a war?" she said.

Damon pinned her like a butterfly on display with his dark laser stare. Right. He definitely hadn't liked her last question.

"I fought in the worst war of all," he finally said.

"World War Two?"

"Wrong. The American Civil War. For the Union."

She was speechless.

"What?" he taunted her. "No smart-ass comment?"

"Um, thank you for your service to our country?" she said.

"Are you being sarcastic?"

"No," she said. "You're the one who specializes in sarcasm, not me." He made no comment, so she asked, "When did you become a vampire?"

"Gettysburg."

"As in the Battle of?"

Damon responded with another curt nod.

She was no expert on that period in American history but she knew enough. "Was it as bad as they say?"

"Worse."

"What happened?"

He was silent for so long she wasn't sure he intended to answer her at all. "If you want an hour-by-hour account, go check out a book from the library. No, wait, you can't go to libraries because the books attack you," he mocked.

"If you don't want to tell me, you don't have to."

"How generous of you," he drawled.

"If it upsets you to talk about it—"

"Who said it upsets me?"

She shrugged. "You were traumatized by the experience."

"Hell, yes."

"You don't have to shout. I understand that you probably suffer from post-traumatic stress."

"I'm a vampire. We don't suffer from anything."

"Including demons?"

"Including demons and witches."

"I don't appreciate you lumping witches in with demons," she said.

"And I don't appreciate you giving me the third degree. I thought witches didn't like inquisitions. Didn't you have enough of them in the Spanish Inquisition?"

"Hey, I was not alive back then. I am not that old."

"Touchy about your age, little witch?"

"I was just trying to figure you out."

"Don't bother," he said.

But she was too curious to give up. "Did you become a Demon Hunter at the same time you became a vampire?"

"Be careful," he warned her. "Curiosity killed the cat."

"I'm not a cat," she said.

"Neither am I," Bella said as she jumped onto the arm of the couch. "Well, I am a cat, sort of. But I'm much more than that. I'm a powerful witch's familiar."

"Zoe isn't that powerful," Damon said.

"I meant to say that I am a witch's powerful familiar," Bella corrected herself.

"Hey," Zoe protested. "I am not a weak witch."

Damon and Bella both gave her a look.

"Okay, on the rare occasion, when a vampire slays the cable guy in my living room, then yes, that does throw me for a moment," she said.

"You shrieked like a little girl," Bella said.

Damon nodded and grinned sardonically. "Yes, Zoe, you did."

"Says the vampire afraid to talk about his past," Zoe retorted.

"Uh-oh," Bella said before beating a hasty retreat.

Damon moved in on Zoe. Okay, he wasn't just moving in on her, he was stalking her again. She was smart enough to recognize the difference. She was also stubborn enough not to back up. She was tempted to protest his use of the word *weak* when describing her but she'd already confronted vampires and been possessed by a demon in her first afternoon in Chicago. Now on her second day, she'd seen a demon dissolve, and it wasn't even noon yet. How much worse could it get? So she just stood there and glared at him, visually daring him to do whatever bad deeds were in his thick head.

Correctly reading her eyes, he said, "You do not want to dare me, little witch."

That was the second time he'd said that to her within the past hour. "I am *not* little." Throwing back her shoulders, she stood tall and proud at every one of her sixty-six inches.

Instead of admiring her stature, his attention became focused on her breasts. She was standing super straight, shoulders back and breasts thrust forward, which highlighted the taut fit of her V-neck top's knit material.

"Hey!" She waved her hand in front of his face. "Eyes up here." She pointed to her face with the universal two-finger sign for "I'm Watching You." She hoped it was also universal in the vampire community, but wasn't sure because Damon's gaze remained fixed on her chest.

Maybe he was contemplating yanking her beating heart out or something nefarious like that. Did Gram's protection spell apply to vampires as well as demons?

"Where did you get those?" he said.

"I grew them myself," she said. "I mean, they are natural. They're mine. My breasts." Every word she said made her feel more embarrassed than the last. "Not that it's any of your business," she tacked on at the last minute. Right, like there was any way to regain her dignity at this point. That ship had sailed, as Gram would say.

"I wasn't talking about your breasts. I was talking about your talisman."

Normally her necklace remained tucked between her breasts, but there was nothing normal about her life lately. The past twenty-six hours had been a wild ride of vamps, panic, fear, panic, vamps, and demons. Any one of those things would be enough to rattle a girl, even a witch.

Her hand flew to her necklace, which had apparently somehow slipped out from beneath her top by way of the V-neck. So the vampire hadn't been admiring her breasts after all. He was only interested in her talisman. It wouldn't be the first time a man had only wanted her for her magic.

Well, it would be the first time a *vampire* wanted her for her magic.

Not that Damon wanted her. And not that Tristin had really wanted her, either.

She supposed she could blame her bad luck in the romance department on the family curse. *No man can make an Adams witch happy.* You'd think a witch would be superstitious enough to listen to things like curses. But somehow hope still sprang, and there were some instances when an Adams witch had been happy.

All of this was intensely personal stuff as far as Zoe was concerned, which was why she quickly tucked the talisman on the single gold chain back beneath her top where it belonged. The vampire knew enough that he hadn't merely described the piece of jewelry as a necklace but instead as a talisman, which it was.

"I asked you a question," Damon reminded her.

"Which I have no intention of answering," she said.

"Why not?"

"Because it's none of your business."

"This makes it my business," he growled before ripping open his shirt and baring his chest.

Had she been a drooling kind of girl, she would have done so, because Damon was definitely drool-worthy. That underwear commercial that David Beckham had done had nothing on Damon. Not that he was only wearing his underwear. He'd merely ripped open his shirt and displayed his six-pack abs.

She managed to clear her mind enough to form a sentence. "Nice chest, but it's irrelevant." *Irrelevant and sexy as hell.*

"*This* is relevant." He pointed to the tattoo over his heart. Tugging her necklace out, he pulled her closer and held her talisman to his chest, practically plastering her against him in the process.

It was hard to think with her nose practically pressed against his nipple. Heat radiated from his body.

"Aren't you supposed to be cool?" she stuttered.

"What?"

"You're hot."

"Don't bother trying to distract me with compliments," he said.

"I was merely stating a fact."

"So you think I'm hot. That's irrelevant. Focus," he ordered her.

"I can't when you're choking me with my own necklace."

He loosened his hold on her. "My tattoo matches your talisman."

"You've got more than one tattoo." He could give

David Beckham a run for his money in the tat department, too.

"I'm talking about this one." He pointed to the elaborate design of a Phoenix rising from the ashes with a shooting star in the top corner. The circle surrounding the image was unique, as it was on her talisman.

"Where did you get that?"

"In New Orleans," he said.

"Wow. What are the chances that you'd get the same design as my talisman?"

"Slim to none."

"Actually the Phoenix is a popular symbol. So are stars."

Damon just kept staring at her, making her nervous, which was why she kept talking. "So were you down there for Mardi Gras? Have you been there since Katrina hit? The city is rebuilding but it takes a lot of time, which is something you'd know about, being a vampire and all. I mean you'd know about time, not rebuilding a city." When Zoe was nervous, she babbled.

"What do you know about Eve Delacroix?" he demanded.

She blinked in surprise at his non sequitur. "Nothing."

"This is her family talisman."

"No, it's not. It's my family talisman. From both my mother's side and my father's side. It's unique," she said.

"You come from her blood." Damon practically spat the words at her.

"Hey," she said, "I can't be responsible for what some tattoo parlor on Bourbon Street gave you during Mardi Gras. Maybe this Eve, whoever she is, saw me wearing my necklace or something. I did go down to Mardi Gras two years ago. Maybe she saw me then."

"I doubt it."

"Why?" she said.

"Because Eve Delacroix is a witch I killed in 1866."

Chapter Eleven

Damon could see the shock in Zoe's witchy bicolored eyes. He could hear her heartbeat speed up with fear. He didn't need to read her mind to know what she was thinking. He'd killed a witch before. He could do it again, and it could be her.

He didn't say anything to dissuade her from that line of thought.

Did scaring the witch make him a better Demon Hunter? Maybe not, but it might make Vamptown a safer place . . . if he could find that freaking spell book and destroy the invading demons. To do the first part, he needed Zoe's help. If she feared for her life, she might be more willing to work with him.

Not that she'd been impossible. In fact, she'd been fairly willing to go along with his instructions, or *orders*, as she'd say. And she'd said plenty when he'd stayed over last night. Thankfully vampires didn't require much sleep. That spending-all-day-in-a-coffin thing didn't work for him.

Not that Damon spent his days running around killing witches, although judging from her expression that was what Zoe was currently thinking.

Strangely enough, he was slightly tempted to reassure her. He didn't know what that was about. He'd already told her numerous times that he didn't care about her emotions. Feelings were a waste of time as far as he was concerned, which was why the vampire lifestyle suited him so well.

"You killed a witch in 1866?" Zoe finally said.

He nodded.

"Why are you telling me this now?"

"You asked."

She nervously fingered the gold chain around her neck. "You're saying she had a talisman similar to mine?"

"Exactly the same as yours."

"Why did you kill her?"

"She betrayed me."

"Was it something to do with the war?" Zoe asked.

"The war of good versus evil, yes."

"And which side are you on?" she asked.

"I'm on the side that fights and defeats demons."

"Some people regard vampires as demons."

"Some people regard witches as demons, too," he said. "But we both know that's not true. Some people also think there's no such thing as global warming but we both know that's not true, either, right?"

"Right. I mean just look at the temperature today. Records are being broken all over the world. But what does global warming have to do with you killing a witch? You're not saying she cast a spell to change the climate, are you?" Zoe demanded.

"No. Eve practiced black magic," he said. "I didn't know that when I first got involved with her."

"How did she betray you?"

"She sabotaged my mission by setting up an ambush with a very powerful demon that nearly got me decapitated. So I killed her." His words were deliberately matter-of-fact although the incident had been anything but.

"What happened to her talisman?" Zoe asked.

"It disappeared."

Reaching out, he tugged Zoe's necklace into view and examined it. Which meant he had to stand really close to Zoe. He could smell her spicy citrus scent. He'd noticed it at their first meeting the instant she'd walked into the bar. Vamps had heightened senses.

Even now he could discern the variation in scents floating down from her workroom on the second floor. Cherry blossoms and vanilla. Bitter orange and tart lemon. Intense pineapple and coconut, a combo that used to make him think of sissy drinks with stupid umbrellas—until now. Not that he'd ever had one of those drinks. They weren't around during his human years. But that combination went right to his head and made him want to pour one of those drinks over Zoe's body then lick it from every inch of her skin.

Taking a deep breath, Damon tried to focus his concentration back on the necklace. He hadn't allowed Zoe to distract him when he'd smelled her scintillating scent in the bar when they'd first met, and he wasn't about to now. He took another breath. Wait, was there an underlying layer of apple in there somewhere with the spice? Was that her version of Eve tempting Adam?

Summoning his willpower, he blocked out all

thoughts of Zoe and studied the necklace. "You must have a record of your bloodline."

Zoe nodded. "It's in the family Book of Spells."

"Get it."

Zoe's grandmother chose that moment to walk into the room with the book. "I had a feeling you might want to take a look at this for some reason." She handed it over to Zoe.

"Thanks, Gram."

"How are you two getting along now?" She eyed Damon's bare chest but made no direct reference to it. "Better?"

"Just peachy," Zoe said.

"Speaking of peachy, I had an idea to blend your peach-scented soap with ginger for a little zing."

Personally, Damon thought Zoe already had plenty of zing, although he wasn't about to say so.

"We can talk about that later." Zoe sat on the couch and set the heavy book on her lap. "I'm looking for the section on our bloodline going back through the generations."

Gram sat beside her and bent over the book.

Damon watched the two of them. His grandmother Sara used to put her hand on his knee the same way that Zoe's grandmother was doing right now. He fought the memories of his own grandmother beside him on the settee before he'd left for the war. His maternal grandmother was a Virginian and on the side of slavery and the Confederacy, which was why his younger brother joined that side. But his paternal grandmother, Sara, was originally from New England and very much for protecting the Union. The damn war had forever split his family in a way that couldn't be repaired.

Looking at Zoe's grandmother, Damon realized she was turning the pages with a wave of her hand. That wasn't anything his own grandmothers would or could have done.

"Why are you interested in our family tree?" she asked Zoe.

"Have you ever heard the name Eve Delacroix?" Damon asked Zoe's grandmother.

"I'm not sure," she replied. "It sort of rings a bell."

"Damon thinks she had a talisman just like mine," Zoe said.

"I don't think it, I know it. I have the proof right here." He pointed to his bare chest.

"A tattoo?"

"He got it after the Civil War," Zoe said.

Zoe's grandmother tugged a pair of magnifying reading glasses out of her pocket and moved in on Damon for a closer look.

"The tattoo is an exact copy of Eve Delacroix's," Damon said. "She had to be of your bloodline."

"That's possible, but she couldn't have had an *exact* copy."

"Why not?"

"Because Zoe's is unique to her, based on the blending of her mother's and father's lines," her grandmother explained.

"Maybe Eve came from the same family lines on both sides as well."

"Or maybe your tattoo isn't an exact replica of hers. Maybe it was a sign that you would meet Zoe and be linked with her in some way," her grandmother said.

"No way!" Damon and Zoe said in unison.

"Or maybe it is just extremely similar to Zoe's but different in some small way," her grandmother said.

"I like that idea better," Zoe said before returning her attention to the book on her lap.

"What's that strange smell?" her grandmother asked.

"Dead demon," Damon said.

"He killed the cable guy," Zoe said. "Who was really a demon in disguise."

"I hate when that happens," Zoe's grandmother said.

Zoe blinked. "When did that ever happen before?"

Her grandmother frowned. "I saw it in a dream once. Or maybe it was in a horror movie. I can't recall exactly now."

"I thought you had no experience with demons," Damon said.

"Not reality-based experience. But a witch's dreams can be powerful things," her grandmother said.

"So you're saying you could have conjured up demons just by dreaming about them?" he said.

"Absolutely not. To quote you two, no way. So what was a demon doing on our doorstep?"

"He was in the living room, actually," Damon said.

"Even worse," her grandmother said. "I hope he didn't leave a stain on the rug?"

"He was on the wooden floor."

"What did he want?" her grandmother said.

Damon shrugged. "He didn't say."

"Did you ask?"

"Demons aren't real talkative," Damon replied.

"Kind of like vampire Demon Hunters," Zoe muttered.

"I'm assuming he came looking for the book," Damon said.

"Which would mean they don't have it in their possession," Zoe said.

"Or it could mean that only a witch can open it," her grandmother pointed out.

Damon wasn't happy with that possibility. He didn't like being dependent on anyone else to get the job done. He was like his sire Simon that way. Simon didn't like working with other Demon Hunters, but he had taken the time after turning Damon to teach him well not only in the ways of vampires but also in the skills needed to successfully hunt demons.

Simon had done more than that. He'd saved Damon from eternal damnation. Eve's betrayal had enabled the demons to haul Damon into the first level of hell. Vampires didn't die there. They were tortured for all eternity. Damon had risked the odds and escaped with Simon's help.

Much of that time was a blur to Damon. His human memories about Gettysburg remained, but thankfully his vamp nightmares of his brief imprisonment were just that: nightmares, not vivid images forever imprinted on his mind.

Simon had been the first to tell Damon about the legend of the Book of Darkness, as he'd called it. A book that could open the gates of hell and let the demons come pouring out en masse. No one had ever actually seen the book or even knew for sure that it really did exist. Until now.

And even now he couldn't be sure. He hadn't seen the book. Maybe the demons had gotten loose through some other means. Not that that seemed likely at this point. He'd been in Vamptown for over two months and there hadn't been a whiff of demon stench until yesterday.

It was no coincidence that Zoe and her grandmother appeared in Vamptown at the same time as this demon outbreak. And things could get worse before they got better if he didn't get this mess under control.

"I found it!" Zoe's exclamation interrupted his thoughts.

"The missing book?"

"No, Eve Delacroix's name. It's in my mother's family tree bloodline," Zoe said.

"Which might explain how she had a talisman like yours from your mother's side, but not your father's."

Damon already knew from the research he'd done on Zoe but he asked anyway. "You don't have any siblings?"

Zoe shook her head.

"Maybe someone from your father's bloodline hooked up with someone from your mother's a century and a half ago."

Zoe made a face. "That sounds kind of incestuous to me."

"But possible," he said.

"Not really incestuous," her grandmother said. "Enough time has passed."

"It still creeps me out that Damon killed a witch that might have been an ancestor," Zoe said. "He claims she was evil. A bitchy witch."

"As opposed to a bitchin' good witch?" her grandmother said. "What? You don't think I keep up on modern terminology? I imagine that must be tough for you, Damon."

"Killing Eve was easy." A lie but he wasn't about to tell the truth.

"I was referring to keeping up with terminology over one hundred and fifty years. Why, when I think about how much things have changed in my sixty-five years—"

"You're seventy-two," Damon said.

Zoe's grandmother glared at him. "Yes I am, but you don't have to make a big deal about it."

"I'd rather make a big deal about the fact that the two of you—descendants of Eve Delacroix—just happen to land in Vamptown and unleash a bunch of demons. I don't believe it," Damon said.

"I don't believe it, either," Zoe's grandmother said. "I mean, what are the chances, right?"

"Right. So are you finally going to tell me the truth?" Damon said.

"I already admitted that I'm seventy-two not sixty-five," she said.

"You can't still think that my grandmother and I are part of some demon conspiracy," Zoe said.

"Can't I?"

"Only if you're an idiot," she shot back. "Look, I want to get rid of these demons as much as you do."

"Really?"

"Yes, really."

"Then prove it," he said.

"How?"

"Find that missing book. Look through your family spell book for something about demons."

"It doesn't come with an index," Zoe said. "It's not like I can just Google a spell. Well, okay, maybe someone can Google a spell, but it wouldn't work."

"How do you know?" Damon demanded. "Have you ever tried it?"

Zoe vehemently shook her head, which made her bangs slide into her eyes. "No witch in her right mind and worth her weight in real magic would do that."

Damon fought the urge to brush her hair away from her face. He already knew how silky the dark strands were; his fingertips vibrated with the memory of touching her. All of a vampire's senses were heightened compared with mere mortals, and that included not only sight, smell, and sound but also touch.

But Zoe was a witch. She was more than capable of casting a spell to throw him off track. Eve had done it. What was to say her descendant couldn't accomplish the same thing?

Damon had told Zoe's grandmother that he didn't need a protection spell. He hadn't told her the reason, which was that he had a few resources of his own as a Demon Hunter to use.

"Googling a spell could make things worse," Zoe warned him. "You may not think they could get worse—"

"Oh, I *know* they can get worse. And they will if we don't get that book back." He paused a moment as a possibility he'd been mulling over in his head took shape. "What if that demon that possessed you had you cast a spell to make the book vanish?"

"I was with you the entire time. You even recorded me on your iPhone. You've got the video of me levitating. How could I cast a spell without you knowing?"

She was right. Unless . . . "What if you did it silently?"

"What about the demon?" Zoe said. "Couldn't he have done something to make it vanish? Or maybe the book had that ability built in?"

"I've got people checking out possible legends about the book," Damon said.

"People?"

"Vampires."

"And they are supposed to be better researchers than a witch with a master's degree in library science? I seriously doubt that," Zoe said.

"You can doubt it all you want," he said. "I don't care."

"You should care if you want those demons stopped."

"I can stop them myself. You saw that." He pointed to the front door where he'd destroyed the cable guy.

"Yes, I did. You seemed to get a kick out of going after him. Maybe you're behind that demon's appearance," Zoe said.

"You witches are behind it."

"All my grandmother did was open a book!"

"And all hell broke loose. Literally. All the demons in hell will be set loose if we don't close the portal," Damon said.

Two hours later, Zoe was still trying to recover from Damon's dramatic declaration. Okay, she was also still trying to recover from being plastered against his body. She would have been fine if he'd just taken off his shirt and she'd merely looked at him and confidently enjoyed the view.

Instead he'd pulled her so close that she'd just about lost it. The memory still left her shaken.

And yes, a better woman would focus all her attention on saving the world instead of harboring secret dark fantasies about a hot vampire. A better witch for sure would have overcome it without blinking an eye.

Zoe had to confess that she did get a kick out of watching the TV classic *I Dream of Jeannie* and seeing Jeannie crossing her arms and blinking her eyes to transport her master halfway around the world. Not that the master thing worked for Zoe, although no doubt Damon would have loved it if it had. He had *masterful* built into his vamp DNA.

With the demise of the cable demon, there was no TV to distract Zoe. She felt guilty even thinking about that. She should be concentrating on the Book of Darkness. She needed to call on her inner librarian, not her inner slut.

Not that she'd ever realized she might have an inner slut until Damon came into her life.

She just couldn't concentrate with him around. And he showed no signs of going away anytime soon.

Refusing to allow her gaze to wander over to where Damon sat in a nearby chair, she kept her eyes on her laptop screen and the grisly illustrations of demons. It was not a pretty picture. She got totally wrapped up in the history, which was why she was so stunned when she looked up and saw the front door swing open and two strange men in suits standing there, pointing at her. "There she is!"

"Demons!" she yelled. "Kill them!"

Chapter Twelve

Zoe stood and glared at the pair of strangers. She had a bad feeling about them. Sure, they were wearing suits, but that didn't mean anything. The last demon to darken their doorstep a short while ago had been wearing a cable guy uniform as a disguise. Why wasn't Damon doing something with that dagger of his?

"They're not demons," Damon whispered in her ear.

"Then why did they come in without being invited and then point at me and say 'There she is'?"

Damon turned to face the two men. "Care to answer that, gentlemen?"

"The door was already slightly open when we arrived. I knocked and the door opened even wider. We were so relieved to have found Zoe. We weren't sure we had the correct address. You scared us by threatening to kill us."

"I wasn't talking about you. I thought I saw a cockroach." In her opinion, just walking in on her qualified these two guys as cockroaches. "Besides, you scared me by barging in without permission. Who are you?" she demanded angrily.

"I'm sorry, I should have made the introductions sooner," the taller of the two men said. "My name is Bob Weaver and this is Tim Simpson. We are followers of Dr. Martin Powers."

"I'm sorry to hear that," Gram said as she joined them.

"You're the one who is going to be sorry," Tim said, speaking for the first time.

"Don't you threaten my grandmother," Zoe said.

"Damn right," Damon agreed. "That's my job."

"We're not here to cause trouble," Bob said.

"Where have I heard that before?" Damon mocked.

"This is all her fault." Bob pointed to Zoe's grand-mother.

"I hear ya," Damon said.

"You seem like a reasonable man," Bob told Damon, who just smiled and nodded.

He's not a man *at all. He's a vampire,* Zoe wanted to tell the intruders but knew she couldn't. She had to bite her lip to stay silent.

"I don't know if you are aware of the fact that Irma Adams is a very disturbed person," Bob said.

"I am aware," Damon said. He put his arm around Zoe's shoulders, presumably to prevent her from hitting someone. He also put an arm around Gram's shoulders, no doubt for the same reason. "What's your beef with her?"

"She came to one of the motivational seminars Dr. Powers was giving back in Boston."

"He's not a real doctor," Gram inserted. "He got his PhD in rhetoric from an online school. He claims that if you use the tools in the Powers Tool Box, you are guaranteed to find happiness. Of course, those tools don't come cheap."

"Dr. Powers has the ability to transform lives," Bob said reverently.

"Yeah, transform them from bad to worse," Gram said. "Unlike other motivational speakers, Powers claims that he is the only one who has the secret to living a perfect life. If you don't buy into his shtick, you will be doomed forever."

Bob shook his head. "That is an extreme exaggeration and a misrepresentation."

Zoe had done some online research about Dr. Powers since Gram's run-in, and it seemed to her that Gram was right.

"Irma created a terrible scene when she stood at the microphone intended to be used to ask relevant questions of Dr. Powers and instead shouted insults at the doctor's followers. It resulted in a huge melee," Bob said.

"Is a melee worse than a stampede?" Gram asked.

"They're about equal," Zoe said.

"And you're here because?" Damon prompted Bob.

"Dr. Powers has indicated that he will forgive Irma providing she goes online to his website and apologizes for her comments."

"When pigs fly." Gram paused, perhaps realizing that she could make that happen. "No way. Not going to happen," she said.

"You insulted Dr. Powers," Bob said, making it sound as bad as breaking one of the Ten Commandments.

"He insulted my intelligence by claiming he could

make your life better just by giving him money," Gram retorted.

"It's not just money," Bob said. "It's his entire Entryway to Enlightenment program in the Powers Tool Box."

"It's a Fast Track to Bankruptcy program," Gram said. "You're talking about thousands of dollars."

Bob's expression was condescending as he looked at them all. "No one is forced to enroll."

"Sure they are," Gram said. "It's called emotional blackmail."

"Nonsense. Everyone has a choice."

"Right," Gram scoffed. "Be miserable or pay me and be happy."

"You are simplifying it in an inaccurate manner." Bob's irritation was starting to show.

Gram waved his words away. "You have no right to come here and bother me. How did you find me anyway?"

"We have our means," Bob said. "And our orders."

"What's that supposed to mean?" Zoe said, not liking the sound of that at all.

"If you don't cooperate, then we are taking legal action against Irma," Bob said.

"If you don't leave our living room right now, then I'll be the one taking action," Gram warned.

Zoe took hold of her grandmother's hand before she could do any witchcraft. "Now, Gram . . ."

"I don't get it," Damon said. "Surely this isn't the first time this guy has been insulted. Why is he making such a big deal about it?"

Bob pointed to Irma. "Bad things have been happening since she started the melee. For some reason, a number of followers have left."

Damon gave Gram a suspicious look, but she shook her head in an indication that she wasn't responsible.

"That's the only bad thing?" Damon asked. "No unexplained sightings or strange events?"

Bob frowned. "I have no idea what you're talking about."

"That's a good thing," Damon replied. "Consider yourself lucky. But since it appears that Irma is not ready to apologize at this point, it would probably be best if you left now."

"This isn't over," Bob said as he and his mostly silent partner headed out. "You'll be hearing from us again."

Zoe took great pleasure in ducking out from Damon's imprisoning arm and slamming the door after them.

Damon did not look amused. "Great. Not only do we have demons to deal with, now we have cult-following humans as well."

"Powers is a motivational-guru con man, not a cult leader," Zoe corrected him.

"Five minutes ago you wanted to kill them," Damon reminded her.

"Because I thought they were demons."

"Which is why you should leave the thinking to me," Damon said. "At least where demons are concerned."

"I thought we agreed that I could do research on the subject," Zoe said.

"We agreed to no such thing," Damon said.

"You don't think there is a connection between Powers and the demons, do you?" Gram asked. "It wouldn't surprise me."

Nothing would surprise Zoe at this point. She turned to face Damon. "And what's with you telling them that you think Gram is disturbed? Your comments were very insulting."

"What? Now you're going to take a page out of Powers's book and demand an online apology from me? Not going to happen, little witch. We have more important things to talk about." He fixed her with an intense stare Zoe could feel clear down to her toes. "I thought your grandmother was the one who started the stampede at their gathering."

"That's right."

"Then why did they recognize you, Zoe?"

"How should I know what they were thinking?" she said. "They clearly weren't acting logically."

"Says the witch who called them demons."

"That's your fault," Zoe told him.

"How do you figure that?" Damon said.

"You vaporize a demon cable guy in my living room and I get a little paranoid. I lost it."

"We can't afford to have you losing it. As far as we know, all the loose demons are now accounted for."

"It's that 'as far as we know' part that has me nervous."

"I have a cure for your nerves," Damon said. "Find the missing spell book."

Three hours later, Zoe was still brooding over Damon's words. She'd spent the intervening time doing additional research on her laptop and going through her family's Book of Spells for any reference to demons. She was also trying to figure out the connection between her talismans and the witch Damon killed a hundred-plus years ago.

So far, all she'd learned was that there was a legendary Book of Darkness said to be able to release demons—but there was nothing beyond a brief mention; no actual sighting or description of it. She kept looking online.

Gram had retired to her bedroom to take a nap while Bella was curled up on a chair, sound asleep.

Which left Zoe basically alone with Damon, who kept looking over her shoulder at the screen of her laptop from time to time, driving her crazy.

"Don't do that," she said in exasperation.

"The Book of Darkness, huh? What do you know about that?"

"This is the only reference I've found."

"Did you Google it?" he asked.

"No. I don't want to get inundated with tons of weird occult spam. You Google it."

"I already did." He didn't elaborate but did add, "I also Googled a photo of your talisman. Our tech vamp is going through the results."

"What did they find out about the Book of Darkness?" Zoe asked.

"Nothing yet," he admitted.

"I told you it was better to have a librarian doing the research."

"Or maybe you knew exactly where to look for it because you owned the Book of Darkness, or your grandmother did."

"We never saw it before," Zoe said.

"Then why did you open it? Do you make a habit of opening strange spell books?"

"No, we don't. It was a stressful day," she said. "We'd just moved here and I'd just discovered vampires are my new neighbors."

"Your grandmother knew Nick was a vampire. She's known for years."

"She didn't tell me."

"I wonder what else she hasn't told you," Damon said. "Or told me."

"Gram isn't like that."

"Isn't she? Come on, who are you kidding? She aggravated those humans enough that they came all the way from Boston to find you."

"You don't know that. Maybe they are local followers of Powers."

"No, they are from Boston. They flew into O'Hare this morning and came straight here. Neville checked it out. He suspects they located you through your website."

"Who is Neville?" Zoe said.

"Our top tech vamp."

"My website doesn't say where I live," she pointed out.

"Maybe not, but your Facebook page for your business has the locator indicator turned on. Neville checked your laptop and found that someone hacked into the site to download a more specific GPS."

Zoe slammed her laptop shut and set it on the coffee table. "Who hacked my computer?"

"We don't know yet. Neville is still following that lead."

"Wait a minute. When did Neville check my laptop? I didn't give my permission for that."

"We don't need your permission," Damon said. "I let you keep your laptop. I never said we wouldn't check it out remotely."

Zoe felt violated all over again, just as she had when Damon had torn through her stuff in her workroom. Her anger rose.

"Are you going to levitate again?" Damon mocked her.

She might not leave the ground but she was about to send some fiery words flying his way when she was distracted by the sound of moans coming through the floor vents in the living room. They weren't happy having-really-awesome-sex moans. No, these were tortured sounds. "What is that?" she whispered.

"Demons!" Bella said as she streaked across the room and dove under the couch.

Zoe was tempted to join her. Not that she'd fit under the denim couch, but still . . . taking cover seemed like a good idea. Unfortunately she wasn't sure where a safe hiding place could be found.

The noise was all around them and became deafening. Zoe put her hands over her ears in an attempt to shut it out.

Damon appeared completely unfazed as he focused his attention on the screen of his damn smartphone.

The moans stopped as suddenly as they'd started.

She looked at Damon. "I thought vampires had better hearing than humans."

"We do."

"Then you heard that?"

"Of course I did," he said.

"How did you make it stop?" she said.

"I thought you did something. You put your hands over your ears like you were doing some sort of witchy spell thing."

"I do not put my hands over my ears when I conjure a spell," she said. "I thought you knew all about witches."

He joined her on the couch. "I know enough."

"Clearly you don't if you think that's how we create spells. Is that how Eve did it?"

He glared at her. "Don't push it, little witch."

"Or what? You've already gone through all my belongings, my work stuff, and my computer. You're already spying on me twenty-four hours a day. What more can you do?"

"This." Reaching out, he cupped her face with his hands and kissed her.

It wasn't gentle and it wasn't polite. It was hot and intense and wicked. He parted her lips and enticed her with his tongue.

This time the moans came from Zoe, and they were signals of her pleasure and not her anger. So this was how vampires kissed. Awesome.

Damon didn't try to overpower her with physical force. He didn't have to. Her eager surrender came as a result of his skill as he took possession of her mouth with the erotic promise of delights to come.

She slid her arms around his neck and melted against him. Her tongue tangled with his. Dark passion flowed throughout her body.

She wanted more. He gave it to her by sliding his hands through her hair and then lowering them to lift her top and seductively sneak his right hand around her side to her breast. The silkiness of her bra provided no protection and instead intensified her pleasure at his caresses. She moaned softly against his mouth and felt as if she might go up in flames.

The sound of evil cackles coming through the floor vents finally brought her back to reality.

She pulled away from him. "The demons can see us! They know what we were doing and they're laughing at us."

"They can't see us," Damon said.

"How do you know?"

"Because I know demons."

The cackles stopped. If the demons couldn't see them, they sure had an incredible sense of timing. Zoe supposed she should be thankful they'd brought her back to her senses. Who knew where she would be right now or what she'd be doing with Damon on this couch otherwise—even with her grandmother in the other room and her familiar hiding under the couch.

"If you're so smart then you should also know that you can't kiss me," Zoe said.

His lips lifted into a mocking smile. "I just did."

"You hate witches."

"So?"

"So?" she repeated incredulously. "So you can't kiss someone you hate."

"I never said I hated you."

"You've accused me of unleashing demons from hell."

"Your point being?"

"Why did you kiss me? What were you trying to accomplish? Were you trying to intimidate me? I don't scare that easily." She looked down at the floor where his smartphone had landed when he'd dropped it to kiss her. "Wait a second. We're being invaded by demons and you're playing Words with Friends? What kind of Demon Hunter are you?"

"The kind who gets things done," he said curtly.

She picked up his phone. "By 'things' you mean thinking *brabbling* is a word?"

He grabbed it from her. "It was in my day."

"How can you play games when all hell is breaking loose? You don't see me fooling around. Other than kissing you, I mean. I'm devoting all my time and attention to this demon situation. I'm not even doing anything regarding my business."

"It's not like you have a real job," Damon made the mistake of saying.

Bella cautiously came out from under the couch to jump on the coffee table and shake her feline head at him. "Bad move, vampire."

"Damn right that was a bad move," Zoe said. "I am an entrepreneur. I may be self-employed but that doesn't mean that I don't have a job. I work hard creating the products for Bella Luna. And I don't use magic to do it. In fact, my workroom is still a mess from your actions yesterday. I need to go fix that instead of wasting my time with you."

"Sure," Damon said with a sweep of his hand. "You go right ahead. What is saving the world compared with making smelly soap?"

"It's scented botanical soap that is vegetable- and fruit-oil-based," she corrected him.

"My mistake. Of course that makes a huge difference. I didn't realize it was vegetable- and fruit-oil-based. Demons can wait. No problem."

"My work is important to me," she said.

"So is mine."

"Then maybe you should focus on doing your work and let me focus on doing mine."

"I'd love to do that," he drawled. "But since you and your grandmother are the ones who released these demons, I need you to be involved."

"You mean you need my help?"

"I didn't say help."

"Would it kill you to say it?" she countered.

"Since I'm an immortal, clearly it would not kill me."

"So are you going to say it? I dare you to. Go ahead," she taunted. "Admit you need my help."

Anger flared in his dark blue eyes. "This is not a game."

"No? Not a Words with Friends game?"

"You're in no position to judge me."

"Right back at you, buddy," she said.

"What did you do back in Boston that got you thrown out?" he demanded out of the blue.

"Where did that come from?"

"I've asked you before."

"And I answered," she said.

"Not really. You were deliberately vague and now we've got angry humans descending on Vamptown."

"You make them sound like an angry mob pounding on the castle doors or something."

"That's not an image that vampires take lightly."

"Witches, either, believe me. But that's the problem isn't it? You don't believe a word I say."

"That's not true. I believe *some* words you say. Just not all of them. You have secrets," he said.

"So do you," she said.

"So do I," a strange voice said. Startled, Zoe turned

to find the hazy hologram-like image of . . . a demon? The astral projection stood there, dressed in strange clothes from another time. His skin was the color of sulfur, and his weird eyes gave her the creeps. Then he smiled at her and said, "Hello, dearie."

Chapter Thirteen

Still amped up on the adrenaline from fighting with
Damon, Zoe didn't scream. So Damon thought she was
a wimp, did he? She'd show him. Cool and collected,
that was her. That wasn't *really* a demon standing in
her living room. It was just the image of one.

"What are you looking at?" Damon asked suspiciously.

"I suspect I'm looking at the astral projection of a
demon. Am I right?" she asked the image.

"Spot on," he replied in an English accent..

Damon shoved her behind him and looked around.
"Where?"

She pointed to the edge of the living room.

"I don't see anything," Damon said.

"Because you're not a witch," she said. "Only witches
can see this kind of projection."

"Allow me to introduce myself," the demon said.
"Silas Milton at your service." He bowed like someone
accustomed to doing so.

"I thought you'd have a lot more scales or something," she said without thinking.

"I'm a demon, not a fish or a dragon."

Zoe stepped out from behind Damon to stand beside him. While the projection didn't terrify her, she was not naive enough to think she had nothing to be worried about. Better to keep a vampire Demon Hunter close at hand when having a conversation with a demonic astral projection.

"Are you the demon in charge?" she asked Silas.

"I am."

"Why are you here?"

"We're not here to bring you harm," Silas said.

"Then why are you here?"

"To right a wrong," he said.

"What wrong?" she asked.

"It's a long story," Silas said. "As you may know, astral projections only last a short time."

"What's he saying?" Damon demanded.

"The Demon Hunter is impatient," Silas said.

"He says you're impatient," she told Damon.

"It's a major fault of his," Silas said.

"I thought the same thing myself," Zoe said.

"You're agreeing with a demon?" Damon said in disbelief.

"On this one matter, yes. But let's get back to this wrong you say you are trying to right, Silas."

"What wrong?" Damon said.

She turned to him in exasperation. "That's what I'm trying to find out if you'd just be quiet a minute." She returned her attention to the demon. "Go on."

"I am being held captive against my will along with two of my associates," Silas said.

Zoe couldn't resist asking, "Which one of you tried to possess me?"

"That was an unfortunate mishap. I know that you now have a strong protection spell surrounding you, your grandmother, and your familiars."

Zoe realized he hadn't answered her question about who exactly was responsible for her possession—but there were more important matters to discuss.

"Give me the short version of the wrong you're talking about," she told the demon. "Is that why you stole that demon spell book?"

"I don't have the book, dearie," Silas said. "If I did, we wouldn't be having this conversation."

"He said he doesn't have the missing spell book," she told Damon.

"I already figured that out," Damon said.

"Who did this wrong to you?" she asked Silas. "Are you here to get revenge?"

"Think about it, dearie. I'm sure you'll figure it out." He tipped his head in a gesture of farewell.

"Wait! Does it have anything to do with my talisman?" she said.

But the projection was gone.

Only now did Zoe realize her knees were shaking. She sank onto the couch. "I've heard about them but I've never actually seen an astral projection before," she said. "And certainly not of a demon. I'm sure he wasn't a warlock."

"No, that was a demon. I could sense that even though I couldn't see him," Damon said. "Maybe it was just a hologram of some sort."

"Then you should have been able to see him."

Damon swore under his breath before admitting, "You're right."

Zoe considered pointing out that this was the first time Damon had ever said those words to her. She really should make a big deal out of it, and she would have if they weren't facing demon demolition.

"He didn't look the way I thought he would," she said.

"How did you think he'd look?" Damon asked.

"More like a scaly goat somehow. Which isn't fair to goats. I mean, I like goat cheese as much as the next person. Or as much as the next witch." She could tell by the look he gave her that he thought she was losing it. "I'm just saying . . ."

"A lot of demons have scales, depending on how long they've been in hell, but demons can take many forms as you found out earlier today."

"He didn't look like a regular human. Not like the cable guy. I mean, Silas had a human form, sort of, but there was something about him . . ." She shook her head.

Damon checked his smartphone. "We didn't get the astral projection on-screen from the cameras."

"I didn't make him up," she said.

"I'm not saying you did. I already told you I sensed a demon presence."

"He said his name was Silas Milton. He was wearing strange clothes that looked like they were made out of snakeskin maybe? His skin was a gray-yellow color. Not a human color. Wait, he didn't have eyebrows. He had a series of bumps over his eyes. Acne maybe? And his eyes . . ." She shook her head. "I can't even begin to describe them. They were red. Like he'd been ass-kicked in the eye but there was no other bruising."

"The bumps represent horns," Damon said. "He had them drawn in."

"I thought he'd have a goatee but he didn't."

"Did he go into any more detail about this wrong he's talking about?"

She shook her head. "Just that I'd figure it out if I thought about it."

"Then do that," he ordered her. "I'll have Neville check on a demon named Silas Milton."

While he did that, Zoe went to speak to her grandmother in her bedroom.

"Gram, the head demon just appeared to me as an astral projection."

"Where?"

"In the living room. But he's gone now. I mean the projection is gone."

"Damn. Why didn't you call me?"

"There wasn't time. He said he was here to right a wrong." Zoe sat on the edge of the bed before hesitantly asking, "Do you think it might have something to do with my mother?"

Gram's expression turned serious. "What makes you say that?"

"She was trying to use dark magic when she died," Zoe said.

"True."

"Did the black magic my mother was conjuring have something to do with demons?"

"I don't know what she was working on," Gram said. "She didn't tell me anything."

"Yet you knew she was dealing with dark magic. How did you know that?"

"I could feel the darkness. I tried to warn her but

she wouldn't listen. There are predators who hunt witches and want us dead. The same way that Damon is a Hunter."

"You think he wants us dead?"

"He wants us gone, but I don't think he wants us dead," Gram said. "I was just using him as an example."

"Of what?" Damon asked as he strolled into the room.

"Of an impolite vampire," Zoe said. "You never heard of knocking?"

"I've heard of it. I just don't believe in it." Damon turned his attention to Gram. "You heard about the projection?"

Gram nodded. "I'm really sorry I missed it."

"Neville checked the video feed from in here to make sure you hadn't done anything to assist with that demon's appearance. You're in the clear."

"Of course she is," Zoe said. "When are you going to believe that?"

"When all this is over," he drawled. "Maybe."

Zoe remained silent, refusing to argue with him over his lack of trust. What was the point? That didn't stop his attitude from aggravating the heck out of her, though. Especially when he got that sly yet intensely sexy expression on his face. She wanted to smack him in both forms of the word—as in kiss him and hit him.

"So neither one of you is familiar with a demon named Silas?" he said.

"I'm not familiar with any demons," Gram said.

"Me, either," Zoe said.

"I heard you ask the demon if he was the one who possessed you," Damon said.

"He never answered that question," Zoe said.

"Of course he didn't. Demons never speak the truth."

"He did say you were impatient and that was true," Zoe pointed out.

Damon just glared at her.

You'd think that a vampire's angry stare would make her think twice, but instead Zoe focused her attention on his mouth. A vampire who kissed like an angel. A fallen angel. Why was she so focused on noticing what a sensual mouth he had? She hadn't felt that intensely about it yesterday, probably because before she'd been afraid she'd find signs of blood dripping from those lips of his.

Ick. That should be a major turn-off. Should be but wasn't. Not that she wanted to see him that way, all bloodied up. But she'd kissed him and knew that he tasted really *really* good and she wanted to taste more of him.

Okay, enough of that. She really should be thinking about something else and not Damon's mouth. She returned her attention to the conversation going on around her.

"What was he wearing?" Gram asked.

"That's irrelevant," Damon said impatiently.

"No, it's not. It might give us an idea of his original time period. Was he dressed in a toga like a Roman or a Greek?" Gram asked Zoe.

"No." She tried to concentrate. "He wore dark brown clothes. A shirt and vest and pants. But not modern. All dark. The vest had long sleeves and looked like it was made out of snakeskin or eel or something. I can do some research into men's attire for the past five hundred years or so."

"Or he could have been wearing that to throw you off," the ever-suspicious Damon said.

"That's possible, too," Zoe said. "Even so, I want to check it out."

"Of course you do," Damon said.

"What's that supposed to mean?" Zoe said.

"That you don't take orders well."

"You're not in the Union army anymore," she said.

"But I'm still fighting," he said.

"You don't have to fight me. We're on the same side."

"Are we?"

"Yes. At least in this demon matter," she qualified. "And I admit I don't take orders well. It's a family thing. None of the Adams women is blindly obedient." She paused before admitting, "It's also a witch thing."

"Yes, well, it's also a vampire thing."

"I noticed," she said.

They shared a look. It was the first time that Zoe felt this sense of sharing. In the past he'd glared at her and she'd glared at him. He'd eyed her breasts. She'd eyed his chest and abs. But this was something new. She didn't even know what to call it, but it felt damn good. Too damn good.

She broke off the visual contact. "I'll go check out that clothing idea."

Her laptop was in the living room so she had to walk past Damon to leave Gram's room. He stepped aside and gestured for her to go ahead of him. He quickly followed.

"I can't think if you are leaning over my shoulder," she warned him as she sat on the couch and picked up the computer.

"Because I'm a vampire?" he surprised her by saying.

"No. Because you're you."

He gave her one of his sardonic smiles.

She stuck her tongue out at him.

Half an hour later, she found what she was looking for. "He was wearing a doublet from the 1600s. You know what that means, don't you?"

"That he's been in hell a long time?"

"It means he could have been around for the Witch Hunt in Salem in 1692."

"You have the date memorized?"

"Every witch does. It's a critical date. Like the date you were turned."

"July third."

"At Gettysburg."

He nodded.

"So this 'wrong' Silas was talking about doesn't seem to be attached to your date but maybe to my family's. Did I tell you he called me dearie?"

"No."

"It wasn't an endearment as much as a veiled threat or warning said in an outwardly courteous voice."

"You're sure there is no reference to a Silas in your family's Book of Spells."

She pointed to the thick book on the coffee table. "Do you know how many pages are in there?"

"No."

"Neither do I. The book is wrapped in magic. Gram and I are the only ones who can access it. But maybe I could do a spell asking the book to find any reference to Silas."

"Do that," Damon told her.

Ex Libris,
Look in the book.

Give us a peek
At that which we seek—

"Don't you have to include what we are looking for?" Damon said.

Zoe flashed him an angry look. "Do not interrupt me while I am casting a spell!"

"Or?" he said.

"Or your privates might fall off," Bella said from the chair.

"Now I have to start all over again," Zoe said.

Ex Libris,
Look in the book.
Give us a peek
At that which we seek.
Silas Milton is the name.
Find the same.

She'd deliberately left the Book of Spells open so the pages could turn easier. They flew back to one of the earliest pages in the book. Over time various generations of Adams witches had added their own variations of spells for everything from bee stings to love potions to hair loss, which accounted for the innumerable pages.

Zoe waited to make sure the spell was complete and this was the right page. Then she leaned forward to pull the heavy book onto her lap. "Don't touch," she reminded Damon as he leaned over the back of the couch.

"Don't touch the book or you?"

"Either one," she said.

She tried to read the old script, but she was no expert on this portion of the book.

"It's in Latin," Damon said.

"I know."

She tugged on her left ear, and the words were translated into English. "A shortcut," she said with a shrug. "We had to translate too many sections to do a spell each time, so we developed a faster way to translate Latin within this book to English."

"What else do you have shortcuts for?" Damon asked.

"Never mind. Stay focused. It says here that Silas Milton had an evil soul."

"That's it?"

"You're interrupting again," Zoe told Damon.

"Then talk faster."

"Or you could be a little more patient," she said.

"Or you could talk faster."

"Silas came to this country from England with a wave of Puritans. He ended up in Salem. Uh-oh."

"Uh-oh, what?" Damon demanded.

"He was one of the accusers of Rebekka Adams, my five-time great-aunt who was hung after being declared a witch." She turned the page to read more but instead found an illustration of a man. "That's him! That's the demon I saw in the astral projection."

"How could you not know that Silas was one of the accusers at the Salem witch trials? You memorized the date and not the names?"

"I don't know everything. I can't remember everything." Zoe felt her control slipping. "I didn't ask for any of this, you know! I didn't practice magic for two years before coming here. And now look at me. I'm casting protection spells left and right!"

"That's a bit of an exaggeration," Damon said.

"I'm having to deal with demon astral projections."

"Something new for you."

"I don't want something new. I want peace and quiet. That's why I came here. To get away from . . ." Her voice trailed off.

"To get away from what?" he pressed.

"Everything."

Zoe welcomed the knock on the front door that prevented her from having to answer further. She wasn't about to admit that by telling her ex-fiancé that she was a witch, she'd broken one of the main rules of their coven. If Damon found out, he might think that she wouldn't be able to keep the fact that she was living among vampires a secret.

Pausing before opening the door, she asked Damon, "Is this another demon?"

"No, it's a friend." Damon reached around her to grab the doorknob. "This is Pat Heller, the owner of Pat's Tats. You need to invite him in."

Pat looked more like a hippie than a vampire. His silvery hair was held back in a ponytail and he was wearing jeans and a Rolling Stones T-shirt.

"Come on in," Zoe said.

"Neville told me you asked him to check out the name Silas Milton." Pat directed his comment to Damon.

"That right."

"He said it was the name of one of the demons?"

"The head honcho demon if there is such a thing," Zoe inserted.

"There is such a thing although the terminology may be different." Returning his attention to Damon,

Pat said, "Do you remember me telling you that there is a cosmic connection between you and Zoe?"

"I don't like the sound of that," Zoe said.

"Neither did I," Damon said.

"Is that why Damon has a tattoo that almost matches my talisman?" she asked.

Pat nodded. "Probably."

"So what is the connection?" Zoe asked.

"That's what we have to find out," Pat said.

"Well, I checked our family's Book of Spells and found that Silas was in Salem during the witch trials," she said. "He made the accusation against one of my ancestors."

"I feared as much," Pat said.

"So they *are* after the witches," Damon said.

"Not just the witches," Pat said. "They are after you, too, Damon. And most likely me as well."

"You?" Damon was clearly surprised. "What did you do to piss off a demon?"

"He wasn't a demon at the time. Just an evil human being who got a thrill out of using fear and torture to wield power."

"So you knew Silas?" Zoe said.

Pat nodded. "We fought on opposite sides of the Civil War."

"On the Union or Confederate side?" Zoe asked.

"The Royalist side," Pat said.

She frowned in confusion.

"It was the English Civil War, not the American one," Pat explained.

"But that was way back—"

Pat interrupted her. "In the 1640s. From '42 to '46 to

be exact. Silas was a Roundhead on the side of Cromwell. Our families were bitter enemies."

"Were you turned on the battlefield?" she asked.

"No. I wish I had been," Pat said. "Then maybe I could have saved my family. After Cromwell came into power, our land was confiscated. My sisters fled to France, and I was thrown in jail for crimes against the Protector."

Zoe wasn't sure what he was talking about. "A vampire?"

"Cromwell. He was known as the Protector but he sure as hell didn't protect me. I managed to escape and was on the run for over a year before I was caught again and put in the Tower. As in the Tower of London. I hated those ravens."

"Cromwell's people?"

"No, the birds. I realize modern researchers say they weren't there until Charles the Second was returned to the throne but I heard them. I was turned while in prison shortly before I was to be hanged."

"Good timing," Damon said.

"Damn right," Pat said. "The transition wasn't easy for me. I went to France and down to Italy. By the time I had my head on straight, the king had regained the throne and Silas had left England for the Colonies. When I arrived in Massachusetts, the trials were over and shortly afterward Silas was dead. Of natural causes they claimed. He was old by then."

"So his grudge against you goes back to the English Civil War?" Damon asked. "When you were both human? It doesn't have anything to do with the fact that you killed him?"

"What?" Zoe looked from one vampire to the other. "What did I miss? Pat didn't say he killed Silas."

"He didn't have to say it. It's written all over his hand." Damon pointed to the tattoos on the back of each of Pat's fingers.

"It is?" She looked closer.

Pat made no attempt to hide his hands.

"Those are Theban symbols," Zoe said. It was also known as the Witch's Alphabet, but she wasn't about the share that info or they'd somehow use it against her. All she said was "Its origins are unknown but it was used as a substitution cipher to encrypt magical secrets."

"Or vampire secrets. The left hand spells out *Silas* and the right *Death*," Damon said.

"Where did you learn how to read Theban symbols?" Zoe asked Damon.

"From Eve," he replied.

"I had no idea Silas became a demon," Pat said. "Not until a few minutes ago when you told Neville the name."

"You never noticed those symbols on Pat's hands before?" Zoe demanded of Damon.

"Of course I noticed them, but usually they aren't facing me," Damon said. "They face him. I'm standing beside and slightly behind him now and it's only then that I recognized them."

"So Silas is after Pat." Her witch's intuition made her add, "Does this all have something to do with the funeral home?"

"Why do you keep asking about the funeral home?" Damon demanded.

"You're vampires living next door to a funeral home.

And now there are demons in underground tunnels. I just put two and two together and got—"

"The wrong answer," Damon said curtly. "Forget about it." He glanced down at the screen of his smartphone then reached out to take hold of Zoe's arm. "You're coming with me."

"Wait a second!" she said. "What are you talking about? Where are we going?"

"There's trouble at the funeral home," Damon said.

Chapter Fourteen

"You and Pat go ahead. I'll wait here for you," Zoe said.

"No, you're coming with me," Damon said.

"Why?"

"Because there's a problem."

"I didn't cause it." Had she? All she'd done was ask to look up something in the Book of Spells. That was a very limited spell that shouldn't have had any impact beyond the book itself. "Besides, a second ago you told me to forget about the funeral home."

"That was before."

"Before what?"

"Before we got a demon possession," he said. "Come on!"

"Wait, why can't Pat go with you?" Zoe said. "He knows Silas."

"The demon wants to talk to you," Damon said.

"What about Gram? I can't leave her here alone," Zoe said.

"Pat is here."

"He's not a Demon Hunter, is he?" she asked.

"No."

"One vampire isn't enough to protect Gram," Zoe said.

"So we'll get another one." Damon opened the door to a slightly heavyset man wearing impeccably pressed gray trousers and a crisp designer white shirt. "Invite him in."

"He's a vampire, too?" she said.

Bruce nodded and smiled.

"Don't worry about your grandmother. Pat and I will take good care of her," Bruce said.

"Fine. Come in, but I still don't understand why can't I stay here," Zoe said.

"Because your services are needed at the funeral home," Damon said.

"I don't like funeral homes," she said. That was putting it mildly. Ever since her father's funeral when she was very young, she'd had a thing about them. "They give me the creeps."

"Too bad," Damon said.

"You can't compel me to go," she said.

"A human's life is at stake."

"Maybe you're lying to get me to the funeral home so you can torture me or something," she said.

Damon responded by lifting her in his arms and moving with vamp speed the two blocks to the Evergreen Funeral Home. Zoe's head was spinning when they arrived. He dumped her back on her feet, but she had to hang on to him a moment until she regained her balance.

"What if someone saw us?" she said.

"We moved too fast for human eyes to see us."

Zoe fixed him with her best angry-witch stare. "Do not just grab me like that again. I do not appreciate being taken places against my will." She looked around. They were in a hallway. "Where are we?"

"In the basement of the funeral home." She belatedly realized that Nick and Daniella were standing farther down the hall.

"What's going on?" Damon asked Nick.

Daniella answered. "It's Phil. He's our embalmer. Well, not mine, as I didn't go into the family business but started my own cupcake business, as you know. Sorry I'm babbling. I do that when I get nervous."

Zoe could sure relate, which was another reason for her to like Daniella.

"Anyway, Phil has been possessed by a demon," Daniella said.

"I can't just kill him like I did the cable guy," Damon said. "If I do, then the human dies. The cable guy was not human. He was all demon. Possession is something else."

"I tried to exorcise him but it isn't a power that I have as a druid hybrid," Daniella said. "His head actually spun around, which can't be good for him. He has back trouble."

Head spinning did not sound like a good thing. "Shouldn't you call for a priest or something?" Zoe said nervously.

"You're the 'or something,'" Damon told her.

"I don't know how to do exorcisms," she said.

"The demon demanded to speak to you," Nick said.

"Can't we do that on speakerphone or Skype or something?" Zoe asked.

"No," Damon said emphatically.

"Phil is contained in the embalming room where we prepare the bodies," Daniella said.

"What about your family?" Damon asked Daniella.

"They don't know a thing about this and we need to keep it that way. They have a big funeral they are arranging with the family of the deceased in the office upstairs. We have to move fast."

"We?" That made Zoe feel better. At least there were four of them.

"You," Daniella corrected her.

"And me," Damon said.

"The embalming room is in here," Daniella said, leading them to a door.

"Do not rush me in there," Zoe warned Damon.

"If you don't hurry, Phil could die. Do you want his death on your hands?" Damon said.

Zoe didn't want anything to do with the embalming room in a funeral home on her hands.

Damon took her hand in his. "Let's go."

He opened the door and entered the room but kept her behind him as he assessed the situation. Zoe jumped nervously as the door slammed shut behind them.

"Who are you?" Zoe asked the man in the white coat. Actually she was asking the demon possessing the man in the white coat.

"Guy." His voice was something right out of a horror movie. "Your time is running out."

"Says who?" she said.

"Says Silas."

"Give me a break. I just met him a few minutes ago," she said. "Talk about impatience. Wait, exactly what do you mean by my time is running out?"

"What I said."

"And you possessed this poor man just to tell me that?" Zoe said, her disapproval evident in her tone of voice.

"Yes."

"Well, that's very rude," Zoe said.

"The Demon Hunter can't kill me or he kills the human," Guy said.

"I'm not a fan of most humans," Damon said, speaking for the first time since they'd entered the room.

"You have your orders and I have mine," Guy said.

"Okay, you delivered your message. Now leave," Damon said.

"No. I'm not done," Guy said.

"What do you want?" Zoe asked.

"A devil's food cupcake. I hear they are very good. I can smell them down below. And a Dr Pepper. Your mother introduced me to Dr Pepper."

"It's a soft drink, not a person," Zoe said. "Wait, what about my mother?"

"She's the reason I am in this position," Guy said.

"Possessing a guy in a funeral home?" she scoffed. "How can you blame that on my mom?"

"She condemned me to hell."

Zoe couldn't believe it. "What? When?"

"Right before she died two years ago."

Was that why her mother had practiced black magic? Was it to send Guy to hell? "Why? What did you do?"

"I loved her."

Zoe shook her head. "I don't believe you."

"May I burn in hell if I am lying. Wait, I am already burning in hell. Not at this exact moment, however." He swung Phil's arms. "It feels good to have human form again."

"Stop doing that. You could be hurting him. Tell me about my mother," Zoe ordered.

"Oops, my master calls. Gotta go," Guy said. "Remember, you owe me that cupcake and Dr Pepper."

Suddenly demon-free, Phil slumped over and would have fallen had Damon not stepped forward to help him to a nearby stool.

"Whaa . . . at happened?" Phil said groggily.

"You passed out," Damon said.

"Low blood sugar," Zoe added, trying to be helpful.

"What are you two doing here?" Phil said.

Zoe tugged on the hem of Damon's black T-shirt. "Something is happening."

"Another possession?" Damon asked

She shook her head. "It's my bangle bracelet."

"This is no time to talk about your stupid jewelry," Damon said impatiently.

"It's not stupid and it's pulling me toward something." Her right arm went straight out at her side, with her fingers aiming at the wall, where several framed certificates hung. But it was the Latin saying that her bangle glommed on to like a magnet to iron.

CORPORA LENTE AUGESCENT CITO EXTINGUUNTUR.

"You shouldn't be in here," Phil said.

Damon looked into Phil's eyes and said, "You will not remember us." Grabbing Zoe's hand, he pulled her from the room.

Daniella was waiting for them right outside. "Is Phil okay?"

Damon nodded. "I didn't sense any lingering demon presence."

"There is a Latin saying framed on the wall that starts with *Corpora*," Zoe said.

"It's a quote from Tacitus."

"Do you know what it means?" Zoe said.

"Bodies grow slowly but are snuffed out quickly," Damon said.

"Bodies grow slowly and die quickly is another way of saying it," Daniella said. "It's been on the wall in there as long as I can remember."

"Why would my bangle be attracted to it?" Zoe wondered aloud. Seeing Daniella's blank look, she said, "Never mind."

"I've got to make sure for myself that Phil is okay," Daniella said.

Once she was inside, Zoe asked Damon, "Can we leave now?"

"Yes."

This time they walked outside at a normal human speed and went around the corner to the bar and grill.

"I need to stop here for a minute." Damon held the door open for her to enter.

She'd barely taken a few steps inside when her bangle once again pulled her toward the wall. This time it was behind the bar where there was a sign, again in Latin.

CINERIGBRIA SERA VENIT.

The sign was higher up than the last one, which left Zoe with her arm raised and her bangle plastered against the sign.

"Let me guess," Damon drawled. "Your bracelet again?"

"It's a bangle, actually, but yes."

"You wear a magic bangle along with your talisman?"

"The bangle never was magical before. I got it from

the Home Shopping Network. It has hand-carved cameos around it, and the writing is from an Italian love letter."

"Written by Tacitus?"

"No. Written by a woman in the twentieth century not—"

"When Tacitus was around in ancient Rome," Damon inserted.

"Right." Using her free hand, she pointed to the sign above the bar. "What does this one say?"

"Fame to the dead comes too late," Damon translated.

At his words, the bond was broken between the bangle and the sign, allowing her to lower her arm. She studied her bangle. "I don't know what's going on here."

"Maybe your grandmother cast a spell on it."

"She wouldn't do that without telling me first."

Zoe was still rattled from her earlier experience in the embalming room. Had that Guy demon been telling the truth about her mother sending him to hell? Or was he lying and trying to besmirch her mother's name? She also hadn't recovered from seeing Silas as an astral projection or from discovering he'd been the cause of her ancestor's death in Salem.

And then there was the whole embalming-room-of-a-funeral-home thing. She needed a drink. Badly. But she was in a vampire bar. Who knew what was on their wine list?

She looked at the bottles behind the bar. "You don't have a lot of alcohol here."

"We have enough," Damon said.

"Do any humans come here?"

"Not many."

"So this is really a vampire bar for the consumption of blood?"

"Could you make your distaste any more obvious?" he retorted.

"I didn't say anything distasteful."

"You didn't have to. That disdainful wrinkling of your nose expressed your feelings."

"Maybe I was just shaking off a sneeze."

"Right," Damon scoffed.

"What if humans wander in and want to order a hamburger or something?"

"We compel them to leave and try their luck elsewhere."

"Do the bottles have blood in them?"

"No. Most do not. Why?" he said. "Are you thirsty?"

"Are you?" she retorted.

"Are you asking me if the smell of blood in the embalming room aroused my appetite?"

Her stomach turned. "There was blood in there? I didn't know that."

"It's an embalming room. You know what they do in there."

"Not the specifics, and I don't want to know. I didn't smell any blood."

"Vamps have an increased sense of smell."

"Bully for you."

"I can smell your fear," he said.

She was sure he was making that up. "What does it smell like?" Wait, she had remembered to put on deodorant this morning, hadn't she? She'd been in such a rush to get dressed, she wasn't sure. "Never mind."

"What are you afraid of, little witch?"

"Demons in funeral homes," she said. "And spiders. I don't like spiders." Damn, she shouldn't have told him that. "I was just kidding about the spiders." She wasn't but she didn't want him to know that.

She also didn't want him knowing the strong desire she felt for him. She was afraid of the way he could get to her with just one look. And then there was that extraordinary kiss—not to mention his hands on her breast. That caress was burned into her memory.

Damon was clearly a master in the art of seduction. He'd had over a century to perfect his moves. She'd had fewer than forty-eight hours to perfect her defenses against him, and there were moments when the walls she'd built were about to come tumbling down.

Even now, Damon was looking at her as if he wanted to lift her onto the bar, peel off her yoga pants and underwear, and have his wicked way with her.

She tried to turn her thoughts away from that vividly sizzling fantasy but it stubbornly stayed in her mind.

Thankfully, she was prevented from doing anything she'd regret by the arrival of a young man wearing broken glasses taped together. Definitely a nerd. Also a vampire? Yep, judging by the way Damon greeted him. So vampires came in all shapes and sizes and personalities. From Pat the hippie who'd actually fought for the English Crown to Tanya whose boyfriend turned her in the 1950s to Damon the darkly sexy vampire who fought for the Union.

"This is Neville," Damon told her.

The nerdy vampire shyly nodded at her.

Was he afraid of her because she was a witch?

Wait, it was coming back to her now. This Neville was the guy who'd hacked her laptop. She wished she was a meaner witch and could do something equally egregious to him. But the poor vamp was probably just following orders. Damon's orders.

He and Damon conversed in such quiet tones that she couldn't hear them. At first she was aggravated, but upon further reflection she wondered if she really wanted to hear what they had to say if it had anything to do with embalming rooms and blood.

When Damon finally returned to her side, she said, "Did he have anything new to add to Silas's story?"

"Nothing we didn't already know. Let's go."

"I need to stop at the Heavenly Cupcakes shop before we go home." It was her home, not Damon's. She wondered where he lived but didn't want to give him the satisfaction of asking.

"Is another Latin saying drawing you there?" Damon asked.

"No, it's the devil's food cupcake."

"For Guy the demon?"

"No, for me."

Zoe entered Daniella's shop for the first time and was impressed by the decor. A Raphael-like angel smiled down on them from the HEAVENLY CUPCAKES sign inside the store. Several other framed prints of angels hung on the pink walls. But Zoe's main attention was focused on the glass case displaying a wonderful assortment of cupcakes. Neon-colored chalk listed their individual descriptions on the glass. They all sounded divine. Black Forest. Chocolate peppermint. Amaretto. Red velvet.

The young woman behind the counter had dark blond hair with streaks of attention-grabbing hot pink throughout. "Hi, I'm Xandra. Welcome to Heavenly

Cupcakes. Happy St. Patrick's Day. We're all out of our Irish cream cupcakes and the mini mints but we have lots of other choices. Have you decided what you'd like?"

Zoe nodded. She'd like for the past thirty-some hours to disappear. She'd like to go back to pre-demon times. She'd like to focus on her lovely soaps and lotions instead of saving the world. But since none of that was going to happen, she needed chocolate.

"I'll have the devil's food," she told Xandra.

"Is that to go or to eat here?" Xandra asked.

"Eat here," she said.

"To go," Damon said.

One look at his expression told her that he wasn't about to change his mind. "Fine. To go then."

Xandra packaged the cupcake in a special box that prevented it from sliding around.

Zoe belatedly realized she didn't have her wallet with her since Damon had whisked her away from home at top vamp speed.

Turning to Damon, she said, "Thank you for paying for my cupcake." Her look warned him that if he refused to pay, there would be hell to pay.

The corner of his wicked mouth lifted in the fleeting hint of a sardonic smile. "You're welcome."

As Zoe stepped back outside, she realized it was the first time she'd been away from their rental house since she'd first met Damon . . . yesterday? She stopped in her tracks. How could that be? She felt as if she'd known him for much longer than that.

She walked past Pat's Tats. Now that she knew Pat was a vampire who had been turned while imprisoned in the Tower of London for crimes against Cromwell, she wondered how many of the other businesses along the street were run by vampires.

She already knew that Tanya's Tanning Salon was one of them. But what about the Happy Times Emergency Dental Clinic?

"Dental care is important for vamps," Damon said, shining his pearly whites at her. "Doc Boomer is a real pro."

"A pro vampire?" she whispered, looking around the street nervously to make sure she wasn't overheard. The sidewalk was empty.

Damon nodded. "He got his nickname from his booming voice and his overwhelming physical appearance. But enough about the doc. If you're done sightseeing, we need to get back to your house."

"I should have gotten a cupcake for Gram," Zoe said, pivoting to return to Heavenly Cupcakes, apparently the only human-owned business on the block. Well, the only hybrid-owned business, she corrected herself.

Damon turned her back. "I had Xandra add another devil's food cupcake for your grandmother."

His consideration surprised her. "That was nice of you. Thank you."

The short walk to her rental house seemed longer with Damon beside her. She could see where super vamp speed might come in handy from time to time. Not that she wanted him scooping her up in his arms again that way.

Doing that took away her power. Well, not her power, but her choice. Apparently her protection spell did not guard her from being whisked off by a vampire on a mission. Not that she was about to point that out to him. Who knew where he might take her next?

Maybe he could only whisk her away within a certain distance from home. Like a few blocks. She'd have to check with Gram when she got home.

Pat was waiting for them the instant they walked inside.

Zoe's bangle started humming. Why was it doing that now? She'd been wearing the bangle when she'd met him earlier.

Instead of aiming at the Theban symbols on his fingers, the bangle glommed on to a tat on his right forearm. NON SUM QUALIS ERAM.

"Sorry about this," Zoe said in embarrassment.

"It's a quote by Horace," Pat said. "I am not as I used to be."

As soon as Pat spoke the translation, the force holding the bangle to the tattoo was broken.

"Her bracelet keeps zeroing in on Latin sayings," Damon said. "First at the embalming room at the funeral home, then at the bar, and now here with you."

"Which sayings?"

Damon repeated them for Pat who asked Zoe, "May I see your bracelet?"

She nervously fingered her bangle. "I can't get it off."

"Maybe the sayings are a sign," Pat said.

"Or a spell," Damon said.

"There seems to be a theme," Pat said.

"A Latin theme?" Zoe said.

"A theme of death," Damon said.

Zoe didn't like the sound of that.

"It's obvious," Damon continued despite her wishing he wouldn't. "Bodies grow slowly and die quickly. Fame to the dead comes too late. I am not as I used to be."

"That last one could be anything," Zoe said. Turning to Pat, she asked him, "When did you get that?"

"I don't recall," Pat said. "Several centuries ago."

"Before or after the tattoos on your fingers?" she asked.

"After, I think."

"Why wasn't my bangle attracted to your tat when I met you a short while ago?" she said.

"It has to be a demon thing," Pat said.

"Really? Why? I mean, aren't these all just famous Latin quotes?" Zoe said. "*Corpora lente augescent cito extinguuntur. Cinerigbria sera venit. Non sum qualis—*"

"Silence!" Gram shouted as she ran to Zoe's side. "Not another word."

Chapter Fifteen

Zoe froze.

"It's black magic!" Gram said. "What you're saying. It's part of a black magic incantation."

"What does it do?" Zoe whispered.

"It's an appeal to the other side to do something bad."

"Something bad like what?" Zoe said unsteadily.

"Release the forces of evil."

Zoe felt light-headed with fear. "I thought it was just a bunch of Latin sayings."

"Or it could just be a bunch of Latin sayings," Gram agreed.

"Wait." Zoe shook her head, which made her dizzier. "I don't understand. It can't be both. Which is it?"

"I'm not sure. My Latin is a little rusty. Most of the spells in our coven are in English now."

"I know. That's why I didn't think this was a spell," Zoe said.

"Where did you find it?" Gram said. "Was it in the family Book of Spells?"

"No. My bangle bracelet was acting like a magnet or something and attaching itself to Latin sayings in various businesses in Vamptown. The first one was at the funeral home."

"You went to a funeral home?" Gram's voice expressed her disbelief.

Zoe pointed at Damon. "He made me do it."

"What's wrong with going to a funeral home?" Damon demanded.

"Nothing if you are a vampire," Zoe said.

"Plenty of humans go to funeral homes. Alive and dead. It's no big deal," he said.

"This particular funeral home is a big deal to you, though, isn't it?" Zoe said.

He made no comment.

"Don't give me that I'm-going-to-fry-you look," she told him. "You need my help dealing with these demons."

"Was there another astral projection?" Gram said. "At the funeral home, I mean."

"No, it was a demon possession," Zoe said.

"Of you?" Gram said.

"No, your protection spell is working," Zoe assured her. She left out the part about Damon whisking her off. She was still freaked about the latest crisis, a possible black magic Latin incantation.

"I should hope so, but still it is reassuring to hear that. So who was possessed?"

"The embalmer Phil," Zoe said.

"How did you get rid of the demon?"

"I didn't. Silas called him back. But before that, he said his name was Guy and that my mother had condemned him to hell. He also said she introduced him to Dr Pepper."

"Well, that may have been true," Gram said. "You know how your mom was about her Dr Pepper."

"Why would he say that about her?" Zoe demanded.

"That she liked Dr Pepper? She did," Gram said.

"No, I mean about condemning him to hell. Witches can't do that. Can they?"

"They definitely can't condemn vampires to hell, just in case you were wondering," Damon drawled.

"I don't remember my mother knowing a guy named Guy, do you, Gram?"

Gram just shrugged and said, "She knew a lot of people. What about Phil? Is he going to be okay?"

"He should be," Zoe said, hoping it was true. "I'm just glad I didn't have to perform an exorcism. I have no idea how to do that."

"You better learn fast," Damon said.

"I don't know that demons would listen to a witch even if I did learn how to do that ritual," Zoe said.

"Silas and Guy both listened to you," Damon said.

"I meant I have no idea if a witch's spell would work," Zoe said. "It could do more harm than good."

"Well, we learned something from all this—the demon today said your mother sent him to hell, which indicates that this demon infestation is personally related to you."

Zoe didn't point out that Guy the demon could have been and probably was lying. Instead she said, "It's also related to Pat and his tats. And to you as the Demon Hunter."

"It's the three of us here in the same place at the same time," Pat said.

"Then maybe we shouldn't hang out together," Zoe suggested.

"It's too late for that now," Damon said.

"I agree," Pat said. "Since you're back, I'm going to return to my place and see if I can figure out a way to deal with this situation. I have a few reference books and sources I can consult now that I know it involves Silas."

Once Pat was gone, Zoe asked Gram, "What is the deal with all these Latin sayings? What do they have to do with Silas and Guy and my mother?" A sudden thought occurred to her. "Do you think it was a spell to bring my mother back?"

"I'm not sure. But even if it was, we can't bring her back," Gram said.

"Because she's dead," Damon said.

"You came back from the dead," Zoe retorted.

"I was immediately turned by a vampire," Damon said. "Your mother has been dead for two years."

Zoe felt the tears coming to her eyes. "I want her back. I miss her."

Damon looked at Zoe in alarm. "No crying. I don't do crying."

"Fine. Then you don't have to cry. But I can and you can't stop me. You can't compel me. You can't kiss me because my grandmother is right here."

Clearly Damon considered that a challenge because he leaned closer. "That doesn't mean I can't kiss you."

But Zoe wasn't about to let him get away with kissing her again. Not until she knew for sure why he was doing it.

"I thought you didn't like witches," she said to Damon.

"I thought you didn't like vampires," he said.

"I don't."

"You just like kissing them, right?" he said.

"Wrong. That's why I stopped you."

He brushed the ball of his thumb across her lips. "You're lying, little witch."

"How long do we have to put up with this?" Bella asked as she strolled into the room. "And where's that cupcake your friend promised me?" She eyed the box that Zoe had set on the table by the door.

"Those are for Gram and me," Zoe said.

"Thank you," Gram said, grabbing the box and heading to the kitchen.

"What about mine?" Bella demanded.

"We've got more important things to deal with," Zoe said.

"Like kissing him?" Bella sat and curled her tail around her body before tilting her head at Zoe. "Seriously?"

"We are not having this conversation now," Zoe said. "You forget, I am the witch, you are the familiar."

"So?" Bella said.

"So I'm your boss."

Bella chuckled. It sounded like a purr, but Zoe knew the difference. Bella had chuckled or even outright laughed at her a lot since she'd strolled into her life. "You are not the boss of me."

"I am so," Zoe said.

"Zip it, ladies."

They turned in unison to glare at Damon.

"This is one catfight I do not want to see," he told them.

"Did someone mention a catfight?" Bruce asked as he entered the living room from the kitchen.

Zoe had forgotten he was still there.

"Don't get your hopes up," Damon told Bruce.

"Catfights aren't my thing," Bruce said. "So what did I miss?"

"Zoe almost conjured a black magic spell to unleash more demons," Damon said.

"That's not true. We don't know what the spell is for," Zoe said.

"Then why did you cast it?" Bruce asked.

"It may not even be a spell. I was just putting together the Latin phrases I found around Vamptown," Zoe said. "One was on Pat's arm."

Bruce nodded. "I know the one you mean. Pat has had it as long as we've been together. We're almost the same age but he's been a vampire centuries longer than I have."

"Bruce used to be a clown in the circus down in Florida before he became a vampire," Gram told Zoe as she strolled in from the kitchen carrying a tray with two mugs and the two cupcakes. "We had fun talking about old times. And he knows some great classic jokes. I've never been good with jokes. I always forget the punch line."

"This is no joke," Damon said with his customary impatience.

"I know," Zoe said. "Black magic killed my mother."

"Yet you were tempted to use it to bring your mother back from the dead," he said.

"Just for a moment."

"That's all it takes," Damon said. "According to you, your grandmother only opened the Book of Darkness for a second—and look at what a mess resulted from that."

"How often are you going to keep throwing that in my face?" Zoe said.

"As often as it takes."

"To do what?"

"To get you motivated to find the missing spell book," he said.

She stood toe-to-toe with him. "Oh, I'm motivated all right."

"Do they do this often?" Bruce asked in an aside to Gram.

"All the time," Gram said.

"You are not helping your cause by aggravating me," Zoe told Damon.

"This isn't a cause," Damon growled. "It's a crusade to get rid of the demons you unleashed."

"There you go again. Placing the blame on me. I feel guilty enough as it is. I don't need you tossing that in my face every two seconds," Zoe said.

They were interrupted by the sound of an organ playing the opening notes from *Phantom of the Opera.*

Bruce's face lit up. "I love this musical. Do you have the original Broadway cast version or a newer version? My fave Phantom is Michael Crawford hands down."

Confused, Zoe said, "I don't have any version."

"It's coming from the floor vents," Damon said.

"They like *Phantom of the Opera.*" Bruce shook his head in amazement. "How bad can they be?"

"Very bad," Damon said. "What part of *they're demons* do you not understand?"

"The part where we have to destroy them," Bruce said.

"*You* don't have to destroy them. I do," Damon said.

"That seems rather harsh," Bruce said.

Damon eyed Zoe's grandmother suspiciously. "What have you been telling him? Have you enchanted him or something?"

"No, I was enchanting before I came here." Bruce's grin faded when he saw the fierce expression on Damon's face. "I was just expressing an opinion."

"A stupid one," Damon growled.

"Don't mind him," Gram told Bruce with a sympathetic pat to his arm. "He's crabby because he really wants to kiss Zoe instead of chasing demons."

"You're all crazy," Bella declared with a swish of her tail. "I need a nap."

"Me, too," Gram said, setting the tray on the coffee table and taking one cupcake and a mug of tea with her.

Zoe figured that was just an excuse to leave them alone. Gram never took as many naps as she had since they'd gotten to Vamptown. But then she'd never had to deal with a bunch of pissed-off vampires before, either.

Zoe knew it was very draining and she was much younger than her grandmother.

"How are you going to sleep with that music blaring?" Damon called after her, but Gram ignored him.

"It's not 'that music.' It is one of the finest musicals ever written," Bruce said reverently. "It's almost as if they are playing it just for me."

"They sure as hell aren't playing it for me," Damon said. Going over to the nearest floor vent, he stomped on it. "Shut up down there!"

Bruce left in a huff. "I'm not staying here with such an unappreciative audience. I'm going to the bar and see if it is playing there."

"You do that," Damon called after him.

As soon as Bruce left, the organ music stopped.

"Finally," Damon said.

"Is 'Dixie' more your kind of song?" Zoe asked him.

" 'Dixie' is a Reb song," he retorted.

Zoe welcomed the ringtone of her smartphone. The number was listed as UNKNOWN. "Hello?"

"Enjoying the show, dearie?" Silas asked.

"How did you get a phone?" she demanded.

"Guy picked one up during his brief time at the funeral home," Silas said.

"That's stealing."

"Which is a sin and I shall be sent to hell for it. But wait, I've already been sent to hell," Silas noted sarcastically.

"Who are you talking to?" Damon demanded. "Something is blocking me being able to hear anything they're saying."

"Tell the Demon Hunter that's a little trick of mine," Silas said before adding, "I hope you both enjoy the next song. I chose it just for you two lovebirds."

Silas hung up before she could say a word.

"What did he want?" Damon said.

"He said that he was using a trick to block you from hearing him speaking to me and that he hopes we both enjoy the next song." She left out the "lovebirds" part. No sense in stirring up more trouble.

She got goose bumps as a male voice started singing "The Music of the Night" from *Phantom of the Opera*.

Suddenly the lyrics took on a new meaning given her current situation. The demons weren't the only darkness. Damon represented forbidden darkness as well. Not evil, but the sexy edge of darkness.

"All we need is a chandelier. And a gondola. And most important of all . . . a mask," Bella said dramatically. "Oh, the stories I could tell you about the masked balls at the Winter Palace. Catherine the Great loved a good party."

The feel of her bangle vibrating against her wrist again distracted Zoe.

Angry at being ignored, Bella took a bite of the devil's food cupcake and ran off with a chunk of frosting in her mouth.

Before Zoe could reprimand her familiar, her arm shot out so that her wrist rested on the small of Damon's back.

"What are you doing?" he demanded.

"It's not me, it's the bangle."

"You don't take responsibility for anything, do you."

His accusation stung and she tried to pull away, but the power of the bangle was too much for her. She couldn't remove the bangle, either. "Take off your shirt."

"This music really does get to you," he said. "Far be it from me to interfere with your fantasies."

She had to tug his shirt out from beneath the bangle.

"You must have a tattoo in Latin," she said. She was facing him, so it was hard to look around him.

"I don't have any tats on my cheek," he said.

She looked up at his face. "I know that."

"I meant my other cheek." He tilted his head downward.

Only then did she realize that her fingers were beneath the waistband of his black jeans and her fingertips were on his butt.

The song went on about savoring sensation before rising in crescendo.

That wasn't the only thing rising. Pressed up against Damon, she could feel his throbbing arousal.

She felt helpless against the powerful attraction flaring between them. She should move her fingers to someplace safer, but the bangle held her captive just as Damon's dark blue eyes did.

She nervously licked her lips.

Damon groaned and lowered his head to lick her lips himself. The touch of his tongue tantalized her into parting her lips to allow him access. He made the most of it by delving into a kiss so passionate, her toes actually curled and her knees almost buckled.

His tongue tangled with hers, touching and exploring with skillful heat. She'd never felt this way before . . . yes, she had. The first time Damon had kissed her. But even that hadn't prepared her for this surge of desire, for the moist need between her thighs, for the erotic fantasies filling her mind.

The song repeated.

Damon cupped her face between his hands as he deepened his kiss.

Was it the music? Was it the vampire? Was it magic? Was it love?

Zoe couldn't turn away. She couldn't resist. She didn't want to. She wanted Damon with an intensity that was undeniable.

His hands shifted to thread through her hair. Tilting his head to one side, he added a new dimension to the merging of their mouths. He moved one hand from her hair down her back to cup her bottom as she was cupping his, tugging her even tighter against his fully aroused body. And when a vampire was fully aroused, he was *fully* aroused. At least this one was.

"The Music of the Night" played on, as did Zoe's fantasies. Damon's naked body hovering over hers on the oh-so-white sheets of her bed as he seduced her with his words and his kisses, tantalizing her with his fingers working their magic all over her body before surging inside her body, focusing his attention on that one spot . . .

Zoe was abruptly brought back to earth by the sound of Bella's voice. "Not again. Get a room."

Breaking off the kiss, Zoe prayed that her familiar hadn't somehow read Zoe's mind and seen those fantasies of the acts that would have taken place in Zoe's bedroom. Ditto re: Damon. She didn't want him knowing how much she wanted him.

She snuck a peek at him, curious to see if he had been similarly affected. Yes, he wanted her. His arousal made that clear. She couldn't move away from him because her bangle still held her hand in place.

"*VENATOR*," he said.

"What?" she stuttered.

"My tattoo. It says *VENATOR*. Latin for 'hunter.'"

At his translation, her bangle released its hold on her so she could release her hold on Damon's butt. She prayed he didn't notice the slight time lag there.

On a trip to Vegas she'd seen a T-shirt at the airport that said GIRLS GO NUTS FOR COWBOY BUTTS.

The T-shirt should have read GIRLS GO NUTS FOR VAMPIRE BUTTS.

She stepped away and put several feet between them.

"No more kissing." Her voice was more unsteady than she would have liked but then given what she'd just been through, it was amazing that she was coherent at all. "We need to stay focused. On desire, I mean on demons. Do you think it's the music?"

"What about the music?"

"Do you think it's responsible for what just happened?"

"*I'm* responsible for what just happened," Damon said. "I don't need music to make you want me."

Damn. What could she say to that? She'd probably come up with a perfect answer in an hour or two, but for now she kept her mouth shut and wished she could blot out the memory of how powerfully intoxicating that kiss they'd just shared was. She wished she could blame it on the music, which suddenly stopped.

Her hometown of Beantown was looking better by the minute, but there was no turning back at this point. She was stuck here in Vamptown dealing with demons and Damon. She had to stay strong and not give in to temptation. She couldn't go to the dark side—the one offered by demons or the sexy one offered by Damon.

She welcomed the knock on the door, but checked with Damon before opening it. He nodded, so she swung the door open.

Bob, Dr. Powers's follower, stood there. He slapped a piece of paper in her hand. "You've been served."

Chapter Sixteen

Zoe stared at Bob in disbelief.

"I'm a process server," Bob said. "I did tell you this wasn't over yet."

She looked down at the official-looking document he'd thrust into her hands.

Zoe had spent hours doing research on demons and hell. She'd had to face a demon in a funeral home and learned that her mother was accused of using black magic to send someone to hell. Then she'd been kissed by a vampire. Twice.

To top it all off, she had almost used black magic herself . . . maybe. Maybe the Latin phrases were black magic, maybe not.

That was enough to upset anyone. Even a witch. Especially a witch.

But Zoe's day had just gotten worse, because behind Bob, Dr. Powers's process server, was none other than her ex-fiancé, Tristin.

He stood there as good-looking as ever. His light

brown hair was a little on the long side and slightly rumpled. That was the only rumpled thing about him. His jeans and light blue shirt were crisp. He was no nerdy absentminded academic. He was a con man . . . who should have forgotten all about her.

Gram had cast a spell on Tristin to ensure that he'd forget Zoe. Or to be more precise, that he'd forget she'd confessed she was a witch.

"These humans are getting on my nerves," Damon muttered for her ears only. Then he focused his attention on Tristin. "Is he with you?" he asked Bob.

Bob nodded.

Damon moved toward Tristin. "Who are you?"

"Zoe's fiancé," Tristin said.

"Ex-fiancé," Zoe corrected him. "And I have nothing to say to you."

"But I have something to say to you. Unless you want me to reveal your secret to everyone?"

Shit. The spell hadn't worked. Looking in Tristin's light brown eyes, she could tell that he still knew she was a witch. She opened the door wider to let him in.

"I thought you'd come around to my way of thinking," Tristin said.

"You thought wrong," Damon said before moving with vamp hyper speed to slam Tristin against the foyer wall and hold him by the throat six inches off the ground.

"You're a warlock!" Tristin gurgled.

"Much worse." Damon bared his fangs at him.

"A vampire?" Tristin stuttered.

"Bingo."

"Are you going to turn me?" Tristin seemed excited by the possibility.

Damon dropped him in disgust. "No way."

Tristin scrambled to his feet. "Why not?"

"You're not worthy."

"What do I have to do to be worthy?"

"There's nothing you can do."

"A vampire." Tristin shook his head in amazement. "Are there more of your kind?"

Damon shot a glance at Zoe. "Is this guy for real?"

"I don't know what she's told you about me—" Tristin said.

Damon cut him off. "Enough to know that you're an asshole."

"I'm a professor of paranormal activity," Tristin said.

"Is that supposed to impress me?" Damon asked. "Because it doesn't."

Zoe turned to find Bob the process server staring at them as if looking into the gates of hell.

She didn't regret the fact that Bob was afraid. After all, the man was making her life more difficult than it already was. But she couldn't afford to have him go out and spread the news about Damon being a vampire. She wasn't confident enough to cast a spell after her last inadvertent incantation had brought up the possibility of dark magic.

Damon moved toward Bob. Looking into his eyes, he compelled him. "Go sit on the couch and be quiet."

Bob complied without a word.

"I'll deal with him later," Damon told Zoe.

"Are you going to drain him of all his blood?" Tristin said.

"No."

"So you're going to turn him?" Tristin pressed.

Damon rolled his eyes. "What is it with you?"

"Zoe couldn't give me any of her powers," Tristin said. "But if you turned me, I'd have your powers. The powers of a vampire. Immortality. I want it."

"Tough shit," Damon said.

"You can't compel me," Tristin said.

"Really?" Damon raised an eyebrow. "And why is that?"

"Because I have a very powerful mind," Tristin bragged. "Tell him, Zoe."

"He's an idiot," Zoe said.

"She's just angry because I dumped her. I'm sorry," Tristin told Zoe. "Upon further reflection, I decided that I was unfair to you. I know your grandmother cast a spell over me but I had anticipated that. So I had a file about you on my laptop. All about you being a witch, and how you helped me. Unfortunately, I didn't know to look for it—hence the lapse in time. I was going through some old files on my computer and ran across the one involving you. It may have taken me a while, but I'm here. And it's not like what I did was that bad. I mean, I could have blackmailed you by threatening to reveal the fact that you're a witch. But I didn't. You love me—"

"Loved you," she corrected him. "Past tense."

"I don't believe you," Tristin said.

"That's your problem," she shot back.

"*I'm* his problem," Damon said. "Because an angry witch is nothing compared with a pissed-off vampire."

"What did I do to piss you off?" Tristin said.

Damon tilted his head toward Zoe. "You hurt her. Big mistake."

"I've acknowledged that," Tristin said.

"Not sufficiently. I can't decide whether to have you

grovel at her feet and beg for forgiveness or bray like a donkey."

"I'll do both those things if you'll turn me," Tristin said.

"Not gonna happen," Damon said. "Get over it."

Zoe finally regained enough presence of mind to ask the questions buzzing in her head. "How did you know where to find me? What's your connection to the Powers people?"

"They came to me," Tristin said. "They Googled you and found our engagement announcement, which included the name of the college where I teach. They said they needed to contact your grandmother, and I said you always stuck together. If they found you, they'd find her."

"Why didn't you come with them when they stopped by earlier?"

"I wanted to see what kind of reception they got," Tristin said.

"He was afraid you'd turn him into a toad," Damon said.

"I waited because I knew Bob would be coming back," Tristin maintained.

"How did you convince him to let you tag along?" Zoe asked.

"I told him that as the man you'd agreed to marry, I could convince you of the error of your ways because you still loved me," Tristin said.

"Talk about being delusional." Zoe shook her head. When her bangs fell into her eyes, she impatiently shoved them aside. "Dr. Powers has nothing on you."

"If I were delusional, I wouldn't have been able to

find you by having a student of mine hack into your social media page and locate you." Tristin preened like a peacock. "Who thinks I'm an idiot now?"

"I do," Damon said.

"Me too," Zoe said.

"Perhaps you don't realize how much trouble you are in or how bad your situation is," Damon said.

"Wait." Tristin held his hand out. "I know why Dr. Powers is so angry. And it's not just because of what your grandmother did at that meeting."

"What are you talking about?" Zoe demanded.

"I did a little research on him. Actually I did a *lot* of research. Did you know he has a degree in rhetoric?"

Zoe nodded. "We know."

"Did you know that his father's maternal grandmother's family goes back to the 1600s in Boston?" Tristin said.

"So? A lot of Bostonians can trace their family trees back that far. Not that all of them are accurate, but they like bragging rights," she said.

"He's a blue blood," Tristin said. "Don't you get it? His family was around for the Salem witch trials. He has a thing against witches."

"Does he think we are witches?" Zoe asked. "Did you tell him or his followers that?"

"I may have insinuated that you had powers he'd find helpful in his line of work."

"He's just a human," Damon said. "Or are you claiming otherwise?"

"Is he a witch hunter?" Zoe said.

Tristin shrugged. "I don't know. I'm just saying it's possible . . ."

Damon moved close to stare directly into Tristin's eyes. "You're just saying that you will forget this conversation and this visit to Chicago. You won't have any further contact with Dr. Powers or any of his followers. You will also forget that I am a vampire and that Zoe and her grandmother are witches. You will forget your belief in paranormal activity and decide to join the Peace Corps and help others instead."

Zoe was surprised that Damon added that last command. Surprised and pleased.

"No witches? No vampires?"

Zoe wasn't sure if Tristin was making statements or forming questions.

"No witches and no vampires," Damon said forcefully. "They don't exist. Understand?"

Tristin nodded.

"Okay, you and Bob are going to get in a cab, go back to the airport, and fly back to Boston."

Again, Tristin nodded.

"Stay there."

Zoe eyed Tristin suspiciously. She wasn't sure if he was faking it or not. She waved her hand in front of his eyes to see if he'd blink, but he retained the same glassy-eyed expression of someone in a trance.

Damon strolled over to the couch and focused his attention on Bob. "You will return to Boston and tell Dr. Powers that Zoe and her grandmother are no longer in Chicago. You were unable to serve the legal document to anyone and you will return it to Dr. Powers." Damon took the paper from Zoe and slapped it into Bob's hands. "Understand?"

Bob nodded.

"Good. Now come join Tristin in the cab heading to

the airport." Damon led both men outside, where a cab magically was waiting.

"How did you do that?" Zoe asked when Damon returned to her side.

"I compelled them."

"No, I meant the cab. It was there without you even calling for one."

"The cabdriver is a vamp from Vamptown. He'll make sure they leave."

"He's not going to kill them, is he?" Zoe asked.

"Why do you care?"

"Because I don't want their blood on my hands," Zoe said.

"You live in Vamptown. You're going to get blood on your hands at some point," Damon said.

"That's not true," Daniella said as she walked in the front door, which was still open. "I don't have blood on my hands. Well, cupcake-icing blood but not the real stuff."

"That was before demons moved in," he said.

As if on cue, the organ music opening for *Phantom of the Opera* rose from the floor vents.

"Wow." Daniella was impressed. "Bruce told me about hearing the music but it doesn't come through our vents at the cupcake shop. I listen to Adele while I'm baking. I like Florence and the Machine, too."

"What are you doing? Making your requests? This isn't a radio station. Those are demons down there," Damon said.

"I know that."

"They can suck out a witch's brains. You don't want to know what they can do to humans," he told Daniella.

"I'm a druid hybrid," she reminded him.

"Which makes it worse for you," Damon said.

"Stop trying to scare her," Zoe said, putting a protective arm around Daniella. "She can do bad things to vampires when she's mad. I want to hear more about that, by the way."

"It won't help you against demons," Damon said. "And hybrids aren't immune. They get the punishment of both a human and a witch. Your beating heart would be yanked out of your chest and then your brains sucked out."

"They're bad. They're evil. They're dangerous. We get it," Zoe said. "Sometimes people use humor as a coping mechanism."

He raised an eyebrow. "People?"

"Hybrids and witches," she said. "To quote one of my favorite TV shows, 'Do not belittle my coping mechanisms.'"

"*Castle*, right?" Daniella said. "I love that show, too. I've been a Nathan Fillion fan since he was in *Firefly*. Did you ever see that series?"

Zoe shook her head.

"I have it on DVD," Daniella said.

"In case you're interested, I just had Neville destroy your ex-fiancé's laptop and any other devices he might have, including thumb drives, so he can't fall back on that to regain his memory," Damon told Zoe. "But don't let me interrupt your girl talk."

"Ignore him," Zoe said.

"I stopped by because Nick is meeting me here for dinner. He's bringing corned beef and cabbage from an Irish pub in an hour or so for St. Patrick's Day. While we wait, I thought you might need some help restoring order to your work space, Zoe. I heard via the grape-vine that Damon made a bit of a mess of it," Daniella said.

"Zoe is a witch. She can fix it with the blink of an eye," Damon said.

"I'm trying not to use magic," Zoe curtly reminded him.

"Yeah, how is that working out for you?" he drawled.

He was trying to get to her. And he was succeeding. "Daniella and I will be upstairs," Zoe told him.

"It would be a good idea to put a protection spell on her," Damon said. "I told you that demons are not kind to hybrids."

Zoe was aggravated that she hadn't thought of that herself. There was also the fact that here she was, forced to use magic again.

"Is it okay with you that I cast the spell?" she asked Daniella.

Daniella nodded.

The *Phantom* music stopped as Zoe quickly cast the spell then shot Damon an irritated look. "Happy now?"

He just gave her one of his sexy smirks that made her lust after his lips . . . and the rest of his body.

She refused to stomp up the stairs as a sign of her anger, but boy she was sure tempted. Remembering how her anger had resulted in her levitating in her workroom, Zoe put a lid on it and focused on the space before her.

"Gram could have gotten things back in order with a spell but I vowed not to use magic when I moved here and it seems like that's all I've been doing. Which is why it's important that I restore order to things myself, without magic," she told Daniella.

"What made you vow not to use magic, if you don't mind me asking? Were you afraid someone would find out you're a witch?" Daniella said.

"My mother died two years ago after using black magic in a spell. After her death, I vowed not to use spells again."

"I'm so sorry for your loss." Daniella hugged her. "I know what it's like to lose your mother. Mine died when I was sixteen but I still miss her."

"Was she a hybrid, too?"

"No, she was human. I was adopted. But that didn't make her any less my mom."

"Of course not."

"She was very smart. Had a lot of common sense, you know?"

Zoe nodded.

"What was your mom like?" Daniella asked.

"People say we looked alike. She was very smart, too. A big history fan. But then the demon that possessed your employee claimed that my mother sent him to hell. The demon, not your employee," Zoe said. "I'm just having a really hard time with all of this."

"I wanted to thank you again for coming so fast to deal with that situation."

"I don't know how well I dealt with it."

"I do," Daniella said. "You were great."

"You weren't in the room."

"Damon texted Nick that you did great."

"He did?"

"You sound surprised."

"I am," Zoe admitted. "Damon isn't exactly generous with positive feedback. Is that a vamp thing?"

"It's more a Damon thing," Daniella said. "Nick wasn't great at it in the beginning, but Damon is worse than Nick ever was."

"You remember that cameras are watching our every move in here and listening to our every word, right?" Zoe said.

Daniella nodded, indicating she got Zoe's unspoken request that they change the subject. "Where do all these soaps go?"

"On the shelves here."

"What made you want to become a soap maker?"

"I've always loved aromatherapy."

"Me, too. There's nothing like the smell of baking cupcakes. Or lemon frosting." Daniella paused to sniff one of the wrapped soaps in her hand. "Mmmm, lemon."

"You can have that one if you'd like. I have a matching body cream." Zoe opened the elegant jar and held it up for Daniella to smell. "I only use pure botanicals. Fruit and vegetable oils. And no magic."

"These smell divine. I love the way you've cleverly wrapped each soap in muslin. I can't get over how many different varieties you have here. Orange and vanilla. Cucumber and melon. Mountain spruce. Sunshine. Revive."

"Along with Sunshine, Revive is one of my most popular scents in the soap line. It helps restore energy with a combination of grapefruit, lime, and lemon as well as a hint of cucumber."

"*Revive* sounds like the perfect name for it. I like the name of your brand, Bella Luna, too. That's Italian for 'beautiful moon,' right?"

"Yes."

Daniella looked around and shook her head. "So Damon made this mess when he was searching your place yesterday?"

"Yes."

"You should have had him clean it up. He can move at vamp hyper speed, you know."

"I know. I saw him do just that today when he scooped me up and took me to the funeral home."

"It was for a good cause. Phil is a really good guy," Daniella said. She grabbed another handful of soaps from the floor. "I notice you've got labels on the shelves all ready for the soap scents."

"My gram did that when she used a spell to set everything in here up for me. She was trying to save me work."

"I also notice the soaps are in alphabetical order."

"Yeah, I keep the bottles of essential oils in alphabetical order, too. Blame it on my library degree," Zoe said.

"You're an ex-librarian?"

"A former librarian, yes."

"When I was in middle school, I used to think that would be my dream job. Sitting around and reading books all day."

"I don't know of any librarian who gets to do that," Zoe said. "It's a tough job. Especially now with people questioning the need to even have a public library when they can use the Internet. American libraries are having a rough time in these economic times. Cities are cutting back hours and staff."

"Is that what happened to you?"

"No. That's a long story."

"One I hope you'll tell me sometime when we're not under observation," Daniella said.

Zoe smiled. "Deal."

"Notice I did not ask you about the ex-fiancé of yours that Damon mentioned downstairs."

"I appreciate that," Zoe said.

"You can tell me about him some other time, too." Daniella paused to look around the room. "This is a beautiful space. You know, legend has it that this house was built to copy the layout of Al Capone's house."

"He lived here?"

"No, but one of the members of his gang owned this house and the one next door. Or that's what I heard growing up. You know about the tunnels, right?"

"That's where the demons are."

"Correct. The tunnels were originally built during the Prohibition era to move bootleg liquor from place to place. They were updated with better lighting thanks to the Vamptown Council."

"Have you ever been down there?"

"Yes." Daniella's normally cheerful voice changed, turning quiet. "I was abducted by the head of a rival group of vampires and held captive down there."

"I'm so sorry. I had no idea."

"It only lasted an hour or two but it seemed like forever."

"Did Nick come rescue you?" Zoe asked.

"Actually, I kind of rescued myself, but I don't want to go into it. I'd rather talk about St. Patrick's Day."

"It's a big day in Boston," Zoë said.

"In Chicago, too. They even dye the Chicago River green," Daniella said. "And the spring equinox is soon. Isn't that important for witches?"

"It's not as important as the solstices, and even then the importance depends on your coven. I haven't celebrated it since my mother's death." Zoe paused as an

ancient belief came to mind. The equinox represented
equal hours of light and dark. A science teacher in high
school had informed her that there was actually still a
difference of a few minutes, but in a witch's perspective
the vernal equinox—also known as the spring equinox—
represented the advent of light starting to overcome
darkness. Her witch's intuition told her that the date
was an important one for obtaining the Book of Darkness. Her train of thought was interrupted by Daniella.

"You said the demon at our funeral home blamed
your mom for him being in hell?"

"Yes, but he refused to give me any details."

"Do you believe him?"

"I don't know what to believe."

"I know what's that like," Daniella said sympathetically. "When Nick told me he was a vampire, I refused
to believe it at first. I thought I'd hit my head and was in
a coma or something. At least you knew Nick and Damon were vampires when you first met them. As for
your mom, well, from what you've told me about her, I
don't see how she would send anyone to hell unless
they deserved to go there. The most likely thing is that
the demon lied. They're not exactly known for doing
good deeds."

"I know. It's just that hearing stuff about my mom—"

"Brings the pain of her loss back," Daniella said.

Zoe nodded, blinking back tears. "Sorry to be a
wimp."

"You are not a wimp." Daniella gave her another
hug. "And neither am I."

"No way. You are a kick-butt druid hybrid who can
protect herself from evil vampires. I wish I could do
that with these demons."

"That's Damon's job," Daniella told her. "As for me being a kick-butt druid, I'm really just a cupcake maker living with a vampire in an apartment above my cupcake shop. Maybe it seems normal to me now because I grew up living above the funeral home," Daniella said.

"Was that strange? Living above the funeral home, I mean."

"Not really, no."

"I don't think I could handle that."

"Why?"

"I have a thing about funeral homes."

"What kind of thing?"

"An avoidance thing," Zoe said.

"It's not a fave hangout for most people."

"Unless they are vampires."

"Even then," Daniella said.

"Damon doesn't like me asking questions about the funeral home."

"I can understand that. But what do you have against funeral homes?"

"I guess it goes back to my dad's funeral. He died in a fire when I was a little girl." Zoe remembered the whispers about the family curse, that no man would be good enough for an Adams woman. "I thought funeral homes crushed you into little pieces. He was cremated. My mom spread his ashes from a sailboat in his favorite cove off the coast per his wishes. But at the funeral there was this urn that someone had put my father in, like an evil genie locking him in there. I'm sorry, but funeral homes kind of freak me out."

"I understand," Daniella said. "We don't have to talk." Reaching for a pad of paper she wrote *What's with you and Damon? I sense sparks there.*

Nothing going on, Zoe wrote.

Do you want there to be?

No way.

Because you're a witch?

Because he's impossible.

Impossible but hot.

So?

So aren't u tempted? Don't lie.

Bella jumped onto the worktable. "What are you doing?"

"Nothing," Zoe said, turning the pad of paper over so Bella couldn't read it. "I was just telling Daniella how aromatherapy centers on the way natural fragrances affect our thoughts and feelings. Lavender is well known as a calming scent. That's why it was often used in sachets or small pillows to help people sleep."

Bella yawned. "Bo-ring."

"It looks like we've taken care of most of the mess," Zoe said.

"It does look much better than it did before," Daniella agreed. While they'd been talking, they'd managed to restore order to the workroom.

Zoe and Bella accompanied Daniella downstairs. "Thanks again for everything," Zoe said.

"There may be just enough time before Nick comes for me to run back to the shop to pick up dessert. I forgot to bring it." Daniella opened the front door. "Oh look, it's Mrs. Seely's Chihuahuas Princess and Coco. She's dressed them up with Irish bowler hats and green bow ties for St. Patrick's Day. Aren't they cute? I wonder what they're doing on your front porch, though."

"Demons!" Bella hissed and tore upstairs as if the beasts of hell were after her.

Chapter Seventeen

"Demons?" Daniella repeated, nervously looking up and down the block. "Where?"

Growling ferociously considering their size, the two leprechaun wannabe dogs raced inside and took off after Bella up the stairs.

"Come back here!" Zoe cried, rushing upstairs after them.

She entered her workroom to find Bella on the worktable. The feline was arching her back and hissing. She looked like a porcupine with her fur standing on end while the dogs scrambled below, jumping up and trying to get at her.

"Bad dogs," Zoe said.

"Demons!" Bella hissed again.

The two dogs turned in unison to face Zoe. They bared their teeth, and their eyes took on an evil glow. "We are the Hounds of Hell."

After the day Zoe had had, there was no way she was backing down from this standoff. She recognized the voice coming from the little dog. "Guy, is that you? Are you possessing Chihuahuas now?"

"I told you this wouldn't work," another voice said through the other dog.

"Who is that?" Zoe asked.

"The other guy."

"I know you're Guy," she said. "I was asking the name of the other demon."

"I'm Guy and he's the other Guy. We're both named Guy."

"But I'm the smarter Guy," the other one said. "I said we should wait until the pit bulls went out for their walk but noooo, you couldn't wait. You possess the first dogs you see."

"You should both be ashamed of yourselves for taking possession of a pair of poor animals like that," Zoe said.

"Actually, they are very pampered," Daniella said from the doorway.

The dogs focused their attention on her.

"Damn, she's got a protection spell around her, too," Guy number one said.

"Get the cat," the other one said.

Bella howled and leapt from the table to a higher shelf, knocking down soaps as she did so.

"Damn," Guy number two said. "Even the cat has a protection spell around it."

Damon was there in the blink of an eye. "What the hell is going on in here?"

"We are the Hounds of Hell," both Guys growled.

Damon frowned. "Why are they dressed like leprechauns?"

"It's St. Patrick's Day," Zoe explained.

"They're demons," Damon said.

Zoe grabbed Damon's arm. "Don't hurt the dogs. It's not their fault demons temporarily possessed them."

Damon sighed. "You're not going to make this easy, are you."

"Why are you here?" Zoe asked the first Guy. "And what are your last names so I don't get you messed up?"

"We're here to deliver a message," he said.

"Another one? I just saw you earlier this afternoon," Zoe said.

"I'm Guy Pettigrew and we were supposed to be more intimidating as pit bulls."

"What's the connection between you two guys?" Zoe said. "Aside from the fact that you are both possessing Chihuahuas."

"We're cousins. And we were both sent to hell by your mother."

"In error," the other Guy said. "I'm Guy Worley, by the way."

"How did my mother send you to hell in error?"

"With her black magic," Guy Worley said.

"Was she trying to send someone else to hell instead of you two?"

"Yes," Guy Worley said.

"Who?" Zoe demanded.

"Our time is up," Guy Worley said.

The dogs froze and then collapsed onto their sides.

"Oh no!" Zoe rushed over but by the time she got to the dogs, they'd stood up and started shaking themselves as if they'd been in a dirty mud puddle.

"Are the demons gone?" she asked Damon.

"Yes. For now."

"Get those dogs out of here," Bella ordered from the top shelf.

Zoe scooped up one dog while Daniella took the other. "They really are sweet dogs. Mrs. Sweeny loves Princess and Coco to bits."

"If she did, she wouldn't dress them up that way," Damon said.

The doorbell rang. "Now what?" Zoe muttered as she took the dog downstairs with her. "Is this one Princess or Coco?"

She opened the door to find a middle-aged woman with spiky pink hair and a nose ring there. She was wearing a KISS ME EVEN IF I'M NOT IRISH green sweatshirt and jeans. "You found them! I don't know what happened. One second they were on their leashes and the next they just took off. I've been going door to door all along the block to see if anyone found them."

"They're fine," Daniella assured Mrs. Sweeny, who put her dogs back on their respective leashes.

"Thanks for catching them," the older woman said. "I hope they weren't any trouble?"

"Tell her they better not come back here," Bella said from the top of the stairs.

"Who was that speaking?" Mrs. Sweeny asked.

"My grandmother," Zoe lied. "She gets crabby without her meds so I better go." She shut the front door.

"I get crabby without my meds?" Gram asked as she strolled into the living room from her bedroom on the main floor.

"Sorry, Gram. I had to say something to cover up the fact that Bella was talking."

"What did I miss?" Gram asked. "I heard a big commotion upstairs."

"Demons possessed a pair of pampered Chihuahuas."

"Why would they do that?"

"They couldn't get to the pit bulls they wanted. It's a good thing that I put that protection spell over Daniella or they might have tried to jump from the dogs to her," Zoe said.

"Ick." Daniella shuddered. "Like fleas?"

"Only a billion times worse," Damon said before speaking into his smartphone. "Neville, research the names Guy Pettigrew and Guy Worley and send me what you find ASAP."

"What do you think it all means?" Zoe asked.

"That the demons are coming up with new ways to make trouble. First possessing you, then the human at the funeral home, now dogs."

"You haven't had demons do those things before?" Zoe said.

"I usually kill them first," Damon said.

"What about an astral projection?" she asked.

"Also something new."

"Music?"

"Ditto."

"What is so special about these demons?"

"The fact that you called them forth," Damon said.

"I need to figure out why my mother would send those two guys to hell, if that's even true," Zoe said.

"Did she keep a journal or anything?" Daniella asked.

"Not that I know of."

"Did she give you your talisman?" Damon asked.

Zoe nodded.

"When?"

"On my thirteenth birthday."

"Did she wear one?"

"Yes."

"Where is hers? Is it back in Boston?"

"No. I have it in my jewelry box."

Daniella held up her phone. "Nick just texted me that he'll be here in a minute with dinner."

"Show her talisman to me after dinner then," Damon told Zoe.

The knock on the front door came a moment later. "That's our secret knock," Daniella said. "It's Nick."

Nick wasn't alone. The good news was that he didn't have any obvious demons accompanying him and the take-out bags of delicious-smelling food he was carrying. The bad news was that Tanya was right behind him with a bag of her own, a designer tote.

"What are you doing here?" Zoe asked Tanya.

"I'm not here for you," Tanya said. "I'm here for Damon. I can't believe how rude you all are to eat in front of him and not offer him anything." She sidled up to Damon and ran her hand up his arm. "You poor thing. When was the last time you fed?"

Damon just shrugged.

"Well, don't worry about a thing. I've got everything you need." She moved her hand to his chest and then down to the buckle of his black pants.

"I'm working," Damon said, lifting her hand back to his chest but not removing it.

"That doesn't mean we can't have a little feast of our own. Look, I brought your favorite. Type O." She lifted the blood bag from the tote and held it up as if it were a prized possession.

What would Damon do? Would he rip it open and start guzzling blood? Would he and Tanya take turns swigging the type O?

"Don't get any of that on my furniture," Gram said.

"You're a witch. You can remove stains," Tanya said.

"Where did you get that from?" Zoe heard herself ask.

The temperature in the room went twenty degrees colder. "We don't talk about that," Nick said as he took the food to the table.

"I already figured out it has something to do with the funeral home," Zoe said, turning to face Daniella.

Daniella shook her head. "My lips are sealed."

"If you two want some privacy, you can go in the kitchen, Damon," Gram said.

Zoe wondered if that was rude, sending him to the kitchen as if he were in a time out for being bad.

"I go where Damon goes," Tanya said, clutching his arm and still holding the blood supply.

"If you'll excuse us." Damon wrapped his arm around Tanya and led her to the kitchen, the swinging door closing behind them.

What if I can't excuse him? Zoe wondered. What if it was too much to take that he was a vampire who drank blood and had a dark side? Was she really in any position to be judging him? It's not like she was Suzy Sunshine. She was a witch whose mother practiced dark magic and may have sent the wrong people to hell.

Witches and vampires made for a volatile combination.

So why did she care what Damon and Tanya were doing in the kitchen? Were they just feeding or doing more? Were they having quickie vampire sex? What would sex with a vampire be like?

"You think too much," Nick told Zoe as he held out a chair for her at the dining room table.

"He used to tell me that, too," Daniella said.

"And I was right," Nick said.

"Vampires don't think?" Zoe countered as she sat down.

"There are times when I wonder," Daniella said with a laugh and a tilt of her head toward the kitchen.

"I've never had corned beef and cabbage," Nick admitted as he helped Daniella into a chair with such gentlemanly courtesy, it made Zoe wonder what it would be like to have that care taken with her.

Nick just did help you into your chair, her inner voice reminded her. *Has Damon ever held out a chair for you?*

She couldn't remember.

He'd kissed her. She remembered that. Hard to forget. Just as Damon was hard to forget. How long were he and Tanya going to stay in the kitchen?

"You're not eating," Gram said. "It's really good. Where did you get this, Nick?"

"From a neighborhood Irish pub just outside Vamptown," he said.

"Are you doing anything special at the bar tonight for the holiday? Green beer on tap or green blood or anything?" Zoe said.

"I fought on the side of the English at Waterloo," Nick said. "So I never celebrated St. Patrick's Day until now. The English and the Irish weren't on the best of terms for much of that time."

"Wow. So you're older than Damon," Zoe said. "He told me he was turned on the battlefield at Gettysburg on the third day of fighting."

"That's more than he tells most people," Nick said. "I'm not the oldest vamp in Vamptown, though. That honor goes to Pat. Of course, age is relative for a vamp. You stay the age you were when you were turned. Most vamps do, anyway."

"But not you?" Zoe said.

Nick looked at Daniella.

"I didn't say a word," she said.

"No, not me," Nick finally said.

Daniella wiped at her eyes. "Nick is no longer an immortal and it's all my fault."

"What did you do?" Zoe said.

"I had sex with him. It made some of his vamp strengths stronger but it meant that he will eventually die."

"But not for a long time," Nick said. "Daniella's aging was also changed by our actions. She is now aging at a slower rate."

"So having sex with a vampire could be an anti-aging technique?" Zoe said.

"I'm not sure all this talk about sex is proper dinner conversation," Gram said.

"What about sex between a witch and a vampire?" Bella asked from the floor where she was seated beside Zoe. Looking up at Zoe's shocked face, Bella said, "What? You know you were thinking about it."

"Familiars cannot read a witch's mind," Zoe stated.

"Anyone could have read your mind," Bella said. "So who is going to answer my question?"

"No one," Zoe said.

"I don't know the answer," Daniella said.

Nick remained silent, as did Gram.

"That corned beef is very high in sodium content

and causes bloating," Bella said. "You'd do better to give some of that to Morticia and me down here."

Morticia mewed her agreement.

"Why does only one of your cats talk?" Daniella asked.

"I don't know the answer," Zoe said.

"Morticia and I communicate telepathically," Gram said. "That's the usual way in our coven."

"But I'm special," Bella said proudly. "Oh shit! There goes that damn spooky organ music through the floorboards again."

"No swearing at the dinner table," Gram reprimanded her.

"I'm on the floor, not the table," Bella said. "What does a familiar have to do to get a little peace and quiet around here?"

"I thought maybe they'd play 'Oh Danny Boy' or something Irish," Daniella said.

"No such luck," Zoe said.

"Maybe we should blast some music back down at them," Daniella suggested. "Maybe some Muse from my smartphone. Their song 'Uprising' would do."

"Would do what? Get rid of the demons?" Zoe asked.

"No."

"That's what I was afraid of." She was also afraid of the answer to those other questions . . . about a witch and a vampire having sex and about what Damon was doing with Tanya in the kitchen.

"Feel better now?" Tanya asked Damon in the kitchen.

Damon wiped his mouth and nodded. Two empty bags of blood sat on the countertop.

"Good." Tanya sidled up against him. "I could make you feel even better still."

"I've got to stay focused on hunting demons," he said.

"It seems to me you're more focused on Zoe the witch than the demons. You do know that witches and vampires are like eggs and water."

"Oil and water," he corrected her.

"Whatever." Tanya thrust her lower lip out in a sexy pout. "I don't like her."

"That's irrelevant," Damon said.

"Not to me it isn't. She doesn't understand you the way I do."

Damon knew that no one really understood him and he liked it that way. This was nothing new to him. Even in his life as a human, he'd been full of contradictions and complications along with a fierce competitive drive. His sire Simon had said that it was one of the reasons he turned him. Nothing got the best of Damon. Not even death.

Yet his memories of that terrible day in Gettysburg stayed in his mind. He'd seen plenty of blood since then, but nothing like that. The hill had been slippery with it after two days of battle, the air filled with the stench of dead bodies and the cries of those mortally wounded but not yet gone. Like his younger brother, Sam, who'd died there. Damon couldn't be sure the voice he'd heard back then was really Sam's, but the possibility haunted him with a powerful persistence and filled him with grief and rage.

He'd tried to become more civilized. Since coming to Vamptown, Damon drank blood from what appeared to be a beer bottle or from a glass. He hadn't chugged it down like a wild beast for some time.

Tanya was excited by his appetite and the sight of the blood. He could see that on her face and in her eyes.

Tanya was right in front of him, ready, willing, and able, yet Damon's thoughts were on Zoe in the other room. His vamp hearing allowed him to listen in on the conversation. They weren't talking about him. Not that he wanted them to.

He was filled with frustration and it showed in the way he crumpled the plastic bag and threw it in the garbage. He let Tanya lick the excess blood from his fingers. Why the hell shouldn't he? Maybe having sex would be enough of a release that he could stop brooding about kissing Zoe and the sweet taste of her mouth.

Eve hadn't tasted that sweet, so it wasn't just a witch thing. It was a Zoe thing. Maybe she'd used one of those creams of hers on her lips to make them so soft and delicious.

Shit, he was doing it again. Thinking of Zoe.

"Yumm," Tanya murmured.

Swearing in Latin, Damon set her away from him.

"What's wrong?" Tanya said.

How could he explain when he didn't know the answer to that question himself? Shaking his head, he said, "Maybe after this demon thing is over."

"How long will that take?" Tanya said.

"Hopefully not long."

"Good." Tanya smiled up at him. "If there's anything you need from me, you only have to ask."

"I know."

"Do you? Do you know how good I am in bed and out of it?" She slipped her finger beneath the buttons on his dark shirt to swirl a fingertip around his navel.

Hell, she was hot all right. So why wasn't he as hot?

Why was he still keeping tabs on Zoe in the other room?

Damon tried telling himself it was to monitor the situation and make sure the little witch hadn't done anything to worsen the demon dilemma. But Nick was out there with her. He should be able to handle things.

Tanya thought so, too. "Why can't Nick stay here and give you some time off?"

He removed her hand from his body before replying. "Nick isn't a Demon Hunter."

"I thought the demons were locked in the tunnel," Tanya said.

"They are."

Tanya did her lip pout again. "Then why do you have to guard the witches? It's because you don't trust them, right? They could be demons themselves."

"No, they're not demons."

"What about that cat of hers?"

"Not a demon either."

Daniella and Zoe walked into the kitchen carrying dirty plates and utensils.

"You should have knocked first," Tanya told them.

"It's my house," Zoe said, dumping the dishes in the sink. "Are you two done in here?"

"Yes," Damon said before Tanya could answer.

"Nick wanted to talk to you," Zoe told Damon.

Damon was glad to leave the women behind. Being stuck in a kitchen with a female vampire, a female hybrid, and a witch was not his idea of a good time.

"Irma went in her room to watch *Jeopardy!* She recorded it," Nick said as Damon joined him at the dining room table.

"I thought they didn't have cable yet." Damon had

killed the cable guy demon and no one had come knocking from the cable company since then.

"She used magic and Neville's tech talents via texts. But I don't want to talk about that. I want to talk about this demon danger. They're getting bolder and figuring out new ways to communicate from outside the tunnels. I heard about the Hounds of Hell," Nick said.

"They weren't that bad," Damon said.

"Demons were here while Daniella was here. I don't like that. What if they'd attacked Daniella or Zoe?"

"Zoe has a protection spell and now so does Daniella."

"Daniella wants to sleep in her own bed tonight and I'm not letting her do that alone," Nick said.

"I'll be fine here," Damon said. "You don't have to stay."

"So you trust the witches now?" Nick asked.

"Enough not to think they are going to call up more demons for the time being," Damon said. "They are both too wiped out tonight to create any more trouble."

"I hope you're right, for your sake," Nick said. "And for Vamptown's."

Chapter Eighteen

Zoe was glad to see Tanya flounce out of the house without saying a word to anyone.

But she was sad to see Daniella preparing to go. Nick was leaving with her.

"You're in good hands," Nick assured Zoe.

"You're sure you don't want to stay a little longer?" she said. "Or we could do something normal like play Boggle? Or Go Fish?"

"I've got to get up before dawn to make cupcakes," Daniella said with a yawn.

Now Zoe felt guilty. "You're right. You need some rest."

"So do you. You've had a hectic day. Possessions at the funeral home and then a visit from the Hounds of Hell," Daniella said.

"Not to mention all that Latin today," Damon reminded Zoe.

As if she could forget her arm around his body or the press of his erection against her.

While saying her good-byes, Zoe told herself that there was no cause for alarm. She'd been alone with Damon all day. And Gram was still in the house.

Her inner panic was merely the result of a horrific day. As Daniella had pointed out, Zoe had had one thing after another happen to her today—most of it involving demon possessions. Then there was Damon and his possession of her mouth and her sanity.

That's what was throwing her. The overwhelming power of the attraction she felt for Damon. She'd always discounted the Adams legend that Adams witches fell in love at first sight. It certainly wasn't true in this case. She hadn't fallen for Damon when she first met him and if she had an ounce of sense she wouldn't fall for him now, either.

She needed to deal with finding the Book of Darkness and getting rid of the demons. Then she could get back to her soap business. That was where her passion lay. Not with Damon.

"You promised you'd show me," Damon was saying.

Show him what? Her need for him? Her naked body? Her fear for the future? Her vulnerability?

"Your mother's talisman," he said.

"Right. Of course. Wait here. I'll go my bedroom and get her jewelry box."

"I'll come with you."

"No!"

Great. Now she'd done it. Damon was looking at her with suspicion.

"Why not?" he demanded.

How could she explain that she didn't want him in such close proximity to her bed? He'd already slept in her room, albeit on a chair and with Daniella present.

But that was before he'd kissed her this afternoon and she'd melted into him.

"What's the problem?" he said.

"I've had a rough day," she said.

"So?"

"So I need some alone time."

"You can have as much alone time as you want when we find the missing book and the demons are decimated. Until then I'm coming with you to get your mother's talisman."

She could do this. She was an Adams witch. She refused to be controlled by a hot vampire.

"Fine." She wondered if Damon had seen the meme on Facebook explaining that whenever a woman said *Fine* the man was in trouble.

But then she wasn't a normal woman and Damon wasn't a man. He was a vampire accustomed to getting his way. And he drank blood in her kitchen with a female vampire. That alone should have shut down any attraction Zoe felt for him.

She was aware of him behind her as she climbed the stairs to her bedroom. She could practically feel his eyes drilling into her back. Glancing over her shoulder, she caught him eyeing her butt. She deliberately sashayed the rest of the way, adding some hip action worthy of Beyoncé herself.

"Can you take it off?" he said huskily.

She almost stumbled over her own two feet. "What?"

"Your bangle. Can you take it off now?"

"Oh." She tried but the bangle stayed put. "No."

She headed for the small jewelry box in the top drawer of the dresser.

In addition to her mother's talisman, Zoe had her

mother's wedding ring and a necklace with a large amethyst crystal in the center plus amethysts along the
side that her mom loved wearing. She used to tell Zoe
that amethyst would bring her calm and bravery. She
said it was her protection stone. After her mother's
death, Zoe had put the necklace in the box and left it
there. The stones hadn't saved her mother's life.

Tears threatened, but Zoe bit her lip and held them
back. She couldn't afford to break down now. The box
also held a few silver items her mom liked—an abalone pin she got from a trip to Mexico, several Native
American turquoise rings from a trip to Arizona, and a
floral ring from an Israeli designer she'd met at a Boston art show.

"I have some silver stuff in here," she warned Damon.

"Only remove your mother's talisman. It's gold like
yours, right?"

She nodded.

She removed the talisman, still on its golden chain.
"My mother's has the Adams family Phoenix rising
plus her father's crescent moon in the top left."

"Show me yours again."

She fished it out from beneath her T-shirt. Her
mother had warned her never to remove it so she had to
stand close to Damon while he bent his head and studied the differences between the two talismans.

As he did so, she noticed the silky darkness of his
hair and longed to thread her fingers through it.

"Yours has the Phoenix rising and the star."

"Right." Her voice sounded rusty.

"And my tattoo has—" He started unbuttoning his
shirt.

"Stop!"

"Why?"

"I've already seen your tattoo. It's hard to tell but I think yours has a shooting star instead of a star."

"Do you know the meaning of the Phoenix?" Damon said.

"Of course. It's a famous legend of the magical bird rising from the ashes to live on."

"Which is why it became a symbol for Atlanta as a sign that the city would be reborn from the ashes of its destruction in the Civil War."

Zoe didn't ask but she suspected that Damon had been there then.

"Why does it apply to your family?" he said.

"Because burning witches is a violent part of our history. Out of those dark times we rose and became stronger than before," she said.

"Kind of like vampires."

"I guess so."

There was a moment of shared silence that she found to be surprisingly emotional. Or maybe it was just the aftereffect of the frantic and dangerous day she'd had.

Exhaustion suddenly claimed her. "I think I'm going to go to bed early. You can go ahead and play your Words with Friends."

She returned her mother's talisman to the jewelry box and closed the lid. She wished she could close the lid on her feelings for Damon with equal ease but doubted that would happen anytime soon.

Zoe was surrounded by darkness. She was trapped with no way out. Beady red eyes glared at her while millions of hands touched her. Sharp claws tore at her skin, ripping it to shreds, while spikes drilled into her bones.

Screaming, she leapt out of bed, disoriented and distraught.

Damon was instantly there to comfort her. "Hold on. You were just dreaming. You're okay."

The only way she could be okay was if Damon was kissing her. So she pressed her mouth to his. Or maybe he did the mouth-pressing thing. They were certainly both actively involved in the tongue-on-tongue thing.

Her body rose as she stood on tiptoes to increase the angle of their kiss. As she did so, the hem of her nightgown rose to skim the tops of her thighs.

Some small lingering semblance of sanity made her say, "This is a terrible idea." She spoke the words against his lips.

"I agree."

"We shouldn't be doing this," she said.

"Probably not."

She looked at him. He looked at her. Zoe's heart was practically jumping out of her breast. Could he hear it? Her lips still tingled from his kiss. Her body, pressed tightly against his, was alive with passion.

The moist heat between her legs indicated the rising level of her arousal just as the feel of his impressive erection indicated the rising level of his. She wanted him with a force that was hard to fight. Impossible to fight.

She saw his hunger darken his eyes and an instant later they were kissing again. Only this time they did pause in between kisses to murmur to each other.

"A witch and a vampire." Damon's voice was husky. "I mean, come on."

"Come on what?" Her voice was husky, too.

"Not a good idea."

"So you already said. Then why are you still kissing me?"

"I'm going to stop," he promised before circling her lips with his tongue.

"Mmm," she purred. "You're mmmm going to stop? When?"

"Soon."

Zoe placed a string of kisses along his jaw and tightened her arms around his shoulders before lifting one hand to slide it through his dark hair. He responded by fondling her nipples, first one, then the other.

"I'm stopping soon," he murmured against her mouth. "No more kissing."

"And your hand on my breast?" she whispered.

"I'm going to move that soon, too."

"Move it a little to the right so your thumb is over my nipple." Zoe was about ready to go up in flames. "Yes. Oh yes! Mmmm."

"Good?" he said.

"Mmm. But we're stopping. Soon. Very soon. Right?"

"Mmm, right."

"Because we can't just have sex," she said.

"Right." He nibbled her ear as he continued to caress her breast. "Tell me why again?"

"Um, because you two are being filmed," a voice from the security camera announced.

Zoe leapt away from Damon. "Is that Silas?"

Damon sighed. "No, it was Neville."

"You mean he saw everything we—" She sputtered into silence, unable to form more words as the realization sank in.

"That would be an affirmative," Neville said.

Looking directly at the surveillance camera, Zoe
warned, "If that ends up as a sex tape on the Internet
I will turn you into a toad."

"Don't worry. That won't happen, right, Neville? In
fact, he's going to erase it right now."

Zoe was pacing the room, embarrassed beyond belief. She paused in front of Damon. "What were you
thinking of making out with me like that when you
knew the cameras were on?"

"What were *you* thinking?" he countered.

"Clearly I was not thinking or I would not have allowed any of that to happen. I was still groggy and
frightened from my nightmare."

"That's as good an excuse as any, I suppose."

"It is not an excuse," she said.

"Chill."

Her mouth dropped open. "Excuse me? Did you just
tell me to chill?"

"You're not familiar with the term?"

"Not coming from a vampire, no."

"What does my being a vampire have to do with it?"

"You're right," she said. "It doesn't. I've never had a
man make out with me and then tell me to chill."

"Because you had sex with them."

"You make it sound like there were tons of men.
And Neville, you better not be recording this!" she said.

"Temporarily suspend surveillance in this room,
Neville," Damon ordered. Returning his attention to
Zoe, he drawled, "You were saying?"

"That I haven't had sex with tons of men. Unlike
you."

"I haven't had sex with any men," Damon said.
"You're confusing me with Pat and Bruce."

"They're gay?"

"Yes. Do you have a problem with homosexual vampires?"

"No. I only have a problem with you," she said.

"Why is that?"

"I wish I knew," she muttered. "You shouldn't be able to get to me this way. You kill witches."

"One witch."

"A relative of mine."

"Apparently a distant one."

"That's no reason to kill her," Zoe said.

"I already told you that she betrayed me."

"Were you hunting demons in New Orleans?"

"Yes."

"How do you know she betrayed you?" Zoe said. "Maybe you wrongly suspected her the way you wrongly suspect me."

"Impossible."

"Why?" Zoe said. "Because you're never wrong?"

"Because she stood beside the demon as he ambushed me."

"Maybe she was forced to do that against her will. Maybe the demon made her betray you. Did you ever think of that?"

"I was rather busy at the time trying to avoid being decapitated."

"So maybe Eve didn't really betray you."

"Oh, she betrayed me all right."

She could tell by his stony expression that she wouldn't get any further information out of him on that subject. "What happens to demons when you find them?"

"You saw what happens."

"You knife them—"

"It's a dagger," he interrupted.

"There's a difference?"

"Yes, there's a difference. And it's not just any dagger, it's a Demon Hunter dagger."

"And then what happens?"

"They disintegrate," Damon said.

"They don't go back to hell?"

"No."

"Then what's to stop them from suicide by Demon Hunter?" Zoe asked. "They taunt you into killing them as a way to escape hell. They simply cease to exist, which might be a better outcome for them than staying where they were."

At his look, she said, "What? You've never had anyone ask you these questions before?"

"No, I can't say that I have."

"It's because I'm a former librarian. I'm logical that way."

"You're logical for a witch, you mean."

"I was born a witch," she said.

"So?"

"So you were born human. What was that like?"

"What was it like being born a witch?"

"I didn't know I was a witch when I was a baby. It's more a process or an apprenticeship. I know the other kids in school whispered about me behind my back. They'd call me a pagan and say my birthmark was the mark of the devil. That was pretty rough."

"What birthmark?" Damon said.

"My mother came up with a cream to make it disappear but it took her a while. She was good with that sort of thing. She didn't flaunt her magic in front of others."

"Unlike your grandmother."

"Gram doesn't flaunt her skills. She likes using them and is accustomed to doing so. But she can be discreet," Zoe said.

"Just not where Dr. Powers is concerned."

"That's true. But even there, she didn't turn him into a monkey or a donkey or anything. Hopefully we've heard the end of the Powers people."

"What about your ex-fiancé?" Damon said.

"What about him?"

"Are you glad you won't be hearing from him again?"

"Absolutely."

"Yeah?"

"Yeah," she whispered.

His deep blue eyes darkened. She saw her own desire reflected in his gaze.

She leaned closer. So did he.

Then he abruptly stepped away. "Neville, turn camera back on."

"Okay," Neville said through the surveillance system.

"Get some rest," Damon told Zoe. "We've got a busy day tomorrow."

Damon faced the new day with resolve. The demons were toying with him and that aggravated the hell out of him. He was a man of action. He'd killed that cable guy demon yesterday morning and felt good that he'd taken care of business.

But this sitting-around-figuring-out-puzzles was not his idea of a good time.

Is having sex with Zoe your idea of a good time?

The answer was yes.

It shouldn't be yes. He was a vampire. He should be able to control things. Vampires didn't have emotions. Some took that to mean they didn't have souls. Damon didn't know about that. He only knew that he was in Vamptown for a reason.

Damon had spent much of the night trying to figure out what was real and what was legend when it came to the Book of Darkness. In between he'd played a few games of Words with Friends on his smartphone. A new player had challenged him and he'd welcomed the mental stimulation.

Because Damon sure didn't need more physical stimulation. Holding a half-naked Zoe in his arms and kissing her welcoming mouth had given him a hard-on that had lasted for hours.

He'd seen the TV ads about calling a doctor for an erection lasting more than four hours. That might be true for humans but not for vampires.

He was sure Tanya would have been all over him in a flash had he contacted her. But he hadn't.

Pat's knock on the front door was a welcome diversion for Damon. Zoe was still upstairs, in her workroom. She hadn't come down for breakfast yet. Not that he cared about such matters.

"I'm here about what happened last night," Pat said.

"Which part?" Damon asked. "The Hounds of Hell?"

"The part that took place in Zoe's bedroom."

"She had a nightmare."

Pat nodded. "That's understandable given the recent events."

"I agree," Damon said.

"What's not as understandable is what happened after that. Come on, don't give me that blank look. You didn't think Neville would tell me what happened between you and Zoe?"

"I'll kill him," Damon growled.

"Calm down. He erased the recording like you told him to. But you didn't tell him not to report what happened to me."

"I should have."

"Not that it would have made any difference. Neville would still have been obligated to tell me," Pat said.

"Why?"

"Because your actions affect us all. Sound familiar?"

"If Zoe and I let off a little sexual steam . . ."

"You could both get burned," Pat said. "I know you like walking on the dangerous side, Damon. But I also know you haven't forgotten what happened to you in New Orleans. Except it wasn't just New Orleans, was it? That incident ended with you in hell."

"Of course it did," Damon said. "That kind of betrayal is always hell."

"I wasn't speaking metaphorically. I was speaking literally."

Damon kept his expression blank but his insides were churning. Yes, he'd been to level one in hell but only his sire had that information.

"Don't try to deny it," Pat said with a strange sort of weariness.

"How do you know this?"

"I've been around a long time," he said.

"What does that have to do with the current events?"

"That's what we are all trying to figure out, isn't it?"

"You're the only one who met Silas before."

"Am I? What do you remember about your time in hell?"

"The torture."

"Do you remember Silas?" Pat asked.

"I never saw those who held me."

"Your sire helped you."

"Yes, Simon helped me get out. I was wrongfully held."

"Like the two demons now claim has happened to them."

"Guy and the other Guy? They lie."

"Do you have proof of that?" Pat asked.

"There's no proof either way."

"So we keep looking," Pat said.

"Time is running out," Damon said. He felt it in his gut. Which was the most important reason why he couldn't afford to focus on Zoe. The little witch could not get in his way or there would be hell to pay.

Zoe heard the sound of Pat's voice even if she couldn't hear the words. She was glad that Pat was talking to Damon downstairs. That kept Damon away from her, tempting her.

She really did need to concentrate on her business for an hour or two. Surely the world wouldn't disintegrate if she just took a little time off.

Zoe practiced some deep-breathing routines that she hadn't attempted since her arrival in Vamptown. They usually calmed her. Especially when she did them in her workroom. She wished she had the time to experiment with some new blends in the kitchen.

But the scents surrounding her worktable were

soothing, especially because she'd deliberately pulled some essential oils that had that property. As she'd told Daniella yesterday, lavender was known for its calming abilities.

Zoe had also dressed the part, wearing her red KEEP CALM AND CARRY ON T-shirt.

She kept her focus on the loaf of cherry almond soap she was cutting with a crinkle cutter. The tool gave each bar a ripple effect that she liked. With her tools, oils, and botanicals around her, she felt more at home than she had since arrived in Vamptown. The digital scale along with funnels and tiny scoops guaranteed that she was adding just the right amount of ingredients. Many of her soaps were stamped with the Bella Luna logo of a crescent moon in a square on each bar. The crinkle cuts didn't allow for that, so the logo was stamped on the muslin in which they would eventually be wrapped.

The sound of footsteps on the stairs jarred her out of her thoughts. "Gram, is that you?"

"It's me." Daniella burst into the room. "I had a premonition that if you and Damon have sex, Vamptown goes up in flames!"

Chapter Nineteen

So much for calm and tranquility. "What are you talking about?" Zoe said.

"I'm talking about sex. With you and Damon. Well, not my having sex with you and Damon obviously. I mean you and Damon having sex."

"Is this about last night?" Zoe said.

"What happened last night?" Daniella demanded. "You two didn't have sex, did you?"

"I thought Damon had the recording destroyed," Zoe muttered.

Daniella frowned. "What recording?"

"From the surveillance camera in my bedroom."

"You two made a sex tape?"

"No!"

"I don't understand."

"I don't either. How can I have this incredibly powerful attraction to Damon yet he aggravates the hell out of me?" she whispered.

"I can understand that. I felt the same way about Nick."

"But he seems nice for a vampire."

"He can be charming when he wants to be. But he was a real pain in the ass when he was opposed to my opening my cupcake store. He said the same about me. This isn't about me, though—except that I'm the one who had the premonition. It's about you."

"I thought you didn't have premonitions."

"I said I didn't have them often but when I do they are usually true."

"Usually?" Zoe said. "What percentage?"

"I'm not good at math. That's why I have an accountant who is also my best friend. Her name is Suz."

"I may need her if my business continues to expand. Is she good with business plans?"

"She's the best. She doesn't know about me being a hybrid druid or anything about Vamptown."

"My lips are sealed."

"Keep them that way. You can't go kissing Damon or who knows where it could go. Okay, we both know where it could go, but it can't."

"Or Vamptown will go up in flames?"

"Right."

"Maybe it isn't meant to be taken literally. Flames in dreams can represent spiritual cleansing or transformation," Zoe said.

"These were real flames," Daniella insisted. "I could see them clearly."

"Was a building on fire?"

"All of them were."

"Including the funeral home?" Zoe said.

"What does that have to do with anything?"

"I don't know. You'd probably know better than I would. It was your premonition, not mine."

"I'm telling you, this is all about you and Damon and sex."

"What about Damon and sex?" Gram asked as she entered the room.

How could Zoe have missed the sound of her grandmother coming up the stairs? Probably because she was rattled by Daniella's announcement.

"You don't have to go all shy with me," Gram said. "You can talk about sex in front of me."

"I had a premonition that if Zoe and Damon have sex, Vamptown will go up in flames," Daniella said.

"Oh my," Gram said. "I've heard rumors that vampires were great lovers but I had no idea they were that great. I'm impressed."

"I'm not talking about vampires being great lovers," Daniella said.

"So they're not?" Gram said,

"I don't know about the rest of them, but Nick is awesome," Daniella admitted.

"We are being watched," Zoe belatedly reminded them. How could she have forgotten? Her brain was mush today. "And don't use magic to mess with the recording," she warned Gram. "You know what kind of trouble that got us into last time."

"I know." Daniella grabbed the legal pad Zoe had been making notes on. *We will write instead of speak out loud.*

Zoe took the pad from her to scribble *I don't think we should write or talk about it anymore.*

Daniella yanked the pad back. *But I have to warn you.*

And you did.

"What are you all up to?" Damon demanded.

Damn, she'd missed hearing his footsteps on the stairs, too, although odds were that he'd used vamp speed so by the time she heard him, he was already in the room. So was Pat.

"Don't all answer at once," Damon said. "What's going on?"

"You and Zoe can't have sex or Vamptown will go up in flames," Daniella burst out. Turning to look over her shoulder at Zoe, she mouthed, *Sorry.*

"Does everybody and their grandmother know about what happened last night?" Damon demanded angrily.

Gram raised her hand. "I don't know what happened. Why don't you fill me in."

"I had a premonition," Daniella said. "I didn't know anything about a recording until I got here and Zoe told me."

"That's true," Neville said via the surveillance system.

"Shut up," Damon growled at him.

"Tell me about your premonition," Pat told Daniella.

"You know I don't have them very often but I had to say something. I had a premonition about my mom's car crash before she died and I never said anything about it. I shrugged it off as a bad dream. But it wasn't. I didn't take it seriously and she ended up dead." Daniella's voice cracked.

"I'm taking it seriously," Pat reassured her. "You shouldn't feel guilty about the one you had concerning your mom's accident. You didn't know you were a hybrid druid then. You didn't realize the gift you have. Now you know. When did you have this latest premonition?"

"An hour ago."

"You were sleeping?" Pat asked.

Daniella shook her head. "No, I was making cupcakes."

"What happened?"

"I closed my eyes for a minute and I got this vivid picture of all Vamptown on fire," Daniella said.

"Maybe it was the demons putting that image in your head. Did you hear any voices that sounded like Darth Vader? Or had an English accent?" Zoe asked.

"I thought you put a protection spell over me," Daniella said.

"I did."

"So now you're saying it doesn't work?"

"I don't know." Turning to Damon, Zoe said, "Can't you tell if she's been affected by demons? Don't you have a demon detector like they have a metal detector at the airports?"

"No, I don't have that," Damon said.

"You're freaking me out," Daniella said.

"I'm sorry." Zoe gave her a hug. "It will be fine. I didn't mean to upset you." The truth was that inside, Zoe was just as freaked out as Daniella, but she couldn't reveal that right now. Keep Calm and Carry On. She couldn't just wear the T-shirt saying that, she had to talk the talk and walk the walk. She could fall apart later. When there were no cameras around. When the demons were gone.

Damn. So much for getting any more work done

today. Not that fighting demons wasn't work, but it wouldn't pay the bills. It might pay Damon's bills because it was part of his job description but it sure as hell wasn't part of hers.

Wait, maybe she shouldn't be tossing around words like *damn* and *hell* even if they remained in her mind and she didn't speak them aloud. Not when demons were around. Maybe she should do what Damon suggested she do last night.

Okay, *ordered* was probably closer to the truth than *suggested*. Damon was good at giving orders, and he'd told her to chill. So maybe she should just chill. The modern version of Keep Calm and Carry On.

"I'm sure this will all work out. I mean, what chance do three measly demons have against an entire community of vampires plus a Demon Hunter and two witches?" Zoe said.

"And a hybrid druid," Daniella said.

"And a hybrid druid," Zoe agreed. "It's no contest. Right, Pat?"

"Right. No contest. The demons would win," Pat said.

Zoe blinked. "What?"

"If the demons get their hands on the Book of Darkness, they win."

"How do you figure that?"

"Because they can call forth billions of demons."

"They can do that by themselves?" Zoe said.

"With the book and a special witch," Pat said.

"You mean Gram?" Zoe said.

"Or you."

"I didn't open the book."

Pat looked Zoe in the eye. "Did you touch it?"

"Yes, but—"

"There are no buts," Pat said.

"We never saw that book before," Zoe said. "Why did it show up here and now all of a sudden?"

"Maybe Silas maneuvered what happened in Boston so you would come here to join Damon and me."

"Why? And how could he even do that?"

"I don't know," Pat admitted. "We're still trying to put this intricate puzzle together, and it's got so many pieces that it is turning out to be quite difficult."

"That's an understatement. And what do all the Latin sayings have to do with this mess? I thought maybe it was a message from my mom telling us how to find the missing spell book but Gram said it was black magic. She stopped me from stringing them together because she said they created a black magic incantation that way. But then on second thought she wasn't sure it was black magic. I figured it wasn't worth taking the risk until we learn more."

"Smart move," Pat said. "We have to be careful not to make a bad situation worse. Which is why I didn't approve of Damon's plan."

"What plan?" Zoe said.

Damon's expression hardened. "The one where I go into the tunnels and simply destroy the demons."

"Except there's nothing simple about this situation," Pat said.

"There never is," Damon said.

"Even you have to admit that Silas is different. He's more powerful than any demon you've ever had contact with before. The readings Neville is getting are off the charts," Pat said.

"What readings?" Zoe asked.

"It's like a Geiger counter for demon strength instead of radiation. That's what Nick told me," Daniella said.

Zoe shot Damon a look that said, *See, some vampires share information with others.*

"The readings could be wrong," Damon said. "This isn't an exact science."

"It's as close to it as we can get right now," Pat said. "And there's still the matter of the missing book. It has the power to release more evil than we can even imagine."

"I don't know. My imagination is pretty good," Gram said.

So was Zoe's, only hers had been filled with images of Damon, not demons. At least since her nightmare last night.

"I need to get back to my shop," Daniella said.

"There are things I need to take care of as well," Pat said.

"Me too," Gram said.

A few seconds later, Zoe was alone with Damon in her workroom. No amount of lavender could keep her calm when he was so close by. Would she be feeling the same way had the adrenaline surge of danger not been present?

Probably. Because Damon had presented an aura of danger before demons were involved. From that very first meeting she'd sensed the threat he'd presented to her peace of mind.

So what now? Other than the fact that she and Damon couldn't have sex, what was the plan?

Find the book, kill the demons. Right. But *how*?

"What now?" Zoe asked.

Damon's deep blue eyes flared with anger. "I have no idea what any of this means and I hate that."

"I'm not real fond of it, either," she said.

"This is not how I work," he said.

"How do you work?"

"Alone." Turning on his heel, he walked out, leaving Zoe alone.

"Fear me if you dare!"

Damon came downstairs to find Bella repeating lines from the animated movie on the TV. She stood with two paws on the arm of the weird chair with the words written on it, her face inches from the screen.

"She's watching *Puss in Boots*," Gram said as she entered the living room. "It's her favorite movie."

"Along with *Magic Mike*," Bella said.

"Where did you get that chair?" Damon asked.

"A beau gave it to me," Gram said. "It's one of a kind from a French designer who has made quite a name for himself in Paris. His work is shown in museums and art galleries. He thinks art is too esoteric so he makes his art functional as well. The feet are carved to resemble pencils."

Damon moved closer to the piece of furniture. The off-white upholstery was filled with a variety of words in different languages and fonts. "Was your beau a warlock?"

"If you're asking if the chair is magical, then no, I don't believe so."

"You don't believe so?"

"One can never be sure about these things," Gram said.

Damon swore in Latin.

"I understood that," Gram said.

"So did I," Bella said. "Go away. You're disturbing me."

"Tough shit," Damon growled.

"I believe they have medication for that," Bella drawled. "Stool softeners or laxatives might help you with your problem."

Damon hated sitting around like this with a smart-ass talking cat and an elderly witch. Being cooped up was driving him nuts. He needed to kick some demon ass.

What if Pat was right? What if Silas was one of the demons who had tortured Damon during his short sojourn in hell? What was his purpose in showing up now after all this time? Eve's betrayal and the subsequent trouble had occurred over a hundred years ago. Why come after him now?

That was assuming that Silas was after him. Maybe that wasn't the case.

Damon tried to remember his time in hell, but it was a bloody blur. He could remember every minute of his time in Gettysburg, which was a hell of its own.

Maybe Simon would know. Damon had tried to get in touch with his sire but hadn't received a response so far. Which wasn't like Simon.

Damon's smartphone beeped, indicating an incoming email. Neville had sent him a transcript of the conversation between Zoe and Daniella from a few minutes ago.

He read at vamp speed. One line stood out. Zoe saying, *How can I have this incredibly powerful attraction to Damon yet he aggravates the hell out of me?*

He had the same question himself. How could he have this powerful attraction to the sexy little witch and her striking eyes when she aggravated the hell out of him?

And what was the deal with Daniella's premonition? He couldn't have sex with Zoe or Vamptown would go up in flames? What was that about?

He couldn't believe Zoe had said what she did knowing that she was under surveillance. But he knew firsthand that it was easier than you'd think to forget. Especially when the distraction was so strong.

This morning, Daniella's declaration about her premonition had probably rattled Zoe. Last night, her nightmare had rattled her. And last night, Zoe had rattled him.

Damon didn't like being rattled. It could result in death for a vampire let alone a vampire Demon Hunter.

As if on cue, Zoe came downstairs. She had her hair tied up in a ponytail; her bangs brushed her eyebrows. Her red KEEP CALM AND CARRY ON T-shirt cupped her breasts while her black pants hugged her hips. She still wore the bangle she'd had on yesterday. The sight of it reminded him of her hands on his body, of her curves pressed against his erection.

"I'm hungry," she said.

Damon was hungry, too. He'd fed on blood yesterday so he didn't need more. He needed Zoe, naked on those white sheets in that big bed of hers, her legs curved around his waist as he drove into her. There was so much he could teach her about pleasure.

She stared at him with those remarkable eyes of hers. One green. One blue. Was she focusing on his mouth?

Was she thinking about him drinking blood or was she remembering their hot kiss in the middle of the night?

The fact that he was a vampire hadn't seemed to bother her then. But the fact that she was a witch hadn't bothered him then, either.

Upstairs in her workroom, he'd been surrounded by so many scents. His vamp senses intensified sight, sound, and smell. Now he associated all those smells with her. Lemon, lavender, cinnamon, apple, and others that he couldn't name, but they all had a certain intoxication.

As did Zoe. He could hear the beat of her heart, sense the blood pulsing through her body. The predator within him urged him to possess her.

The opening notes of *Phantom of the Opera* floated up from the vent in the floor. A second later the music abruptly stopped and flames shot up from the vent.

"Fire!" Bella howled and flew upstairs.

Neville's voice came through the surveillance system a moment later. "It's happening all over Vamptown."

Gram stood and immediately cast a spell.

Fire, fire, this is dire.
Magic and lore,
Flames no more.

The flames continued.

Gram frowned. "That should have worked. Zoe, you try."

Zoe repeated the spell. The flames continued and were getting dangerously close to the drapes.

The possibility of the house burning down was not one Zoe was willing to accept. There had to be another way . . .

Zoe pictured the item needed in her mind and a moment later it appeared. A fire extinguisher.

Damon grabbed it and aimed it at the flames.

"What about the rest of Vamptown?" Zoe asked.

"The vamps all have fire extinguishers."

"Daniella's cupcake shop?"

"Has extra fire extinguishers," Damon said.

Gram opened the windows to let the smoke out and the fresh air in.

Pat was in their living room an instant later. "This is getting dangerous."

"The flames were put out," Damon said.

"This time." The words came from Tanya. She stood just inside the doorway with two vampires by her side. "Who knows what will happen next? We can't take the chance. The witches have been called before the Vamptown Council for immediate action."

Chapter Twenty

"I don't like the sound of that," Gram said.

"What does 'called before the council' mean?" Zoe asked.

"It means you are both to haul your asses over there immediately," Tanya said.

Zoe shot a nervous glance at Damon. "You're not going to grab me at vamp super speed, are you?"

"No."

"And no other vamps are going to try to grab us and do that, right?"

"There won't be any grabbing going on," Pat said.

"Unless you fight the order." Tanya looked like she was hoping Zoe and her grandmother would do just that.

"We're not fighting. I'm just trying to understand what is happening," Zoe said. "Where are we supposed to be going?"

"For security reasons we will be having the meeting in Nick's bar," Tanya said.

"Where is Nick?" Zoe demanded.

"Waiting for us in the bar," Tanya said. "Along with the rest of the Vamptown Council."

"How many are in this council?" Zoe asked.

"You'll find out soon enough. Stop stalling." Tanya nodded to the two vampires by her side. "Take them."

Damon stepped in front of Zoe. "I told them there would be no grabbing. They can accompany you without force."

Zoe saw Bella and Morticia in the shadows at the top of the stairs.

Stay here. She sent the telepathic message to Morticia and prayed that Bella would pick up on it as well.

"This isn't really my going-outside outfit," Gram said. She turned, and her colorful caftan was replaced with the knockoff vintage Chanel suit she'd worn when they'd first met Nick and Damon. The magic only worked between that particular caftan and that suit.

Tanya was not impressed. "You'd think a witch could come up with a better outfit than that. What about you?" She directed her question to Zoe. "Are you going to use your magic to change clothes, too?"

"No," Zoe said curtly.

She had no intention of wasting magic on appearances. She might need it for something more urgent later on.

"Let's go."

Zoe shot a look at Pat, but he seemed intent on avoiding her gaze. His expression was serious, and that was enough to worry her a lot.

The walk from their rental house to Nick's All Nighter Bar and Grill seemed to take no time at all.

They entered the bar to find the normal tables gone and two rows of chairs set up in a court-like arrangement.

Gram got the same vibe. Maybe it went back to their ancestor's experiences in the Salem Witch Trials, but being called in front of this kind of tribunal was not a good thing. Back in Boston, their coven had deliberately avoided any setup that might mimic a trial. Instead they'd gathered in a circle even as they reprimanded Zoe for revealing the fact that she was a witch to a human.

Gram looked around nervously. "Courts give me the creeps the same way funeral homes give Zoe the creeps. I can't even watch *The People's Court*."

Tanya sauntered up to Zoe. "Where's your magic wand and fairy dust now?"

"I'm a witch, not freaking Tinker Bell."

"I doubt that Tinker Bell could raise hell the way you have. And I'm not saying that in a good way." She paused to give Zoe the once-over before adding, "Besides, you're not thin enough to be a fairy."

"Let me give her some warts," Gram pleaded. "On her nose and forehead. And a few boils on her neck."

"No, we are not stooping to her level." Bending closer, she whispered in Gram's ear, "We are in enough trouble as it is."

"All right. But when this is all over I plan on giving her warts."

"We'll discuss that later," Zoe murmured. "We need to focus on the current problem. Come on, let's sit down." She chose the two seats closest to the exit.

She recognized Nick, Pat, and Bruce as well as Neville but there were several other vampires there she did not know. Damon had once mentioned that Doc Boomer had a booming voice, so she identified him. She didn't know the two vampires who had come to the house with Tanya.

"Put the two witches up front," Tanya said.

"We're fine right here," Zoe said.

"When you are called before a vampire clan council, you go where we tell you," Tanya said. "Isn't that right, Nick?"

"Unfortunately, that is true," Nick said. "Come on, I'll get you both some chairs up front."

"They need to stand to face their accusers," Tanya said.

"I don't like the sound of that," Gram said once again.

Zoe didn't either. She searched the small crowd for Damon. Where was he? He couldn't just bring them and dump them here, could he? Would he desert them like that? Apparently the answer was yes.

"Damon isn't a council member," Tanya said triumphantly. "He can only be called as a witness."

"Or to vouch for character," Nick said.

Right. Like that was going to happen.

"We could be in hot water here," Gram said, taking hold of Zoe's hand and eyeing the small crowd anxiously.

"Nick won't let anything happen to us," Zoe said with more confidence than she felt.

"Nick only has one vote," Tanya said.

"Daniella—"

"Is not a vampire," Tanya said. "She is not a council member."

"Why isn't Damon a council member?" Zoe said.

"He hasn't been in Vamptown long enough. There is a one-year residency requirement."

Great. Zoe knew the only reason Damon would save them was to get the Book of Darkness. At this point she didn't really care what his motivations were. She just wanted to get out of there.

"Let's get started," Tanya said. "I will turn the procedure over to Pat since he is the oldest."

The regret she saw on Pat's face was not reassuring. Surely he knew that Zoe was a necessary part of the plan to get the spell book. Not that there actually was a plan per se. Maybe that's what this was all about. They wanted to hear the plan.

Okay, then she'd better think of one fast. Hard to do when standing before a group of angry vampires, but not impossible.

"I think this has something to do with the equinox," Zoe said. "It's coming soon. The day after tomorrow, in fact. It's the official beginning of spring but it's also the day when there are equal amounts of light and darkness. The demons represent darkness."

"Next you'll be saying they are the cause of global warming," Tanya scoffed.

"No, humans are responsible for that." Zoe took a deep breath, trying to gather her thoughts. "If the number of daylight hours increases, then that should weaken the power of the demons."

"I didn't find any scientific evidence of that in my research," Neville the Nerd said.

Doc Boomer held out his hand. "Wait, are you saying that the demons could turn the world dark?"

Okay, that sounded worse than she'd hoped. "No, I'm not saying that. Definitely not saying that."

"Then what are you saying?" The vampire dentist was clearly impatient.

She didn't know what the hell she was saying. She was starting to panic, and that was never a good start for logic.

She just knew that the equinox was coming and the demons had to be defeated by then. *Before* then would be even better.

Zoe closed her eyes for a moment, trying to regain her composure. Instead she got a vision of herself and Gram in black garb reminiscent of seventeenth-century Salem as someone put a noose around her neck.

She immediately opened her eyes and quickly looked down. Her KEEP CALM T-shirt was still there. Her hand flew to her throat. No noose. Just the chain holding her talisman.

Okay. Things would be okay. She just had to stay calm.

"You both have been accused of being a danger to Vamptown," Pat said.

Accused? That didn't sound good.

"Flames were reported coming from every floor vent in Vamptown," Neville said.

"Every *vamp* floor vent," Bruce pointed out. "Not the humans'."

"This time," Neville said. "What if that isn't the case next time?"

"The flames came from the demons," Zoe said. "Not us."

"The demons are here because of you," Tanya said. "You released them."

"Damon is going to get rid of them," Zoe said.

"But you can call forth more," Tanya said. "You own the book that released them from hell."

"We do not own it. We never saw it before, right, Gram?"

Her grandmother twisted her fingers nervously. "Well, I may have seen it once as a young girl."

Zoe's mouth dropped open. "What?"

"There," Tanya said triumphantly. "You heard it, fellow council members. The older witch brought the book here to release demons upon Vamptown and destroy us."

"Hold on a second. Gram, did you see it or dream you saw it?"

"I'm not sure," Gram admitted.

"The old witch is senile," Tanya said.

"Not senile enough that I can't put warts on your face," Gram growled.

"She threatened me," Tanya said. "Allow me to get rid of her."

"Damon has made it clear that we need the witches to retrieve the demon book," Nick said.

"We don't need them both," Tanya said.

"We do," Nick said.

"Then let's separate them." Tanya snapped her fingers, and the two vampires who had accompanied her earlier moved toward Zoe and her grandmother.

"Wait, you've got something on your face," Gram told Tanya, who immediately whipped out a compact mirror to check her appearance.

Grabbing Zoe's hand, Gram pointed to the mirror, which flew from Tanya's hand to the wall beside them. Then Gram rapidly recited,

Mirror on the wall
Who's the ugliest vampire of them all?
Mirror, mirror
Get us the hell out of here!

Zoe didn't have time to ask where they were going, but she soon found out. The tunnels.

"Welcome, ladies." Silas bowed. He looked just like his astral projection—only now she not only sensed his malevolence, but could actually feel it crawling over her skin. "How kind of you to grace us with your presence."

This time Zoe cast the spell.

We're in trouble
Take us back on the double.

In the blink of an eye they were back in front of the Vamptown Council. Only this time Damon was there.

"What's going on?" Damon demanded.

"The witches tried to escape," Tanya said. "They must be punished."

"Shut up!" Damon growled. "Everybody just shut up." He turned to face Zoe. "You won't be hurt."

"Or Gram. And we won't be separated," Zoe said fiercely, already thinking of a spell to take them to someplace safer than the vampire bar or the demon tunnel.

"Neither you nor your grandmother will be hurt by us," Damon said. "You have my word on it as a Demon Hunter."

To leave or not to leave?

"I trust him," Gram said.

"And we won't be thrown into vampire jail or anything," Zoe said.

Damon stepped past the other vampires to stand before her, so close she could feel his breath on her cheek. "Trust me, little witch," he whispered. "Stay or all will be lost."

In the end Zoe trusted her gut, and that told her he was telling her the truth. She nodded her agreement.

For one brief second, Damon looked like he wanted to touch her. Instead he pivoted to face his fellow vampires. "Listen, everyone. The demons are behind all of this. They wanted you to try to get rid of the witches. That's why they created the flames. So you'd either banish the witches or scare them into leaving."

"We can't have flames shooting out of the heating ducts," Doc Boomer said. "I don't mean to be a downer. I'm just stating the obvious."

"I know that," Damon said.

"So what do you plan on doing about it?" Doc Boomer said.

"The demons are right below us. I am not going to say anything to warn them of their destruction."

"I say we take a vote now about these witches," Tanya said. "Remember, Damon, you do not have a vote. All in favor of getting rid of the witches say 'Aye'. Let me be the first. Aye."

"Aye," Doc Boomer said regretfully.

Neville cast a nervous look in Damon's direction. "Aye."

"Nay," Nick said.

"Nay," Pat said.

"Nay," Bruce said.

Zoe cast a nervous look at the two vamps that Tanya had used to bring them to the bar.

"They can't vote," Damon said. "They haven't been in Vamptown long enough. So it appears we have a tie."

"And no motion can be carried without a majority," Nick said. "Which means Irma and Zoe stay. And they continue to work with Damon on locating the missing Book of Darkness. This meeting is formally adjourned."

"I'm so sorry about that," Pat said. "I feel responsible. I should have spoken up about my connection to Silas."

"No," Damon said. "Keep that to yourself for the time being."

"Bruce knows. And I told Nick already," Pat admitted.

"Told me what?" Nick said as he joined them.

"Let's continue this in your office," Damon said.

The five of them barely fit in the small office at the back of the bar. "It's soundproof," Nick said.

"I don't think we should tell anyone else about Pat's connection to Silas at this point," Damon said. "You saw how paranoid everyone got."

"Not everyone," Bruce said. "We voted nay."

"Let's explore this equinox connection further," Damon said. "Pat, can you check your personal library of ancient books?"

This was the first Zoe had heard about the older vampire having a specialized library.

"I received a few illuminated manuscripts dating back to the Dark Ages from my sire. He had a strong connection to mystical powers in ancient times," Pat said. "I've never had cause to consult the volumes before, but this is definitely a time for it. I'd already started when I heard this meeting called."

"After the flames nearly burned the Moroccan rug I had near the floor vent," Bruce said.

"Keep those manuscripts safe," Damon said.

"I will. And you keep the witches safe," Pat said.

"I don't need to tell you that time is running out," Nick said. "Vamptown could have gone up in flames today."

"And Damon and Zoe didn't even have sex," Gram said.

"What?" Nick's voice was curt.

"Daniella said she had a premonition that if Damon and Zoe had sex, Vamptown would go up in flames," Gram said. "Was I not supposed to say that?"

"I know about the premonition," Nick said.

"You can't blame the flames on Zoe," Gram said. "Or Damon."

"I wasn't going to," Nick said.

"I was surprised how modern your spell was," Bruce told Gram. "I was expecting something more along the lines of Shakespeare's witches from *Macbeth*."

"'Eye of newt, and toe of frog,'" Gram quoted.

Bruce nodded. "That's right."

"Not my thing," Gram said. "Although I have used the 'hell-broth boil and bubble' line on occasion."

"Where did you go when you disappeared?" Bruce asked.

"Listen, they've had a rough time," Damon said. "Let's get the details later. For now, I think we should head back to the house."

"Good idea," Nick said.

The moment they were in their house, Gram headed for her room, citing the need for a nap.

"Where *did* you go when you disappeared?" Damon asked Zoe.

"To the tunnels."

"Your grandmother sent you both to the tunnels? Why?"

Zoe put her hand to Damon's mouth. "Keep your voice down." She quickly pulled her hand away. Her fingers tingled, but she couldn't think about that now. She had to stay focused, as in focused on demon demolition and not sex with Damon. "It wasn't deliberate on her part. She panicked and didn't specify a destination."

"How do you know you were in the tunnels?"

"Because Silas was there to welcome us. I saw two shadowy figures behind Silas that I'm assuming were the two Guys. We didn't stick around long enough to find out."

"Did Silas say anything?"

"He said welcome and something about how kind it was of us to grace them with our presence."

"What else did you see? Any weapons? Anything else?"

Zoe shook her head. "We were only there a few seconds. I'm sorry. My only thought was to get us out of there."

"You did good."

Zoe couldn't believe her ears. Had Damon just given her a compliment? That had to be a first.

She'd experienced more firsts since coming to Vamptown than she could count. She couldn't even focus, she was feeling so burned out. "I need a few minutes alone."

"I understand."

Zoe didn't see how Damon could understand when she didn't. What was happening to her? Why had she had that flashback about Salem? Why had Gram's spell

resulted in them landing in the tunnels? What did the
impending equinox have to do with anything? Where
the hell was that damn demon book?

So many questions, so few answers.

And then there was the intensely personal question.
Why, despite everything, did she want to hurl herself
into Damon's arms and kiss him? Why did she long for
him, lust for him? Were those thoughts enough to have
sent flames shooting through the floor vents throughout
Vamptown?

But the biggest question of all was this—was she
falling in love with Damon? Because that would be the
most dangerous thing of all, at least as far as her heart
was concerned. Dealing with demons was bad enough.
Dealing with a broken heart should pale in comparison. It didn't.

Dammit, dammit, dammit.

Chapter Twenty-one

"I'm so glad you are back," Bella greeted Zoe at the top of the stairs and followed her into Zoe's bedroom. "I was looking for something or some way to help you and I think I've come up with it."

"What is it?" Zoe said.

Bella stretched her paw under the bed and pulled out Zoe's mother's amethyst necklace. Picking it up in her mouth, she jumped onto the bed and dropped it beside Zoe with the pride a normal cat might show at capturing a mouse.

Zoe frowned in confusion. "How is my mother's necklace supposed to help me?"

"As you know, I never met your mother. I came to you after she passed."

"Yes. So?"

"So I didn't know about this necklace until today. You never showed it to me even though you showed it to Damon."

"I didn't show him the necklace. I only showed him her talisman."

"Well, that explains it then," Bella said.

"Explains what?"

"Why the Demon Hunter didn't tell you about the power of this. Look." She nudged it closer to Zoe. "Look carefully at the carving on the pendant part of the necklace."

"It's some sort of animal. A cat?"

"A bear. Carved in amethyst. It's a protection amulet said to put demons to flight," Bella said.

"Wait a second. How do you know this?"

"I Googled it." Bella lifted her head with pride.

"So you're saying if I put on the necklace, the demons will disappear?"

"It could happen."

"Or maybe it's a trap. If my mother had a protection amulet, she would have told me about it."

"Maybe she never got the chance to."

"The necklace didn't protect her from death." Zoe's voice cracked.

"I never said it would protect you from death. Only from demons. Was she wearing this when she died?"

Zoe nodded.

"Then her death wasn't caused by demons," Bella said.

"Or it was, and the necklace didn't work," Zoe said. She took several deep breaths, trying to regain her control and keep the tears at bay. She didn't know how much more she could take. Part of her just wanted to curl up in a little ball and pull the covers over her head. But her inner witch wasn't having any of that.

No guts, no glory. What if black magic was the only way to get rid of the demons? If they'd killed her mother, she'd be willing to jam Damon's dagger into Silas's throat herself.

"What are you girls doing up here?" Gram asked, joining them on the bed.

"I thought you were going to take a nap," Zoe said.

"I couldn't sleep."

"Did you know that Mom's amethyst necklace had a bear carved into the pendant?"

Gram studied the necklace. "A protection amulet."

"I don't remember it having a bear carved into it," Zoe said.

Gram held the necklace in her hands and closed her eyes. "I don't sense any evil or black magic. I sense your mother's aura."

"You didn't sense that the spell book was evil," Zoe felt compelled to point out.

"Boy, one little mistake and no one trusts you anymore." Seeing the look on Zoe's face, Gram sighed. "Okay, that demon spell book thing was a big mistake and we knew that the instant I opened it."

"What did you mean when you said earlier that you may have seen the Book of Darkness when you were a child?"

"I can't be sure. I felt no sense of recognition when I saw the book here the other day. Maybe I just heard stories about it."

"Do you remember the stories?"

Gram shook her head. "I was very, very young. I didn't hear stories about the demon book when I got older or I would have remembered. This entire thing is a mystery."

"Do you think it's tied to the Salem witch trials?"

"I have the feeling it goes back much further than that," Gram said. "But speaking of the witch trials, I had the strangest experience in front of the Vamptown Council."

"Me too," Zoe said. "When I closed my eyes, I saw the two of us in black dresses dating back to that period."

Gram nodded. "And I heard sobs and smelled sweat. And someone was putting nooses around our necks."

"I thought maybe it was just me," Zoe said.

"No, I had the vision, too. Perhaps it was collective memory from our ancestor. Or a warning of what the vampires wanted to do to us."

"Not all the vampires."

"I'm so sorry I got you into this mess," Gram said. "Maybe we should never have left Boston."

"We didn't have much of a choice."

"Then maybe I shouldn't have gone to hear Martin Powers speak," Gram said. "But I didn't go there looking for trouble. Witch's honor. I saw a brief interview on the TV and there was something strange about his aura. Still, I kept an open mind at the motivational seminar until he started talking about how he could solve everyone's problems and how he had the secret to happiness but would only share it if paid a large sum of money. Even the most powerful of witches can't guarantee someone's happiness. But Powers was doing that, teasing the people there with promises he couldn't keep. Even so, I should have walked away. I shouldn't have created a scene. If I'd just kept my mouth shut then that mass exodus wouldn't have occurred. I didn't use any magic to cause that," Gram said. "I just spoke the truth."

"I know."

"I'm sure there are other motivational speakers out there who help people with self-awareness and confidence and that sort of thing. Martin Powers just wasn't one of them."

"Tristin thought Powers has a thing against witches because one of his ancestors was involved as a judge in the Salem witch trials. He admitted that he might have told Powers that we have special powers."

"That's not possible. I cast a spell to remove your confession of being a witch from Tristin's memory," Gram said.

"Which lasted until recently, when he found the file he'd put on his computer just in case we did something to make him forget."

"When did you learn all this?"

"Tristin was here yesterday."

"What? Why am I just hearing this now?" Gram demanded.

"Because it's been crazy around here. The bottom line is that Damon took care of Tristin."

"He killed him?"

"No, he compelled him and sent him packing. He also had Tristin's computer files destroyed. I think we've heard the last of him," Zoe said.

"What about Powers?"

"Damon also sent Bob back to Boston after compelling him to forget about finding us."

"But if Powers thinks we are witches—"

"We don't know that that is the case. Maybe he ignored Tristin's comments."

"Let's hope so."

"Let's hope what?" Damon said, strolling into Zoe's bedroom as if he owned the place.

Zoe pointed to the surveillance camera on the crown molding. "Read the transcript or watch the recording."

"Look, I know you're stressed out—"

"Damn right, I mean *darn* right I'm stressed out." Zoe leapt to her feet. No way was she staying in bed with Damon in the room.

"Zoe just informed me that you took care of Tristin for her," Gram said.

"For her and for Vamptown."

"Thank you."

"No thanks necessary," Damon said.

"Then will you accept my thanks for sticking up for us at the trial?" Gram said.

Damon shook his head. "Again, no thanks necessary."

"Would it kill you to just accept her thanks?" Bella said with an impatient swish of her tail.

"He's immortal," Zoe said, repeating the words he'd said to her. "So obviously it wouldn't kill him."

"You wouldn't know it by the way he's acting," Bella said. "Show him your mother's necklace."

Zoe reluctantly did so. "It's amethyst."

"Catherine the Great's favorite stone," Bella said.

"And I care about that because?" Damon said.

"Because the necklace has a bear carved into it."

"A protection amulet against demons," Damon said.

"See?" Bella said. "I told you he'd know what it meant."

"Does it work?" Zoe asked.

"It's an old wives' tale. A myth," Damon said.

There was no reason for Zoe to be disappointed. She

already had a protection spell. She didn't need an amulet.

"You look exhausted," Gram told her. "Try to get some rest. Take a nap."

Great. So it had finally come to this. Now Zoe had to nap before she could kick demon butt. She had never needed a nap before. A sniff of peppermint essential oil and she was usually ready to go.

But then she'd never dealt with demons before. Or hot vampires. What happened to vampires being cool, pale, and all shimmery? Was the hot thing unique to Damon?

Gram was right. Zoe was exhausted. And thinking about hot vampires wasn't helping, which is why she made no protest as Gram and Damon left her alone to rest. Alone . . . with Bella.

The gray cat sat beside her on the bed. "Lie back and I'll tell you a bedtime story about how I became a familiar."

"You never talk about that," Zoe said.

"Be quiet and listen. Once upon a time there was a beautiful, brilliant woman who married a count and became a countess who was a close confidante of Catherine the Great. They didn't have Viagra in those days so the marriage with the much older count was a bust. But this countess was smart enough to make good connections and not get caught up in the backstabbing and the espionage taking place on a daily basis at court. I avoided any mention of the king of Prussia like the plague. Not that he *had* the plague, although Catherine's husband, who had a similar problem getting it up, had smallpox before they were married. He was

German as was Catherine, whose birth name was Sophia. But this isn't about them. It's about me. I had a great life until an evil witch turned me into a familiar and I had to do her bidding. The end."

"That's it?" Zoe said.

"What? You were expecting *and then they lived happily ever after*? Didn't happen. When she died, I became the familiar to her daughter and so on until finally we left Russia for London before the Revolution. From there we traveled to Boston first class. The witches became more and more difficult and my life sucked until I was sent to you."

"Why did the witch turn you?" Zoe said.

"She was jealous of my beauty and brains."

"That's sad."

Bella eyed her suspiciously. "Are you hormonal or something?"

Zoe blinked back tears. She didn't know why she felt sad, she just did. Like she needed a reason after what she'd been through lately.

"I could use some pet therapy," she said.

"Get a dog," Bella said.

Zoe's lips trembled.

Bella shook her head but moved closer until she was curled against Zoe's side. Once there she started purring. "Better?"

Zoe smoothed her hand over Bella's head. "Yes, thank you."

"Go to sleep."

Zoe woke in time for dinner. She felt guilty wasting time that way and tried to make up for it by spending the rest of the evening alternating between going through the Adams Book of Spells and the Internet searching for a connection between the equinox and demons or any reference to the Book of Darkness.

The closest she got was a reference in their Book of Spells with drawings of demons with claws surrounded by flames. She'd never seen this page before. That was the problem with magic. Things had a way of appearing and disappearing at awkward times. Sometimes there were meanings behind it, or messages trying to be sent. But trying to decipher it all was not an exact science by any means.

Gram, still shaken from the Vamptown Council meeting, had been unusually quiet during their meal and had retired to bed early.

Damon focused on his phone.

"Anything new?" she asked.

"Not yet."

Her cell phone rang. It was Daniella. "I'm so sorry about Tanya calling you and your grandmother in front of the council. I'm sorry I couldn't be there for you."

"They told me you couldn't attend because you're not a member of the council."

"Because I'm a hybrid."

"Did you have flames at the cupcake shop?"

"No. You know, I may have been a bit off on my premonition. It could have been the flames through the floor vents and not that the entire neighborhood would be incinerated. Not that I saw anything incinerated. I didn't mean that."

"So what are you saying? That the precipitating event you listed before may not be a problem? That it's okay to . . . you know."

"You're asking if it's okay to have sex with Damon?"

"Yes."

"That's your call. I do know there is a very powerful bond between you two. Maybe it's fate. Maybe it's your destiny."

Daniella's words stayed with Zoe long after she'd ended the call.

It wasn't logical but Zoe was dealing with legends and magic, not logic. She was also dealing with demons, darkness, and doom.

She wasn't someone who used sex like chocolate to feel better after a bad day. At least, she never had been in the past.

Maybe when this was all over, if it went well and the demons were demolished and good won over evil then . . . maybe then . . .

Oh, who was she kidding? There was no guarantee that good would win over evil. Even Pat said the odds weren't in their favor. Zoe wasn't giving up, but would it be so wrong to . . .

Yes, it would. Anything that didn't directly apply to destroying the demons and the book that called them forth was a distraction. It was wrong to think or speculate or fantasize about anything other than those goals.

"Something is wrong," Damon said.

"Ya think?" Demons were threatening and she was thinking about sex with Damon. Hell yes, something was wrong.

"I haven't heard from Simon. He hasn't responded to any of my attempts to contact him."

"Who is Simon?"

"My sire. The Demon Hunter who turned me."

"How did he do that?"

"Simon used his fangs to open the vein on his wrist

and then held it to my mouth, urging me to drink his blood. I did and that created an irrevocable bond between us. Because when you are turned, the first blood you get is from the vampire that turned you. He taught me how to survive the transition."

"Survive it? I thought vampires are immortal."

"You aren't a vampire until you survive the transition. I did. Some don't. After that, Simon taught me how to hunt."

"How to hunt demons?"

"Yes."

"And humans?"

Damon nodded. "Vegetarians mostly."

"Whaaat?"

"They're healthier. You get more vitamins that way." He reached out to close her mouth, which had dropped open. Brushing his thumb over her lips, he said, "I'm just teasing you, little witch."

He was teasing her all right. Her lips were humming and hungry for the touch of his mouth on hers. Passion rose within her like the flames had risen from the floor vents.

"I need a cold shower," she muttered.

Damon instantly released her. "Go ahead. The surveillance cameras are off in the bathrooms now."

Zoe fled upstairs, but there was no escaping her desire for Damon. No amount of cold water could cool the heat and no amount of lathering with Sunshine soap could remove the memory of his touch. She tried, she really did. But when she stepped out of the bathroom wearing only a towel around her body and saw Damon waiting for her she wanted him as much as she had before. Maybe more.

"I had the camera turned off in here," Damon said. "You don't have to fear me. You don't have to run from me the way you just did."

"You thought I ran because I was afraid?"

"Weren't you?" he said.

"I ran because you touched me."

"And that turned you off after hearing how I became a vampire."

"It turned me on. Not the vampire stuff. Your touch. You, Damon." Her trembling fingers caused the towel to accidentally slip.

Damon was there in half a heartbeat. His fingers rested just above her breast. Gazing down into her eyes, he moved her hand away from the towel.

"I want you." His voice was hoarse.

"I want you, too," she whispered.

He removed her towel and with it any chance she could hold back the wave of desire coursing through her naked body.

Moving with vamp speed, he yanked off his black shirt and pants and underwear. Now he was as nude as she was and she couldn't get over how good he looked without clothes. Yes, she'd seen him shirtless, but wow. The vampire was built. And he was aroused.

So was she. Dampness pooled between her thighs and it wasn't because of the shower. It was because of Damon.

Still, she felt she had to warn him. "There's a curse that says no man can make an Adams witch happy."

"I'm not a man," Damon said. "I'm a vampire, and I can make you very happy."

He moved in and took possession of her mouth, parting her lips and dueling with her tongue. Then he licked the roof of her mouth with such delicate strokes she thought she'd go crazy. His kiss scorched her in a carnal way.

Lowering his hand, he slipped his fingers down past her abdomen to slide them through the curls at the gateway of her vagina. Now his *touch* scorched her in an incredibly intimate and carnal way. His erotic caresses down there were beyond anything she'd ever experienced.

When her knees gave way, he scooped her in his arms and carried her to her bed. Did she want him to take her with vamp speed? Did she want it all to be over in a split second?

He dragged his teeth over her bare breast. No fangs. Did vampire sex involve fangs? Maybe she should have asked a few questions ahead of time. But could she when her entire focus was on the intense pleasure and anticipation he was creating? No way. Let him ask the questions.

"Do you like that?" he said.

"Yes," she moaned.

He remembered the way he'd touched her before, the night she'd had the nightmare, and repeated the caress.

"How about this?" Now he added the new element of laving his rough tongue over her nipple.

"Definitely." She threaded her fingers through his hair and held him in place. While his mouth focused on her breast, his talented fingers moved lower, sliding over her pelvis and homing in on her clitoris. Once there, he took his time, brushing his thumb over the tiny bud that was such an intense erogenous zone.

Zoe arched her back as shards of raw hunger pulsed through her body. Kissing his way down her body, his tongue replaced his fingers as he stroked her there with warm laps and wicked lunges. She came hard and fast. Not once but twice . . . three times.

Lifting his head, he smiled that sexy smile of his. Lifting his body, he positioned himself between her legs. Zoe couldn't fathom how she could possibly climax again and she tried to warn him not to be disappointed . . .

He drove into her with one powerful slide. She closed around him as his thrusts created a friction that was both blissful and insanely wild.

Her vagina clenched as her orgasm took over, increasing to a mind-blowing ecstasy. He stiffened in her arms and within her body as he reached his climax. It was magical, it was raw and reckless.

"It was over too fast." Zoe didn't realize she'd actually whispered the unsteady words aloud until Damon smoothed her bangs from her eyes.

"That was just the beginning," he said.

"Really? I mean, I wasn't complaining. It was incredible. Just the beginning, huh?"

"Oh yeah. There's lots more. Let me show you." And he did.

Damon sat straight up in bed. Something was wrong. He was alone in Zoe's rumpled bed.

It was barely daylight. Too early for night to have completely given up its darkness. Where was she? And why had he fallen asleep? That never happened to him. Vampires didn't need much sleep. Did it have something to do with her being a witch?

Damon grabbed his pants from the floor and moved at vamp speed. There was no sign of Zoe on this second

story of the house. The scents coming from her workroom didn't allow him to focus on finding her that way,
but a quick search confirmed she wasn't in any of the
upstairs rooms.

He looked down from the top of the stairway and
saw Zoe's grandmother standing there, tears streaming
down her face. "Zoe is gone. She's been taken!"

Chapter Twenty-two

"That's not possible," Damon said. "You had a protection spell around her."

"Yes, but she's immune to magic now," Gram said.

"She had sex with you," Bella told Damon. "That made her lose her powers. You kept yours but she lost hers."

"Do you still have your powers?" Damon asked Zoe's grandmother.

"Yes, but I can't save her. She's immune. *You* have to save her. You killed a witch once. Now you have to save one."

"Where is she?"

"The demons have her in the tunnel," Zoe's grandmother said.

"How do you know that? The surveillance cameras were off. Did the cameras down here show who took her?" Damon said.

"Uh, that would be a negative," Neville said through the surveillance system. "And I now see three demons and one witch on the scan of the affected area of the tunnels."

"You're going to need help, Demon Hunter," Bella said. "You can't do it alone."

"Watch me."

"The cat is right," Pat said.

Damon hadn't even realized that the older vampire had joined them, that's how stunned he was by the news that Zoe was a captive. He had to get his shit together or all would be lost. He couldn't focus on the fact that having sex with him had left Zoe vulnerable to attack.

"I should have had her wear her mother's amethyst necklace with the bear carved into it," Damon muttered.

"You said it was a myth, that it wouldn't help her," Zoe's grandmother said.

"That's when I thought she had the protection spell. Maybe the amethyst amulet thing isn't a myth," Damon said.

"It doesn't matter," Pat said. "Even if normally it may have protected Zoe from demons, it wouldn't do so once her magic was gone. There was nothing you could do. If anyone is guilty, it's me for not finding the passage about this sooner."

"What are you talking about?"

"About the part where you having sex would make one of you lose your powers," Pat said.

Damon shook his head, trying to make sense of it all. "The cat said that."

"I'm not a cat. I'm a familiar," Bella said. "And I only know because it suddenly appeared minutes ago in the Book of Spells written on a page that was previously blank."

"What, that having sex with a vampire would make a witch lose her powers?" Damon said.

"It's only true for you and Zoe in particular. It's all tied up with the Book of Darkness. Touching the book made her vulnerable in a way none of us could have anticipated," Pat said. "I only discovered all this when I found a passage copied from a papyrus dating back to the great library in ancient Alexandria. You remember I told you my sire had given me some illuminated manuscripts pertaining to mystical powers in ancient times? I'm so sorry I didn't find this information about you and Zoe sooner."

Damon was tormented by the thought that Silas had Zoe. He felt as if the demon had reached into his chest and ripped his heart out. Not that he had a heart. Or emotions. Or fear. Until now.

How could this be happening? The fact that he'd had sex with Zoe had changed everything, including him.

"The only silver lining, if there is one, is that there is a way to reverse the curse and get Zoe's magic to return," Pat said. "At least that's what it says in this illuminated manuscript. The original sources go back thousands of years."

"The demon book didn't look that old when I saw it," Gram said.

"Yes, well, the Book of Darkness has the ability to mask itself and to appear and disappear," Pat noted.

Gram threw back her shoulders and faced Damon. "There is a silver lining, as Pat said. There is a way to save Zoe and restore her magic."

"I have to get Zoe back," Damon said. "Whatever it takes." He checked his smartphone to see if Simon had answered or sent a message via Words with Friends, which had been their secret means of safe communication. Instead he saw one word. DEARIE.

Shit. The demon had been playing the online game with him. Damon was going to eviscerate him.

Damon felt his fangs emerge as he went full vamp. He could feel his eyes darken. He needed to go into warrior mode.

"Do you love Zoe?" Gram demanded out of the blue.

Damon looked at her in disbelief. That was the last thing he'd expected to hear her ask him. "What does that have to do with anything?"

"It's critical," Gram said.

"I've only known her—"

"Time is irrelevant," Gram said. "We're talking about a vampire and a witch here. Do you love her?"

"Why does it matter?"

"Because it may be the only way to break the curse and restore Zoe's magic to her."

"I have to rescue her first and then destroy the demons. The rest can wait."

"No, it can't. You can't rescue her without breaking the curse."

"The one about no man being able to make an Adams witch happy?" Damon said.

"She told you about that?"

He angrily pointed to his fangs. "I'm a vampire, not a man."

"Exactly," Gram said. "You alone can save her. But only if you love her. Do you?"

Did he? How else could he explain this gaping emptiness he felt without her? The way she'd gotten to him from the very beginning, aggravating him and arousing him at the same time. The little things he noticed about her, like the way her bangs fell into those stunning eyes of hers or how she would swirl her hair around her finger or the way she smelled or the distracting questions she'd ask him.

Did he love her? Shit, yes. It wasn't wise, wasn't logical, wasn't anything he'd planned. Sometimes karma was a bitch. Or maybe his karma was a witch.

"Do you love Zoe?" Gram repeated.

"Yes, I do," Damon said.

"Then you can bring the magic back to her."

"How?"

"Simple. You kiss her," Gram said.

Damon waved her words away. "This isn't some stupid freaking fairy tale."

"No, it's not. It's a nightmare."

"Zoe and I can't have a future together—"

Gram waved his words away. "We'll work out the details of that later. For now you have to save her and part of that is—"

"Kissing her. I get it," he said impatiently.

"Bring the magic back."

"And no kissing her on the cheek and no tongue, either," Bella said.

"She's right," Gram said. "A simple kiss on the mouth, but you must love her in your heart or all is lost."

"Then we're in deep shit because I don't have a heart," Damon said.

"Yes, you do, Demon Hunter," Bella said. "You may not have before, but you do now. You need to believe."

"I believe what I can see," he said curtly.

"You couldn't see the connection between Zoe and you, but you felt it," Gram said. "You fought it but I know you felt it."

She was asking him to feel while he fought, and he'd never done that. Not since Gettysburg. Not since he'd become a vampire. Not since he'd become a Demon Hunter.

Loving Zoe was a problem, not a solution.

"I wouldn't have believed love was possible had I not seen it between Daniella and Nick," Pat admitted.

"Nick has more humanity than I do," Damon said.

"True. But you are strong enough that love would not weaken you. This is your destiny."

"Does that ancient manuscript of yours say how this turns out?" Damon said.

"No," Pat admitted. "But it does say that the equinox plays a role in this. That the demons' powers are getting stronger while there are more hours of darkness than light."

"It's always darkest before the dawn," Gram said.

Damon's eyes were drawn to the weird chair with the writing on it. Amid the cursive French phrases, two words in Latin in the middle of the seat stood out. They seemed to glow. AD FINEM—to the end.

He refused to believe that this was the end. He was a vampire Demon Hunter and he would succeed or die.

"Welcome to our humble abode, dearie," Silas told Zoe.

"Did you bring Dr Pepper?" the first Guy said.

Zoe tried to make sense of her situation, but her mind was hazy. The last thing she remembered was cuddling in her bed with Damon. How did she end up here? Where the hell was she?

The tunnels. She was in the tunnels, wearing a tattered red dress. A tattered red Victorian ball gown like something out of *Phantom of the Opera*. She was lying on something cold and hard. Her hands were bound above her head. Her ankles were bound as well, and she wore sparkly ruby shoes that looked remarkably like those worn by Dorothy in *The Wizard of Oz*.

"I apologize for the lack of amenities," Silas said. "We couldn't get out to the embalming room at the moment, so we brought the embalming table to us."

Zoe could feel the cold metal of the table through the tissue-thin silk of her dress. Not *her* dress. The dress Silas had put on her.

"Mirror, mirror, get me out of here," Zoe said frantically.

"No mirror in here. Not that it matters," Silas said. "It's no good casting spells, because you've lost your magic. Tsk tsk. Such a shame, dearie. You really should have listened to that hybrid when she warned you that having intercourse with the Demon Hunter would result in Vamptown going up in flames."

Her protest froze in her throat as she got her first good look at the tunnel walls. Or more specifically, what was *on* the tunnel walls. Spiders. Millions of them. Rappelling down from the ceiling and the walls.

Silas waved his hand toward the insects. "Ah, I see you've noticed our little friends. I understand they are not faves of yours?"

"What do you want?"

"I'm supposed to say world peace, right?" Silas laughed. It was not a pleasant sound. "I want the Book of Darkness, of course."

"I don't have it," Zoe said.

"But you can get it."

"If I could get it I would have already done so."

"You just needed a little assistance, dearie. That's where I come in. I'm here to help you."

"By holding me against my will?"

"It's a ritual requirement. Hence the dress and the shoes."

"Ritual?" Zoe did not like the sound of that.

"Had you kept the Book of Darkness open longer, you would have learned all about this. Your ancestor, the witch Rebekka Adams, cursed me and sent me to hell."

"You accused her of being a witch."

"I spoke the truth. She was a witch."

"She wasn't hurting anyone."

"That's immaterial. I need the youngest witch from her family tree to assist me with the book."

"You just said I've lost my magic."

"That doesn't change anything," Silas said.

It sure changed a hell of a lot for her.

"You're still a witch. Losing your magic merely made my job that much easier. I'll have to thank the Demon Hunter for that."

"He'll come for me." She wasn't sure about that, but it was worth a shot.

"I'm counting on it, dearie. I'm going to kill him and your little cat, too."

More *Wizard of Oz* references. Zoe struggled against the chains restraining her. She even tried tapping her shoes together and muttering, "There's no place like home, there's no place like home."

"Don't waste your energy," Silas said. "You're going to need it for the ritual."

Zoe kept one eye on Silas and the other on the spiders. She needed a plan. Looking down, she realized the dress barely covered her breasts. She didn't want to know how Silas had put her in that dress. Some things were too awful to think about right now. She just needed to stall him long enough to devise a plan.

He pulled out . . . an iPad. "Before we begin, here's a short informational video about the ritual."

"I can't see anything laid flat out like this," she said.

Laid out on an embalming table, she silently continued. *Keep calm and carry on.* The table was cold and hard and very uncomfortable but it wasn't slimy with blood or anything. That was a good thing.

She needed to figure out why Gram's protection spell had stopped working and then figure out how to regain that protection. If she really had no magic, then what were her other options? *Slim to none* was her first thought, but she refused to surrender to the panic circling inside her. If she couldn't use her magic, she'd use her mind.

"What do you know about my mother?" she said.

"I know she couldn't protect you from all this, although she did try."

"What do you mean?"

"That dark magic she was working on? She meant to direct it toward me. But that didn't work. Ditto for the spell your witch coven cast to keep you away from books. They never told you that, right? They are the reason those books all talked to you in the library. You've always had sensitivity to books. Which is another reason the Book of Darkness sought you out."

Zoe tried to register what he was saying. "You killed my mother?"

"No, dearie, she did that herself when she used black magic."

"But it was you. She was trying to get rid of you!"

"Trust me, you've got bigger problems at the moment," Silas told her. "It's time to start the ritual."

Zoe yanked at the bonds holding her.

Silas held the iPad in front of her face, mere inches from her nose. "Watch this."

Zoe squeezed her eyes shut.

Silas pinched her nipple hard.

Her eyes flew open. "Ouch!"

"Don't be a coward, dearie. No one likes a coward."

"No one likes demons, either."

Silas took a step back with mock horror before laughing. "Sticks and stones may break my bones, but words will never hurt me."

Zoe wanted to break every bone in the evil demon's damn body.

"Anger is a good thing," Silas said. "You should direct it against the Demon Hunter for putting you in this untenable position. Had he kept his vampire pants zipped then you wouldn't have lost your magic."

There had to be a way out of this. Zoe just had to find it. But it was hard to think when there were spiders everywhere and Silas was forcing her to watch the gruesome video. Couple that with the memory of Damon warning her that demons sucked out a witch's brain and Zoe was freaking out. While brain-sucking wasn't shown in the video, there was a lot of slicing and dicing of body parts in a ritual that represented all things evil and depraved.

Blood, guts, and gore were not her thing. They made her sick. Everything here in the tunnel made her sick.

She couldn't afford to throw up. She could choke and die on the table.

He plans on killing you on this table anyway, her inner panicky voice said.

Shut up. Can't you see I'm trying to stay calm here?

Good luck with that.

Great. Her inner wimp had a sarcastic streak. Just her luck.

This demon was the reason her mother had resorted to black magic, resulting in her death. Zoe couldn't afford to let panic blind her. Her mother wouldn't want that.

"If you kill me, then I can't open the book," she said.

"I don't have to kill you. I can carve you up, as you saw in the ritual video. A charming witch's circle on your left breast, a delightful pentagram on your right. And maybe that Phoenix of yours on your tummy." He held up a scalpel. "The Book of Darkness will appear if you express enough emotion. Fear is a powerful emotion. And pain makes the fear even greater. A win–win situation."

"I want my Dr Pepper," Guy said.

"I'll get you a truckful if you help me," Zoe implored.

Silas laughed. "Not going to happen, dearie."

"Why not? I sensed some good in both Guys."

"Only because I wanted you to. I thought there was a chance they could get you to remove them from hell and that you'd find a nerdy demon was more approachable and relatable. But there's no need for that illusion any longer. I don't need these Guys."

Moving to the foot of the table, Silas gestured the two Guys to his side. Flames rose around them as he pulled them close until they merged into one demon. Silas. Now she could see his horns. And his scales. His fingers had turned into blackened claws. The spiders scuttled closer, onto the table at her feet.

"What did you do?" she whispered, too scared to scream.

"I just took back what was mine."

"Just like I'm going to take back what is mine," Damon said from somewhere behind her head.

"So glad you joined us, Hunter," Silas said. "Let the festivities begin."

Chapter Twenty-three

Screw keeping calm. "Get the spiders off me!" She could feel them crawling along her ankles and her calves. She froze. Maybe they'd go away if she didn't move.

Wrong. Instead they scuttled farther up her leg.

Zoe was terrified.

Something heavy dropped onto her stomach. A giant Godzilla spider? No, it was the Book of Darkness. A split second later Bella was sitting on the book. She wore Zoe's mother's amethyst necklace wrapped several times around her neck like a collar.

"You have angered the cat, demon," Bella declared, her tail switching back and forth.

Silas was startled by Bella's appearance and was distracted by the sight of the book so near at hand.

Before the demon could take advantage of the moment and grab the Book of Darkness, Damon moved with vamp speed to stand beside Zoe and lean over her.

Looking deep into her eyes, he said, "I love you."

Zoe was speechless. She couldn't talk anyway because his mouth covered hers for a kiss.

Despite her desperate circumstances, she still felt the powerful bond linking her to Damon. And then she felt something else.

Her magic was back.

While he'd been kissing her, Damon had released her hands from the chains holding her.

When Silas made a grab for the book on her stomach, Zoe held him back with her hand outstretched. She also dispatched all the spiders to a land far far away.

"Bye, gotta go," Bella said. She disappeared and took the book with her.

"No!" Silas howled.

Sitting up, Zoe wanted to undo the bonds holding her ankles but she couldn't waste a second. Time was very limited.

The protection spell could only do so much when she was mere feet from an über-demon like Silas.

"Your magic can't save you now." Silas's face was contorted with fury. "And neither can your vampire lover. I put you in hell before, Hunter, remember?"

Silas tilted his head toward the left side of the tunnel, which turned into a projection of Damon writhing in agony on a slab of some kind. The rack. He was being tortured on the rack.

"I did it to you before and I can do it again," Silas said. "Your dagger won't work on me. Not here, not now." He spread his arms apart. "Go ahead, try throwing it at me."

"I don't take orders from you," Damon said.

"He's three demons in one. It's going to take both of us to defeat him," Zoe told Damon.

"How sweet. You need a girl to help you," Silas mocked. "She's a stupid little bitch."

"No one calls my witch a bitch," Damon growled and leapt at Silas.

While Damon was slashing and dashing, Zoe used magic to undo her ankle shackles. She stood. She was wobbly but upright.

She'd never seen Damon in vampire Demon Hunter mode before. His face was etched with rage as he bared his fangs. Using his demon dagger, he sliced Silas's arms. The demon lashed out with his claws, but Damon was too fast for him. With a single move, he ripped the demon's throat open.

Silas gurgled and fell to the ground, dead.

Damon returned to Zoe's side.

Silas leapt to his feet. "Nice try."

"The power of the pen is stronger than the sword," Zoe said. Ever since her magic had returned, she'd sensed a strong message coming from her mother telling her to use the Latin words to destroy Silas.

She started reciting the Latin sayings. She wasn't sure how she remembered the exact wording, but she did. And Damon, translating her visual message, recited them with her.

Zoe had never spoken so fast in her life.

Corpora lente augescent cito extinguuntur.
Cinerigbria sera venit.
Non sum qualis eram.

It only took a few seconds but it felt like years to Zoe.

Cocky from his survival after Damon's attack, Silas

just stood at the foot of the table, grinning at them with malicious intent. "Words will never hurt me, dearie."

Damon had his dagger in hand, ready to attack Silas again.

Zoe reached out to touch the tattoo on the small of Damon's back.

"*Venator,*" she said.

"*Ad finem,*" Damon added.

Bam, Silas went up in flames. It happened so fast that Zoe couldn't believe it was real. But the smell of sulfur was nearly overwhelming.

Her tattered red dress was suddenly replaced with the clothes she'd worn when Silas had taken her, which was the nightgown she'd put on in the middle of night. The ruby-red shoes were gone and she was in her bare feet . . . on the ground where spiders had crawled.

Zoe thought she was going to pass out. She started to sway, and her ears started to ring.

"Don't wimp out on me now," Damon told her.

She blinked away the black spots blotting her vision and turned to face Damon. "I am not a wimp! I've just been chained to an embalming table with an über-demon threatening to cut me in pieces. And I had spiders on me." She shook so hard her teeth chattered. "I hate spiders!"

"We've got to get out of here."

"Ya think?"

He scooped her into his arms and leapt straight up through a vertical shaft she hadn't noticed before.

"You can fly," she whispered.

"Only when I have to," he said.

"Same here." By the time the words were out of her mouth, they were in the living room of her rental house.

Gram was waiting for her with open arms as Damon released her from his hold.

"Are you okay, honeybun?" Gram said.

Nodding, Zoe got tears in her eyes. Her grandmother hadn't called her honeybun since she was a little girl. Zoe rushed into Gram's arms for a much-needed hug.

"Is the book here?" Damon said.

"Of course it's here," Gram said as she released Zoe. "Bella and Pat have been guarding it."

"We have to destroy it," Damon said.

As a former librarian, Zoe was opposed to destroying books. But she could see where it would be necessary in this case.

"Bella has been telling us what happened." Gram engulfed Zoe in another huge hug. "I'm so sorry you had to go through that."

"The demon is gone," Zoe said. "We destroyed him with the Latin phrases. Damon and I recited them together. I don't know how I remembered all the Latin sayings but I did. It was as if I could feel my mother's presence and she was guiding me."

"Maybe she was," Gram said.

"I need to sit down," Zoe said unsteadily before sinking onto the couch.

"Let me bring you up to speed," Pat said.

"Let me help," Bella said. "Zoe, you and Damon had sex last night and that made you lose your magic. We didn't realize that until a very short time ago, when it suddenly appeared in the Adams Book of Spells."

"What did? That Damon and I had sex?" Zoe said.

"No, of course not," Pat interceded. "That if the witch who touched the book had sex with a Demon Hunter, one of them would lose their powers. The warning also appeared in an illuminated manuscript on the occult in my library. The information about the Book of Darkness actually dates back thousands of years to a papyrus manuscript in the library in ancient Alexandria."

"The world's first library," Zoe said in awe.

Pat nodded. "It needed all three of us near for the book to appear."

"From where?" Zoe demanded. "Where did it come from? Did Gram have it all along but didn't know it because it was cloaked? Did my mother see it and use it in error? Where has the damn book been? In an alternative universe? Or in the demon stratosphere?"

"Hell, it could have been in the Doctor's TARDIS for all we know," Bella said. "Yes, I watch *Doctor Who*. But we can discuss that later. Right now we need to get rid of the book before it disappears again."

"Right. Irma and I think we've come up with the way to destroy the Book of Darkness," Pat said.

"We have to move fast," Gram said. "Let's go to the kitchen. I already have the big spaghetti pot out. It's the largest container I have."

Zoe pointed to the fireplace. "We can put a cast-iron cauldron in there."

"Right," Gram said. "I should have thought of that. I left our cauldron in storage back in Boston but I can get it in a sec. First let me get a fire going."

Flames
Take aim
Into this fireplace
Please make haste.

The fire was lit.

"Good," Gram said. "That worked. Now for the cauldron."

> *Cauldron of mine*
> *This is the time*
> *To come forth onto the fire.*
> *I said I could do it, don't make me a liar.*
> *Appear*
> *Here.*

The cauldron appeared, hanging on a stand over the fire.

"Quickly now," Gram said. "First off, I need a strand of hair from you, Zoe, as well as Damon and Pat. And a cat whisker from Morticia."

Gram put each item in the cauldron. "This last one is tricky. I need the urine of a Russian aristocrat."

"Where the hell are we supposed to get that?" Damon said.

Bella raised one paw. "Hello? That would be *moi*. But I'm not peeing into a fire."

Zoe produced an empty plastic bin large enough for Bella to jump into and take care of business. The bin was brand new and had yet to be used. It certainly wouldn't be used after this little episode. Zoe poured the liquid into the cauldron.

"One final thing." Gram nodded to Pat, who added a raven's feather.

"I happened to have it from my Tower of London days," Pat said. "Irma warned me I might need it."

Gram turned to Zoe. "As the youngest witch in our line, you must throw the book into the cauldron. Don't touch it until I point to you. Understood?"

Zoe nodded.
Gram held out her hands.

Book of Darkness, hear my call
Your time is done and that is all.
Hell-broth, boil and bubble
Begone this evil harmful trouble.
Be short be swift. Give hope a lift.
Close the door to hell
And destroy this evil book as well.

Gram pointed to her.

Zoe's inner librarian still hated the idea of destroying a book, especially one as old and rare as this one. But her inner witch knew that it had to be done. So she quickly did it.

The contents of the cauldron went up in a burst of wild flames that were a strange inky black color.

"Are you sure we got it? What if it just went somewhere else?" Zoe said. "We don't even know where it was while it was missing."

"Do you feel different?" Pat asked Zoe.

"I'm sort of buzzing all over. Like when your hand falls asleep," she said.

"Me too," Gram said.

"Me too," Bella agreed.

Morticia nodded as well.

"Then that is all the confirmation we need that the book was destroyed forever," Pat said.

"What are you talking about?" Zoe said.

"It's written here." Pat showed her the illuminated manuscript he had on the coffee table.

"I'm not fluent in Theban," Zoe reminded him.

"Whomsoever shall destroy the Book of Darkness shall enjoy immortality," Damon translated.

"Holy Toledo," Gram said.

"Holy shit," Bella said.

"Sweet," Morticia said.

Zoe stared at the calico cat in amazement. "You can talk!"

"Because all of you contributed to the ingredients to the spell that destroyed the book, you all became immortal. That's what the buzzing is," Pat said.

"Or it could be the flu or something," Zoe said.

"You're afraid to believe in the magic," Damon said.

"Can you blame me?" she said.

"No," Damon said. "The good news is that you will have an eternity to learn to believe."

"Did you know about this immortality issue beforehand?" Zoe asked.

"I'd heard legends about the possibility. This is the first time I've seen it in writing," Damon said.

"Why didn't you tell us?" Zoe demanded.

"That's on me," Pat said. "I couldn't risk the chance that you might not want to be immortal and therefore not do the spell to destroy the book."

"Who doesn't want to be immortal?" Gram said.

"You'd be surprised," Pat said.

"Does this mean I'm stuck in a cat's body forever?" Bella grumbled.

Zoe was having a hard time processing what she was being told. She'd already been abducted by a demon, held captive in a tunnel filled with spiders, and had a vampire Demon Hunter kiss her after telling her he loved her. Now she got the news that she was immortal and it wasn't even noon yet.

She needed to be logical about this. She needed to fill in the blanks, although there were some she didn't want reviewed. She didn't want to know how Silas had gotten her into that red dress. She was going to pretend it had happened in the blink of an eye.

Which reminded her, she was standing in her bare feet and nightgown. "I need a shower," she said.

But before she could reach the stairs, the front door burst open and Daniella ran in with Nick and Bruce close behind her.

"You poor thing," Daniella said. "Nick just told us what happened. That the demons are gone and the book, too."

"And Dr. Powers back in Boston has been compelled by a vampire friend of mine to forget and forgive everything regarding Irma. So, everybody okay now?" Nick said.

"Obviously not." Bruce pointed to Zoe. "The poor girl is still in her nightgown."

"I need a shower," Zoe said.

"I brought a box of a dozen cupcakes," Daniella waited for Pat to remove the illuminated manuscript and set it inside the Victorian armoire for temporary safekeeping before setting the goodies on the coffee table. "I brought a lemon ginger and a salted caramel as well as your fave red velvet. Oh, and a couple of maple bacon ones, too."

"Bacon?" Bella's ears perked up. "I love bacon almost as much as caviar!"

Daniella handed Bella a piece of bacon from the top of the cupcake and gave one to Morticia as well.

"Thank you," Morticia said politely.

Daniella's eyes widened in surprise. "Both your cats talk now?"

"And we're immortal," Bella added.

"I'm taking that shower now," Zoe said and headed upstairs. She did not want to try to explain anything. It was beyond her. Gram and Pat would have to do that, accompanied by Bella no doubt. Too bad. Zoe was done for the moment.

Once locked in her bathroom, she tore off the night-gown and cursed it so it dissolved. She never wanted to see it again as long as she lived. But wait, that would be . . . *forever.*

She turned the water on full tilt and stepped in for her shower. She used the strongest soap she had but still kept washing, trying to scrape the memory of Silas touching her from her skin, not to mention those damn spiders. It was a very, very long shower. She only stepped out when the hot water ran out.

She'd washed her hair as well. Reaching out, she wiped the steam from the old-fashioned mirror above the sink. She didn't look any different. One eye was still green, one still blue. But everything had changed. She'd had sex with a vampire and, well . . . that part had been awesome. The trauma came after that. She'd gone from having no magic to being immortal. Talk about a change in circumstances.

Zoe wrapped a big bath towel around herself and stepped from the bathroom into her bedroom.

Damon was sitting on her bed, waiting for her.

She hadn't expected that.

"What are you doing here?" she said.

"Waiting for you. We need to talk."

"Right." She tightened the towel around her body. "I have questions."

A smile lifted the edges of his lips. "You always do."

"How did you know to add those last two words in Latin to get rid of Silas?"

"*Ad finum*. To the end. They were on that weird chair with the words on it you have downstairs. They were on the seat where the cats usually sit, and the words were glowing."

"What about the images on the tunnel wall of you being tortured? Were you really in hell?"

"Only the first level."

"What happened?"

"You remember I told you about Eve?"

Zoe nodded. "The witch you killed because she betrayed you."

"Her betrayal resulted in my being ambushed. I ended up in hell. Silas hated that I was the one who got away. No one gets away from hell."

"He did."

"And the two goons that were his Guys. But only because of the book."

"He did that deliberately. They weren't two Guys, they were really just a part of him. He just did that so that I might take pity on them. Their story about my mother sending them to hell was a lie." She took a deep breath. "That dark magic my mother was working on when she died? She was directing it at Silas. Somehow she knew and was afraid of what would happen. So did our coven. They cast the spell that was the reason all those books in the library talked to me. They were trying to keep me away from books although they never told me that. I'm not sure why. Perhaps they were forbidden by the rules of magic. They didn't tell me. They didn't give me a choice. Just like you didn't give me a choice. Didn't the vampire Demon Hunter who turned you give you a choice? Weren't you asked if you wanted to be turned?"

"You weren't turned. You're not a vampire. You're still a witch."

"Forever."

"What, you were hoping to come back in your next life as a cat?"

"No. But I was hoping I'd be reunited with my mother on the other side someday," Zoe admitted quietly. "She's the one who charmed my bangle so we'd find the Latin chant to destroy Silas. I know she was."

"You could be right. At least you've got your grandmother forever. I didn't have any of my family. In fact, my brother died on the same battlefield I did."

"You never told me that before."

"I know, and I realize we've only known each other a few days." He stood and came close to brush her damp bangs away from her eyes. "But we've got forever now."

"Did you really kiss me and say you love me?" she whispered.

"I did."

"Were you telling the truth?"

"I was."

"Do you still love me now that I may be immortal?"

"I'll have forever to prove it to you."

"Or you could do a vampire pinkie swear," Zoe said.

"How about an immortal pinkie swear?" Damon murmured against her mouth.

He linked his pinkie with hers.

"Are you swearing to be mine?" she asked.

"Are you swearing to be mine?" he asked in return.
"Yes."

"Then there's only one more thing left to be done." He whipped the towel from her body.

Grinning, Zoe shoved Damon back so he landed on her bed. She lowered herself onto him. He'd removed his clothes in that millisecond.

"I showered. Downstairs," he said.

She straddled his thighs and propped her hands on his chest before leaning in to lick droplets of water from his collarbone. "I've got you now, vampire."

"Yes, you do." He lifted her hips and brought her down on his erection. "And I've got you."

His tumescence filled her. She rocked forward and then back before pausing. "Is this going to rob me of my magic again?"

"No, that was a onetime thing. This . . ." He reached down to thumb her clitoris. "This is not a onetime thing."

His caress was direct and forceful yet tender and tantalizing as well. He was so erotically skillful, introducing her to new avenues of bliss.

Her earlier fears and misgivings scattered, blown away by the intensity of her increasing pleasure. She rode him and he guided her so that his long steady strokes created maximum ecstasy.

Her vagina clenched around him as she climaxed. He made her come again as his hips surged up, driving ever deeper into her welcoming depths.

This wasn't just awesome hot sex. Damon loved her. He didn't just drive her mad with his stubbornness, he drove her mad with his lovemaking. He'd saved her. They'd saved each other.

There was no holding back. She shattered in his arms, wild pulses of bliss oscillating through her.

She collapsed, unable to speak for a long time. "I love you, Damon," she whispered against his throat.

"It sure took you long enough to say the words."

"There's no rush." She ran her fingers down his chest past his navel to his vampire privates. "We've got forever."

He grinned. "True enough, little witch."

"Admit it." She held him in her hand, her fingers gently caressing him. "You're glad I came to Vamptown, aren't you?"

"Damn right!" He flipped her onto her back and slid his fingers into her moistness. "And you're glad you're here, aren't you?"

"I'm more than glad. I'm over the moon." She ran her fingers over his tattoo so close to her own talisman. "A shooting star is only in the sky for a brief period of time." She touched the talisman around her neck. "A star is there until the end of time. Just like us."

Her eyes flickered from the fiery joy he was creating with his caresses—but before they closed, she saw his tattoo shift so that the shooting star became a star. Magic. Pure magic.

"Just like us," Damon murmured. "Just like us."

Read on for an excerpt from Cat Devon's next book

LOVE YOUR ENTITY

Coming soon from St. Martin's Paperbacks

When Sierra Brennan opened the door to her new house in Chicago, she didn't expect to find a naked man standing there. A very hot, sexy, well-built, and well-hung man, looking like he was hung-over. He made no attempt to cover up while she made every effort to keep her eyes on his face and not his privates.

"Thank God you're here," a woman wearing a corset and little else said from right beside Sexy Naked Guy. Sexy Naked Trespassing Guy. "What took you so long?"

"What do you mean what took me so long?"

"Who are you talking to?" Sexy Naked Guy asked. His voice was low and rough.

"Your girlfriend," Sierra said.

"I don't have a girlfriend," he said.

"Look, I don't care what your relationship is with her, but you are both trespassing so you need to leave right now. As soon as you get dressed, I mean."

"I'm the only one here," he said.

"Clearly that's not true as I am here as well." She punched 911 into her smartphone.

He moved closer and looked deep into her eyes. He had chocolate-brown eyes and thick lashes. His chiseled cheekbones made his face as sexy as the rest of his chiseled body. "You don't want to do that."

"You really don't want to do that," the corseted woman said.

Sierra already knew what she didn't want. She didn't want to screw up her chance to inherit this house. Several others had tried and failed to fulfill the thirty-consecutive-days residency requirement. She'd only met her great-uncle Saul Brennan once yet he'd listed her in his will. Yeah, he'd listed two older cousins of hers before her, but here she was anyway. They hadn't stayed in the house. She would. Because she had a huge advantage.

Sierra was not afraid of snakes or spiders or things that went bump in the night. Especially things that went bump in the night. That was her specialty.

Sierra saw things most people didn't. Yes, maybe it was a cliché, but she saw dead people. Ghosts. Spirits who for one reason or another didn't or couldn't move on to the other side.

Which was why she was able to write such good paranormal novels. *Write what you know.* That's what all the pros said, and it was what Sierra did. Her S.J. Brennan books featured a vigilante ghost hunter and the challenges she faced in finding justice and punishment where needed.

Yep, she saw ghosts, and she was seeing them now as the corseted woman moved closer and shimmered with translucency. Which meant Sexy Naked Guy was a ghost too, right? She put out her hand to check. Her fingertips rested on his bare chest. His *solid* bare muscular chest.

"Why aren't you leaving?" he growled.

She yanked her hand away as if burned. "Because this is my house and you are the squatter."

"The house is mine," he said.

"In your dreams," she said. "Who do you think you are?"

"I know who I am," he said. "I'm Ronan McCoy. Who are you?"

"Sierra Brennan, the owner of this property."

"Since when?" he said.

"Since yesterday."

"Forget him. I need your help," the ghost said. "My name is Ruby, in case you were wondering."

"One thing at a time," Sierra told Ruby. "Get dressed," she told Sexy Naked Guy. Wait, his name was Ronan.

He looked deep into her eyes once more. "Get out."

Sierra shook her head. "No way."

She saw the confusion there before irritation took over. "Leave!" he bellowed.

"You leave," she bellowed back at him. She'd driven her U-Haul truck nine hours across three states and she was beyond exhausted. She had PMS and she was not a happy camper.

"How long has he been here?" Sierra asked Ruby.

"Who are you talking to?" he demanded.

"He's been here a few days," Ruby said. "I've been here for decades and decades."

Sierra frowned. If Ronan was a recent arrival, then he couldn't be the reason Ruby hadn't crossed over. He obviously couldn't see Ruby. She should have realized that Ruby was a ghost faster than she had, but Sierra chalked that up to the fact that she was so tired. Usually she could tell a ghost from a human but nothing about this Saturday had been usual.

She'd done a book signing at nine this morning in Ohio. There had been a good turnout, but a majority of the audience had wanted her to pass on messages to their departed loved ones. Sierra had had to tell them that she wasn't a clairvoyant, she was a writer.

Yes, her books revolved around ghosts but that didn't mean they were real. That was her story, and she always stuck to it. The rest was between her and the ghosts she helped to the other side. She wasn't about to reveal her ghost whisperer side to the general public. She knew all too well the stigma that carried, the mocking laughter when as a child she'd told friends that she saw ghosts. She'd been labeled weird and ostracized. Ever since then, she'd been careful not to reveal her hidden talent.

Sierra would deal with Ruby the Ghost later. First she needed to get rid of Naked Ronan. "Look, I don't know why you think you have a right to be here," Sierra told him, "but I'm telling you that the previous occupants did not fulfill the requirements of the will."

Ruby raised her hand and had a sheepish look on her translucent face. "That may have been my fault."

"I had a feeling," Sierra muttered.

Ronan frowned. "You had a feeling about what? No, don't answer because I don't care."

What kind of man stood there so arrogantly while so naked? An extremely ripped one. Not in a bodybuilder-weird kind of way but in a six-pack, shoulda-been-in-the-movie-*Magic-Mike* kinda way.

Sierra was finding it increasingly difficult to keep her gaze above his neck. Okay, she'd sneaked a peek down to his navel once or twice. And maybe she'd mistakenly looked even lower.

Right, who was she kidding? She'd seen him in all his glory. His nudity rattled her.

Keeping her own self-preservation in mind, she had her phone in one hand while her other hand was in her purse, her fingers curled around a can of Mace. Because the bottom line here was that she was facing an angry naked guy and that was not a positive in the security department.

A knock at the door at her back startled her. She yanked it open to find a man standing there, flashing a badge of some kind at her.

"That was fast," she said. She must have pushed the 911 button without realizing it and they'd used the GPS on her phone to locate her. "Come in."

"I'm Damon Thornheart. Is there a problem?" he said.

"*He's* the problem." She turned back to Ronan to find that he'd donned a pair of jeans. That was also fast, but it didn't change the fact that he didn't belong in her house. "Get rid of him, please."

Ronan McCoy couldn't believe this was happening to him. He'd spent the past century waiting to come home and now that he had, this woman with the bad attitude and great breasts was getting in his way.

Which was why Ronan welcomed the arrival of fellow vampire Damon Thornheart. Ronan wasn't sure why he hadn't been able to compel the woman to leave. Maybe it had something to do with the fact that he'd been an indentured vampire for the past one hundred years.

Ronan had been turned on the battlefield in World War I in 1914. The trench warfare had been brutally bloody. Hundreds of thousands had been injured, Ronan among them. But his torture hadn't ended with his death. It had only begun.

He ruthlessly shut those thoughts down. He refused to let his past dictate his future. His immortal future.

Yes, Baron Voz had sired him but unlike most vampires, Voz had kept Ronan indentured to him for a century, forcing Ronan to do his bidding and his killing.

But Ronan was done with that now. When he'd left Chicago to head off to war in Europe, he'd promised his sister Adele that he'd come back. He was keeping that promise. Her letters had kept him going for the months before his death.

So here he was, home again. The returning warrior. Yeah, right.

"She won't leave," Ronan told Damon.

"Damn right, I won't," she said. "The house is mine. I have the paperwork to prove it." She dug in her purse. "No, wait, it's here. I could have sworn . . . Yes, here it is." She handed over the forms. "These prove I am the owner of this property."

"Of the house, yes, but not the property," Damon said after looking over the paperwork.

"What do you mean?" she said.

"That you have apparent ownership of the house, but not the land it sits on or is surrounded by."

"You mean the small front yard and back yard?" she said.

Damon nodded. "That's right."

"How is that possible?" she demanded.

Damon shrugged. "You'll have to take it up with your attorney."

"He's just left on a two-week cruise to Antarctica. I can't contact him while he's away."

"Then you'll have to wait until he comes back."

"No way," she said.

"Why not?" Damon said.

"Because the clock starts ticking today."

"What clock?" Ronan demanded.

"Never mind. You still haven't said why you're here. Where is your proof that you have any right to be here?" she asked Ronan.

Her glare at his still-bare chest let him know that she wanted to add, Where is your shirt? Hmm, maybe he could read her mind and could get rid of her that way.

Ronan concentrated on Sierra, taking in everything about her from her shoulder-length auburn hair to her green eyes to her great breasts. She had a cute nose and a stubborn chin. She grabbed her documents from Damon's hands with slim fingers.

Ronan wondered if she'd be so confrontational if she knew she was facing a pair of vampires.

Reminding himself that he was supposed to be trying to read her mind, he refocused his attention. She was angry. She was tired. She was concentrating on the papers and then looking over his shoulder. What was she looking at?

He turned but saw nothing there. He returned to Sierra. She was wearing black pants, a lime green top that hugged her breasts, and a pair of Cladaugh earrings.

With her coloring, the auburn hair, pale skin, and green eyes, he figured her heritage was Irish. So was his. But she was a mere human while he was not.

Ronan breathed her in. All his senses were powerfully heightened to vampire strength. Her scent was tantalizing. He could hear her pulse swishing through her body. He focused in on the slight quiver of her carotid artery in her neck.

As an indentured vampire, Ronan had had to kill more humans than he wanted. But that was over. He'd worked hard to develop his vampire self-control. That didn't mean he wasn't tempted, not only by her artery but also by her curvy body. His afterlife would be much simpler if she just obeyed his compulsion.

He didn't sense anything different about her from other women he'd come in contact with over the decades. Mind-reading was a talent he'd developed over time, but even that skill was difficult where she was concerned.

He sensed all kinds of strange thoughts in her head. Writing deadlines, cover ideas, iceberg images, a woman in a corset. Whoa. Where had that last one come from? Maybe he'd mistaken Sierra's earlier appreciative looks at his body. Maybe that wasn't her thing. Maybe women in corsets were her thing.

Not that it mattered. Sierra's sexual orientation was irrelevant. She had to go and she had to go now. Ronan needed the house to himself. This was his family's home, and therefore it was his if he wanted it according to Vampire law. And he wanted it. Badly. The secret to saving his sister's soul was somewhere in this house.

Besides, the house was located smack-dab in the middle of Vamptown, a Chicago neighborhood inhabited mostly by vampires. This was no place for a human woman, even if she was one with courage and a surprisingly strong stubborn streak.

"She has to go," Ronan told Damon.

Nodding, Damon stepped closer to Sierra and looked into her eyes. "You need to leave."

"No way!" She narrowed her eyes, her increasing anger and frustration very evident. "I don't think you are being an impartial person in this situation. In fact, I want your badge number so I can report you to your superior."

Frowning, Damon looked at Ronan. His message was clear. Damon hadn't had any better luck compelling her than Ronan had. Which on the one hand, made Ronan feel like he wasn't incapable after all. But on the other hand, it meant they were stuck with her for now.

"You two work it out," Damon abruptly told them before turning on his heel to walk out.

As Head of Security in Vamptown, Damon was no doubt going to check out every detail about Sierra Brennan. Meanwhile, Ronan had a situation to handle.

"What kind of cop are you?" Sierra shouted after Damon.

"He's the kind with fangs," Ronan drawled sarcastically. "Welcome to the neighborhood."